SHADOW ROAD

Michael Donovan was born in Yorkshire and now lives in Cumbria. A former consultant engineer, his first novel *Behind Closed Doors* won the inaugural Northern Crime competition.

By the same author

Praise for Michael Donovan's writing

'At a time when there seems more competition than ever in the crime-writing genre, Donovan's debut novel is a real winner...'
Lytham St Annes Express

'... a wonderful debut novel in a hugely competitive market ... an enthralling novel ... deliciously complex ... make(s) the readers hair stand on end. Donovan ... succeeds in breathing life into a host of warm, witty and realistic characters.'
Cuckoo Review

'Eddie Flynn is part Philip Marlowe, part Eddie Gumshoe, a likeable wisecracking guy but with a temper when roused ... humour ... violent confrontations ... well recommended.'
eurocrime

'... good old-fashioned detective work. A slick, dynamic mystery...'
Kirkus Reviews Recommended Book

'... one of the best novels I have read this year. Brilliantly absorbing ... escapism at its best.'
Postcard Reviews

'For many thriller fans, one read may not be enough.'
Best Thrillers

www.michaeldonovancrime.com

SHADOW ROAD

MICHAEL DONOVAN

HOUSE ON THE HILL Publishing

CHAPTER ONE
Burke and Hare would approve

The shop was on a back street behind Balham High Road, an oasis of calm clear of the commercial frenzy. Its bare display windows reflected our grey silhouettes, hiding the interior. What was on sale wasn't for the casual passer-by. Everyone needed the place but didn't want to be reminded. Lucy stood alongside me, checking the facade, and I sensed doubt for the first time. But what's doubt but a P.I.'s adrenaline? It floods in before most action. I grinned down at her.

'Show time,' I said.

Lucy's eyes showed nothing behind her dark glasses. Her voice was kind of quiet.

'Yeah,' she said. 'Let's do it.'

I dropped my grin in case anyone was watching and opened the door for her.

We went in. There was no chime to announce our arrival. Just still life and quiet. A bare room, teak floors and counter, a display of memorial stones along the wall. A maybe-plastic potted plant. The lighting was subdued to give a sense of eternal overcast. And the silence once the door had closed was a deep silence. Even the minuscule street noise had gone. If I'd had a pin I'd have dropped it just to raise hell.

But this was not the time for frivolity. I looked at Lucy's sad face and snapped my own into a matching set and we waited.

After a minute I began to wonder if anyone was going to come out. There was no desk bell, and the solid door behind it gave no clue about whether anyone was back there. Lucy looked at me. I threw her an encouraging smile and shrugged. The heavy silence felt like it might last all afternoon. Then just as I'd decided to go out and come in again with a good slam of the shop door I heard footsteps in the back.

The rear door opened and two men stepped smartly through as if they'd just hurried along a mile-long corridor. My guess was that we'd tripped a buzzer on the way in, and since the premises weren't a mile wide the delay was probably simple decorum. Funeral businesses don't like to project haste. Dignity is all. Emphasis on the long-term.

The two men wore identical black suits and ties under their wesk'ts but they'd beamed down from different planets. One was ancient, with a tall frame that exuded the leathery sadness of an ancient carthorse. He watched us with glistening eyes that had the melancholy of a wet Sunday, broadcasting a solemnity developed over a lifetime of digging. He was the comforting hand you needed close by when you buried a loved one, though I guess you'd avoid him on dark streets. The younger guy was a foot shorter and thirty years fresher and sported a comb-over to get Bobby Charlton rolling in the aisles. His face was padded by too-good living that left his shallow grey eyes projecting their simple cunning from out of baby fat. He'd be marching up front with the baton when they did the ceremonial cortege, the picture of dignity and sorrow, but whistling like nobody's business by the time he got the cheque to the bank. Whatever his act, you knew right away it would lack depth.

He was the one who spoke.

'Mrs Gallagher?' His mouth shot sparks of gold across the shadows.

Lucy dabbed at her shades.

'Please come through.'

He stood aside to let the old guy lead us through the door and down the corridor. We followed, sandwiched between them, and entered a small chapel of repose. The two stopped outside.

'Come back through when you're ready,' Baby Fat said. He reached and closed the door.

We waited a few seconds until they were clear then Lucy took a last dab at her eyes and pushed her glasses up.

'Jeeez, Eddie,' she said, 'this is creepy.'

I grinned at her.

'Part of the job,' I said. 'Creepy. Devious. Reprehensible. Stay with it and you'll be out of adjectives before you know it.'

She threw a shudder and walked over to the casket. The thing was nice. Ornately carved in an expensive wood I couldn't name. A top of the line model for sure, though you wouldn't want to be the passenger. I joined her and we looked down at Tom Gallagher, slumbering peacefully. Either Tom had mandated high-end in his will or the casket was simple exuberance on the part of his executor. With Tom's reputed wealth and no surviving family a little exuberance by that executor – who was his long-time lawyer – was in order. As far as we knew he was the only person Tom had talked to regularly in the last five years, a solicitor called Jimmy Diamond whom I'd met and quite liked. I didn't see the guy working cheap though.

The home had done a good job on Tom. His cheeks were so rosy he looked set to jog to the cemetery. He lay back in creamy silk upholstering, peaceful and sad in his absolute healthiness.

It was warm outside but I'd needed my jacket buttoned as we came through. I opened it now and pulled out the equipment. Started with the mike. Lucy leaned over to watch.

I cut a slit in the lining by Tom Gallagher's feet, close to the staples. Pushed the mike and its transmitter in. The transmitter was half the size of a matchbox and held the electronics and a lithium-ion pack. It disappeared amongst the foam padding like a mouse in a duvet. The mike sat right by it. I set the transmitter switch and stretched a six-centimetre wire out under the silk. The receiver-relay would be staying in this room and when they rolled the casket back to the rear I needed the transmitter to be good for seventy-five feet. When everything was set up I superglued the slit and dropped the pleats back over. The equipment was invisible. I pressed the area. Felt nothing. I leaned close and sneezed. Good and loud. A detonation to give the unwary a heart attack. Testing one-two-three.

Two LEDs in the relay I was holding flowered into life. Amber confirmed that the two-minute transmission was coming in from the mike and green said that the relay's own signal was going out fine.

Next I went round the casket and clambered over a backdrop of fake petunias onto the windowsill to Blu-tack the relay behind the pelmet. Skipped back down. I wasn't going to win any prizes for subtlety but the funeral home wasn't going to be sweeping the chapel for bugs.

The tricky job was the cam. I needed a good field of view, and for various reasons neither the silk lining nor Tom Gallagher's suit jacket were going to work. Harry had made a suggestion that was entirely reasonable and practical but depended on the fact that he wasn't the one doing the job. His recommendation was to use the shoes. I was hoping for other options but just in case we needed to go with that one Tom's niece, aka Lucy May, had ordered that he be laid out in a pair of his favourite brown leather brogues that were just right for the job with their convenient lace eyelets. Lucy had also requested a simple laying out: just Tom in his suit and shoes. No quilt cover to scupper the cam view. But to bug a shoe meant getting the shoe off. I'd handled cold bodies in my time but the idea of wrestling with a dead guy's foot seemed less attractive to me than it had to Harry. And funeral people usually have to fight like hell to get the shoes on in the first place. I didn't see it being easier now. I searched the casket again for a more favourable location but the conclusion was clear: Harry's idea was the only idea.

I loosened the lace on Tom's left foot and got the brogue off with a bit of muscle and a few horrified clucks from Lucy. I grinned viciously. In any reputable business it would be the apprentice doing the dirty work. I re-threaded the lace to by-pass one of the eyelets and prised out the plastic collar to give me a two-millimetre hole. Then activated the cam and taped it behind the eyelet. Punched mini staples through the tape to hold it in place. Then taped the shoe tongue behind the cam to protect it and slid the footwear back on. This involved more contact with cold socks than you'd want but I heard that chiropodists spend years training with dead feet and look at the cars they drive.

I pulled the lace tight and re-tied it. Apart from a small bulge under the leather you'd never notice. The cam had a rated field of view of sixty-degrees. This was cut to maybe forty-five by the eyelet but with Gallagher's foot resting against the side of the casket those forty-five degrees were pointed right where they should be. And the field of view was not likely to be disturbed. Whatever action went down, Coffin Cam would get it. Lucy leaned to check out the shoe in what I interpreted as admiration. I threw her a modest shrug. This one had to be a contender for some kind of sleuthing prize. I'd remind Lucy to get the forms.

The cam was activated by a light-sensitive switch. As long as light was hitting the lens the camera would snap one black-and-white frame per second and store it in a two-Gig flash memory. It was a nice bit of kit with the only downside being that it had no transmitter. If you wanted the pics you had to retrieve the cam. The delights of this job were far from exhausted.

I checked my watch. Eight minutes, start to finish. I threw Lucy a grin. Enough grieving. Time to go. I gave Gallagher a comforting pat on the shoulder and Lucy gave me one of her looks and pulled her shades back down. Then we opened the door and went back out. Walked through to where the two guys were waiting in the shop. The old one stood to stooped attention and observed us with a look of profound gloom. Baby Fat stood formally in the middle of the floor, hands clasped in front of him and a glint of impatient sympathy in his eyes. He rocked on his feet. Worked up a sad smile.

'Will Mr Gallagher be receiving any more visitors?' he asked.

Lucy shook her head. Spoke in a faint voice.

'Mr Gallagher has no other relatives, Mr... ?'

'It's Stephen,' he said. He proffered his first name as a comfort.

All part of the act you pay for. Or, in this case, Tom Gallagher was paying for.

If Stevie was already aware that Gallagher had no other relatives he didn't let on.

'Then we shall see you next Wednesday,' he said. He looked at his old guy who turned to open the door. We thanked him and went out.

~~~~~

When you drive to Balham you don't expect to park but the funeral shop had some kind of deal with the council. Had its own space reserved for business hours. Good for one smallish car. The hearses loaded up round the back. The smallish car of the moment was a Frogeye Sprite with a brindle Staffie waiting on the driver's seat. The dog was Herbie, my sometime footslog assistant and company mascot. Lucy hopped in and Herbie shifted to her lap. I jumped in and pressed the button and we moved off.

The dearth of parking might have been a problem but Harry knew a guy ran a timber and DIY business down the road. We drove down under the railway and pulled in through reinforced gates to where a rust-specked Mondeo was parked by the fencing. A big guy in a leather-patched herringbone jacket was leaning on the wing watching the clouds.

Harry Green, our tech guy. Out taking the sun.

We pulled alongside. Jumped out.

Harry quit his cloud-gazing to give me a gimlet look.

'Whassup?' I said.

'You going down with a cold, Eddie? Or has the dead guy got hay fever?'

Lucy pushed up her shades. Smiled at Harry in that "you know how it is" way.

'Next time you're gonna sneeze like an Italian on pepper-spray give me some warning,' Harry said. 'Save my eardrums.'

I grinned.

'You want me to go "testing-one-two-three" in a chapel of rest? What kind of respect is that?'

'How about respect for my eardrums?'

'These people might have been listening. I figured natural was best.'

Harry shook his head. 'You called that natural? Sounded like you were taking a choking fit. I'd have run round to put a Heimlich on you if I didn't know Lucy was there.'

'Heimlichs I can do,' Lucy said. 'If you ever choke give me a call.'

'I take it the reception's good,' I said, back to the point.

'Loud and clear,' Harry agreed. 'Is the cam in?'

'As per your advice.'

Harry's turn to smile.

I slid into the Mondeo and he dropped into the other seat. Leaned over to lower the glove compartment flap. The receiver and flash memory were taped inside, powered by a lead from the fag lighter. The device would stay live for a week if need be, assuming no one decided that the Mondeo was worth climbing the security fence for. Which was unlikely on balance. The receiver and flash were safe. Harry would be visiting the car twice a day. When the mike tripped we'd have the alert we needed to back in for the cam.

Harry locked the Orion up and we went over to squeeze into the Frogeye. Lucy was heading off for her afternoon gig at her uncle's Bethnal Green shop which was lucky since the Sprite doesn't fit three. She threw us a breezy wave and headed off for the Northern Line. Herbie waited until Harry had got the Sprite's door closed then vaulted it. The springs creaked and Harry grunted as twenty kilograms touched down. I jumped in myself and backed out. Gave Lucy a toot and headed for the river.

Harry spoke over the wind roar.

'What's next, Mr Hare?'

'Burke,' I said. 'You got the wrong one.'

'Sure. I'll be Hare. You're Burke. Both our names are mud if it gets out we're bugging stiffs.'

'We do worse.'

Harry thought about it.

'You gotta point,' he said.

'What's next is wait and see. Gallagher's funeral is next Wednesday. If nothing breaks by then the operation's a flop.'

Harry and Herbie both grinned. We'd talked about this after we'd signed the contract. The job had sounded pretty easy before the ink dried. But the reality was that all the gadgets had to work flawlessly and someone had to open that coffin lid or we'd have nothing.

Still, look on the bright side.

Bugging stiffs.

Worst case, we'd have a new line to add to our services portfolio.

CHAPTER TWO
Legal smoke

We crossed back over the river and drove up through Fulham. Raindrops started hitting our foreheads. I kept an eye on the sky, wondering if we were going to beat the downpour. Summer in London. Harry was making the same calculation, probably wishing he'd brought his umbrella. His only protection was from Herbie, sitting upright in his lap. I put my foot down and swung east towards Paddington.

'You think they'll bite?' Harry said.

'The bait's juicy enough.'

Harry grinned. Stayed hunched down to let Herbie soak up the shower.

'Is it Unwin?'

Stephen Unwin: the business owner. Baby Fat.

'The guy's the type. Inherited the family firm, believed not too enamoured by the business but too sluggish to sell up and try something else. Sympathy and service aren't his thing, I'd say. It must put his blood sky high to fake the empathy. He looks good to me.'

We parked behind Chase Street and went round. Normally I'd have taken thirty, grabbed a sandwich, but Lucy had left an appointment on my desk that was dangerously specific on time. That's Lucy: there when she's not there. We went up and I rooted out a pig's ear for Herbie then went to search the clutter on my desk.

No need.

Lucy had planted the Post-it on the exterior of the pulled-down roll top. The appointment was one-thirty. Someone called Leach and Howling who had the sound of a legal firm. An address over in Islington. I dropped into my seat and raised the top. Grabbed my laptop and checked online.

Confirmed my hunch. Leach and Howling were actually Leach & Howling Solicitors LLP whose service list covered everything modern man needed. Family law, immigration, property disputes, criminal defence, financial crimes and sexual misdemeanours. The gamut. You do it, they've got your back. But there are always legal activities that need a P.I. to dig out who actually did what and whose back needs stabbing. This firm was new to me. I checked their address and estimated that thirty minutes would get me there, of which I had twenty-eight left. I told Herbie to fetch his lunch and left Harry to lock up. Jogged back down and drove across the city.

The firm had offices in a grey brick commercial building on Islington Green, squeezed between estate agents and salons, bookies and cafes with vacant outdoor seating. Where Leach & Howling stood out was in their special touch: they'd put up an entrance surround of low-relief fluted columns supporting a blocky lintel that clashed magnificently with the brickwork. The lintel displayed the firm's name in gold but the columns sounded hollow when I rapped them, like those structures on film sets. Probably a message in there somewhere.

The tiny reception dispensed with the ostentation. Just a plain room with five chairs on coarse commercial carpet, a desk with a heavily decorated receptionist behind it. She raised her falsies and threw a smile. I gave her my name and she stood to escort me up to the top floor. The building didn't run to lifts so the senior partner must have plumped for the height on the basis of the view up there. My chaperone huffed her way up three flights as if she was resigned to this – I guess it saved on gym fees – and tapped on a door with the name Rupert Leach up on it.

For a small jobbing firm the boss's office was decked out impressively. Teak and reproduction 18th Century oils everywhere. A room fit to impress the most opulent client, though my guess was that Leach met most of them downstairs: it's hard to be impressed whilst you're receiving CPR. I crossed the green and gold Axminster to shake the hand of a tall, sixtyish guy in a sober wool suit who'd stood from behind his desk. His mop of prematurely white hair and fresh vacation tan gave him the air of a semi-retired salesman, but the gleam of his teeth as he gripped my hand flagged a guy who was still swimming with the sharks. The grip was short before he turned to introduce me to a young woman who was also rising from a seat beside his desk.

Her name was Susan Abbott and apparently we were here to talk about her business. She was about my height, thirtyish, with a pretty, thin face framed by the stylish cut of her short red hair. I shook her hand and wondered. Legal jobs rarely put P.I.s in touch with the end client. We're brought in as helping hands, back-room operatives digging out the stuff the lawyers can't get by more linear methods. The end client and their issues are usually of no relevance. We're hired to go out and gather, bring back the goods, cash the cheque. Seemed this was one of those rare cases when we'd be in the know. Leach invited Susan to sit again and gestured to a second chair then sat himself back down.

I ignored the chair. Jabbed my hands in my pockets and went to check out the front window. More or less what I'd anticipated. A prime view of Upper Street's commercial fronts. Rooftops and high rises behind. We were facing the wrong direction for the City skyline. The damn climb was for nothing. I turned and smiled at Susan.

'How can we help?' I said.

Leach twisted to keep me in view. Struggled to hide annoyance. Business conducted with a wrenched neck was not the normal protocol.

'Ms Abbott has a family problem,' he answered for her. 'Her brother is missing. I recommended the services of your firm.'

He stated this like a warning. We've done you a favour here. You'd better shape up.

I nodded. Missing persons we do. Although when people go missing their nearest and dearest tend to come to us directly. No need for the legal angle.

I looked at Susan.

'How long has he been gone?'

'Two years,' she said.

Quite a while.

'You've heard nothing from him in that time?'

'No. He's completely vanished. He hasn't been in touch and we've not been able to contact him.'

'Has it ever happened before?'

'No. He's always done his own thing, might not call us for a few weeks. But he'd never lose contact entirely.'

'What was he doing at the time?'

'He'd just finished university and was thinking about careers. He'd decided to take a break, tour the country.'

'By car?'

'Hiking. Hitching.'

'And he went off to do that?'

'We thought he'd just gone up to Town for a few days. He hadn't told us specifically that he was on his way. But the UK trip was his plan so we assume he went straight out from London.'

'Two years ago.'

'Yes.'

'Could he have extended his tour? Decided to cut contact for a while?'

'That would have been way out of character. He'd know we were worrying.'

'So when did you decide he was missing?'

'After a few weeks without contact. He didn't get in touch and wasn't answering calls. There was obviously something wrong.'

'Did you talk to his friends?'

'The few we knew, but none of them knew anything.'

'Did you inform the police?'

'Yes. But there was nothing they could do, especially since Chas had stated his intention of taking time for himself. They told us to get back in touch if he didn't reappear and that was it. And when we did go back to them a year later they still couldn't do anything. They just had him on a list in case any reported incidents came in that might relate to him.'

The story was familiar. The police handle around two hundred thousand missing persons reports a year and most of those can be categorised as own-initiative, clear up after a few days or weeks. And the couple of thousand that stay unresolved are assumed to be mostly people who don't want to be found. A university graduate taking time out to kick things around wasn't going to trip alarms. I turned back to my view. Rain spattered the windows and the high rises dissolved into unbroken grey. A wet afternoon coming in.

'I recalled a similar case you took on a year ago,' Leach said. 'With impressive results.'

I stayed watching the sky. Grinned. Half truths and flattery. Because unless Susan's brother was a child then this was not similar. And Leach's remark, set against the result we got, had to be either flattery or delusion.

'How old is your brother?' I said.

'Twenty-three.'

'And let's be clear: this would be way out of character?'

'Yes. I guess.' Susan searched for the right words. 'He could be thoughtless sometimes. Moody, directionless. If something grabbed his attention he might wander off without telling anyone. But not for two years. And what really upset our mother was that our father died six months ago and Chas doesn't know.'

I nodded, still wondering why Susan had involved a lawyer in this.

'What did your brother study?'

'He'd graduated with a business degree at Exeter. By July he was back home in Alton considering options.'

'Meaning what?'

I turned.

'Chas was conflicted. He was never really interested in the business degree but Dad pushed him into it. He'd barely scraped through and decided that his career lay elsewhere.'

'What kind of elsewhere?'

'He had ideas. Some of them pretty wild. Farming; wildlife warden; setting up a wind farm; maybe living off the land – he mentioned a friend up in Scotland who was into crofting. Stuff like that. Chas was kicking it all around and getting into fights with Dad.'

'Why's that?'

Her chin came up. Her eyes glittered in the light.

'Dad was disappointed. Didn't see great job prospects for Chas and was annoyed that he didn't even seem to be looking.'

'Okay. So what happened prior to his leaving?'

'He was home kicking around, disappearing for odd days to stay with friends in London. Then he announced he was going to take some time, maybe a year. Travel around. That's when he and Dad had a row. Dad told him to do as he damn well pleased but he'd be paying his own way. And the next day Chas grabbed his rucksack and left. That was the last time we saw him.'

'He didn't call?'

'We called him but his phone was always off and he didn't reply to messages. It got to weeks then months. That's when we reported things to the police. But nothing happened and the months just stretched out. When our father died our mother was devastated that Chas wasn't at the funeral.'

Rupert Leach sighed and shook his head. Stood slowly and came over to the window to check out his view himself.

'It's always family affairs that are most upsetting,' he told me.

And most lucrative. The gleam in his eye wasn't tears. I stayed focussed on Susan.

'Did your brother have any issues? Vulnerabilities?'

'Only in the sense of being a little lost in life. My brother's not an alcoholic or drug user, if that's what you're asking.'

'Got it. So now you've decided to take some action.'

'We can't wait another two years.'

Leach spoke beside me.

'Let's not dismiss the possibility,' he said, 'that Chas *may* have a vulnerability. Perhaps his life took a downward turn after he left. Two years is a long time. Who knows what might have happened?'

He turned to cast a doleful frown Susan's way. Looped back to his seat and sat with a sigh then strained his neck again to see me.

'It's better to have him found, Mr Flynn.'

I didn't disagree, though why a lawyer was making the sales pitch I couldn't see. What was in it for him? At best some kind of finder's fee for rustling up a detective service, unless Susan had paid these people a hefty fee up front to do a job they could afford to subcontract. But Susan Abbott didn't look the wealthy type.

'What do you do?' I asked.

'I'm an interior design consultant.'

So maybe a little wealth. But I didn't get the sense she was naive enough to throw money at a lawyer when there were a hundred agencies in the directory all claiming a speciality in locating the lost. So maybe Leach was just her personal solicitor. She'd sought advice and he was taking the finder's fee. I let it go.

'What about Chas' friends?' I said.

'We've talked to his old friends from home. They know nothing. And we don't know his university or London friends. All we have is two names. One friend in London, one Scottish girl he met at university.'

'Is Alton still his registered address? Does he get bank statements and phone bills there?'

'Yes. We've opened them all. There's nothing. His bank account and phone haven't been used in two years.'

Which was bad news. If her brother had left no paper or social trails he could be deep under the radar.

'Does Chas drive?'

'He didn't have a licence.'

Nix that line of enquiry too, though we'd make a quick check.

Without paper or electronic trails getting to Chas was going to take legwork. We could be talking weeks or months and Susan would be looking at a hefty tab. I walked across finally and sat down to give her my thoughts. Explained the financial aspect. Susan shrugged them off.

'Whatever it takes,' she said. 'Just find him.'

'Another thing,' I said, 'is that we'd be working for you, not your brother. If he doesn't want to be found we'll find him anyway and you'll have something he's trying to keep from you. You may have to live with that.'

'We'll deal with the consequences,' Susan said. 'Chas doesn't have the right to put his mother through all this. We want to know what's happened to him. After that it will be up to him.'

'Just find the young man,' Leach said. 'That's all we want.'

Spoken like a venerable uncle, sharing the pain. A good lawyer suffers right along with his client until the final cheque clears. I watched him. He still had that sad gleam in his eyes and I was still wondering what was in it for him.

Then he answered the question. He stood to bring over a form which was a contract covering our services. A retainer and weekly fee already inked in. The figures were pretty reasonable. The guy had done his homework. And his cut would be fifty percent on top, which would explain his sincerity.

Unfortunately we don't do subcontracts.

I grinned at Leach and handed the paperwork back.

'We have our own contracts,' I said. 'And we work directly for the end client in cases like this. If that's a problem, Ms Abbott can tell us now.'

Ms Abbott looked at Leach. I waited for him to start warning her about the dangers of going without legal oversight, but the guy just smiled and planted the contract back on his desk. Held up his hands.

'That's absolutely fine,' he said. 'I was simply trying to expedite things. Ms Abbott will be happy whichever way you work things. I'll only ask her to give me a glance at the contract before she signs. Just for her peace of mind.'

I held the grin. The guy could glance at the contract until he got migraine as long as he didn't try to change it. I'd just have to get Lucy to check the form before she printed it out. Make sure there were no long words or obscure terminology. Right now the only two bits of paper that mattered were the Retainer form that I had in my pocket and Susan Abbott's cheque that would cement our agreement. I pulled the form out and pushed it onto Leach's desk for his due diligence check.

The form said basically: I hereby retain the Eagle Eye Detective Agency at a non-refundable advance of _____ to act as my agents in the matter of _____ under conditions laid out in contract reference

_____ .

Of which the key legal jargon was the "non-refundable" bit.

In matters of high urgency we sometimes skip the form, take an informal cash payment and let the contract catch up. But since we were all here and armed with pens and chequebooks, and since Chas Abbott had been absent for two years, rush didn't seem appropriate. Leach read and double-checked the wording and I inked in the details, informed Susan of the weekly fee and explained about expenses and escalation hours if we needed more manpower. Then she penned her signature and we were done.

'We'll start tomorrow,' I said. 'I'll call in at Alton. If it's convenient then both you and your mother should be there.'

'That's fine,' she said. She sighed and I saw the weight come off her shoulders. After two years of worry something was happening. P.I.s are like dentists in that respect. Capable of bringing instant relief, the anaesthetising effect of the retainer.

Leach copied the form and I pocketed the original and shook Susan's hand and she smiled for the first time. Thanked me again.

'Thank us when we find Chas,' I said.

Leach's grip was strong and sincere. Almost as if he'd be involved in the day to day of this.

Which he wouldn't.

Though I was still wondering about him.

CHAPTER THREE
No refunds

I called in at Chase Street next morning to clear paperwork and leave me free for the Chas Abbott job. Lifted the roll top to check how big the clearing job was. When I saw how much I pulled the top back down and locked it securely. It could wait until I'd found the boy. A minute later I heard a muscle car growling behind the building. My windowsill hid the view so I watched the railway tracks as the growl surged and burst into two final barks as someone stamped the pedal. A minute later Harry came up the stairs whistling *The Dambusters* theme. He was driving Shaughnessy's car whilst his Mondeo was standing listening-post duty in Balham. Shaughnessy was strictly a bike guy. The car was hobby stuff, a souped-up eighty-five quattro that came out when he needed something weatherproof to ferry his daughter about or for occasional bad weather stakeouts. The vehicle also came out when we needed extra wheels. Harry wiped his grin and went back to pretending he'd drawn some kind of short straw here. According to Harry, quattros were too flashy even back then, but the way he pedalled the engine every time he changed gear told a different story. Truth is, the Audi was the perfect street-cool vehicle for a P.I. If I didn't own a Frogeye I'd have made Shaughnessy an offer myself.

I topped up the coffee machine whilst the forces of good and evil battled it out in my head over whether I could leave the paperwork. Finding Chas Abbot might take two days or two months. Did I want the stuff preying on my mind the whole time? If I attacked the paperwork now, scrimped on words, I could have two reports closed and invoices out when I headed out. Maybe I could do it. Maybe coffee was the answer.

Harry planted his mug and reached for the kettle. Harry's a tea guy.

'You check the mike?' I said.

'As I came through. We've just one trip, which was the lid going down and the casket shifting to the back room. A little background conversation.'

But nothing from beyond. I guess that might take a few days. I shovelled coffee into the filter.

'The sooner something comes through the sooner you get your wheels back,' I noted.

'Can't be soon enough,' Harry said. 'You know the damn mileage on the Audi?'

'Somewhere around twenty to the gallon.'

'Eighteen in urban. Damn thing's costing me a fortune.'

I flicked the coffee switch on and off. Looked for signs of heating. Harry could boost the Audi's economy any time he wanted by holding back on the foot-stamping every time he pulled up but I didn't bother to point that out.

Then Shaughnessy came in, holding the door for Lucy so she could sprint through with her thoughts on yesterday's job. It had killed her for sure riding in on the Tube. No one ever talks to you down there.

'Hiya fellas,' she said.

We looked at her. The mourning outfit had gone. We were back to orange hair and Day-Glo mini skirt. Brown midriff. No shades in sight.

'Any messages from the dead? she asked. 'You checked the ouija boards? Have the police called?'

See?

Smart-isms stacked a mile high. As if she hadn't been playing the leading role yesterday when Act One of Uncle Tom's Last Ride played out.

And just like that the paperwork didn't sound so bad. I headed back to my room.

'See what you can do with the machine, Luce. And yesterday was legal. Remember that.'

'Sure, Eddie. *This* side of the Styx. But there's gotta be rules somewhere. They don't say Rest In Peace for nothing.'

'Tom's resting. We didn't disturb him.'

Though if Lucy hadn't dressed down for the job I suspect that an eye or two would have opened. I went through. Over in my visitors' chair Herbie had opened his own eye and was dropping to the carpet to go chum-up with the refreshments supervisor.

I flopped into my Miller and slid the roll top back up. Two hours was doable once the coffee arrived. I swivelled the chair in the interim to get the window view, contemplate blue skies and the stimulating breadth of a P.I.'s job description.

~~~~~

The home from which Chas Abbott had disappeared was a town house on an executive development snaking up a hill near the centre of Alton. I pulled onto its forecourt and told Herbie to sit tight. Hopped out.

Susan Abbott opened the door and took me into a spacious lounge smelling of air freshener and beeswax. She introduced her mother, Patricia, a somewhat startled woman with white curled hair sitting uneasily in a high backed armchair.

Patricia knew why I was here but she was still uneasy. Her son's two-year absence was burning her up but it was a private pain, nothing to concern the world outside. And if a private detective was only here because they'd invited him it was no less an intrusion. Maybe barely less so than if the media had shown up. I shook her hand and saw it all in her eyes as I sat down.

I asked her about Chas to get things moving.

She hesitated as if she'd not understood but Susan sat on her chair arm and took her hand. Her mother sighed finally.

'There's nothing *to* tell. He's a boy like any other.'

The same as all mothers' sons.

I rephrased. Went for specifics. Teased out a picture of an ordinary schoolkid, ordinary interest, ordinary friends. An ordinary university student just about scraping through.

And then gone, as if he'd never existed.

'I understand that your husband was assertive on the subject of higher education,' I said.

Patricia paused. Searched for truth in the sheepskin rug at her feet.

'Chas needed a push sometimes.'

'But a business degree was not his preference?'

'Chas seemed happy enough.'

Susan squeezed her mother's hand.

'He wasn't really happy,' she said. She looked at me. 'Dad's view was that Chas should just suck it up and get his qualifications and a job would follow. Then he'd recognise the security of a career, an income.'

Patricia shook her head.

'I never knew what he thought,' she said.

'I understand he came back here after his degree award.'

'Just for a few weeks whilst he decided what to do. He left mid July.'

'You told me Chas stayed with London friends sometimes.'

Susan replied: 'The only name we recall is Ralph. And we know nothing about him. Not even where he lives.'

'But he mentioned that girl at university,' Patricia said. 'Heather.'

Susan concurred.

'She was the one had him talking about moving to Scotland. Taking up crofting or whatever.'

'Any details about her? Is she a crofter herself?'

'We don't know. It sounds unlikely for a university student. My guess is that it was just talk. Something that interested Chas.'

'And you've no last names for Ralph or Heather?'

They shook their heads.

'Did he mention any places in Scotland? Maybe a crofting community?'

If Chas had been bent on going off grid a remote croft would do it.

'He mentioned a village,' Patricia said. 'But I don't recall the name.' She frowned down at the rug and shook her head in frustration. 'Something like a brand of vodka.'

A Scottish place sounding like vodka. No name sprang to mind but Highland geography has never been my strong point.

'Any other friends? University? London? Mention of any particular places?'

'No. He just had ideas of travelling. Taking time out. Then he was gone. I never imagined we'd not see him again.'

'The friction between Chas and his father. Tell me more about that.'

'They were fighting whenever I was here,' Susan said. 'Dad wasn't happy about Chas' Ordinary degree or him kicking around here, or his plans to waste a year travelling.'

'He had Chas' best interests at heart,' Patricia said. 'But your father was never much of a pragmatist. The degree didn't matter. Only what Chas did with his life.'

'What was Chas' mood? Did the uncertainty get him down or was he excited by the possibilities – the wildlife warden, farming and so on?'

'It's hard to say,' Patricia said. 'Sometimes he was up, sometimes down. But I suppose he felt the pressure.'

'He was mixed up,' Susan said, 'if that's what you're asking.'

'You mentioned a fight with his father after he announced his travel plans. Are you sure that triggered his departure?'

'I think the row was the final straw,' Patricia said. 'I thought he'd gone off to Town to let things cool down but after a week we'd heard nothing and realised he'd gone.'

'When exactly did you last see him?'

'We all saw him the morning he left,' Susan said. 'He walked out with his small rucksack, headed for London we assumed.'

'A friend of mine saw him walking into the station,' Patricia said. 'That was the last sign of him.'

She stopped as the thing rushed back in. Susan gripped her hand.

'We'll find him,' she said.

Patricia watched the floor.

'I'm not sure,' she said.

Resignation. Prepared for the worst. Maybe the resignation dated back to her husband's death when any hope of reconciliation died.

'Did he take his stuff with him? Phone? Computer? Documents?'

'He took his phone and a few clothes,' Susan said. 'That's it.'

'Was his service operating when you called?'

'Yes but calls went to voicemail. I assume the phone was switched off.'

'It still is,' Patricia said. 'I call nearly every day.'

Susan looked at her, surprised.

'Of course I do,' Patricia insisted. 'I'm still hoping he'll pick up one day.'

'Is the rest of his stuff still here?'

'All of it.'

'Does postal mail still arrive?'

'Occasionally. His bank statements come monthly. One or two periodicals continued until the student subscriptions ran out.'

'You told me you'd checked the statements?'

'Yes,' Susan said. 'They show a cash withdrawal in London shortly after he left and then nothing. He's not used his card in two years.'

'Was there money in the account?'

'A little. But there've been no more withdrawals or credits.'

'Be good if I could take a look.'

Susan took me upstairs to Chas' bedroom. It was a bright, pristine room with a large bay window giving a view down over the town. But the bed was stripped and the boy's gear had been stashed with a neatness that told the story. The room was dead. A relic of someone gone. The boy's old books and CDs were stacked neatly on their shelves, nothing out of place. Two walls were covered in posters: Guns N' Roses; Earth Crisis; The Sword; other artists. One wall sported an old half-million topographic flying map of the UK with "Restricted" stamped on it. Marginally legal on a civilian wall. Maybe filched from an Air Cadet student friend. The books on Chas' shelves were a mixture of academic texts – business and economics – and general non-fiction: a history of Roman Britain, travel and adventure. Books on wild camping and trekking, ecology and wildlife.

A small desk beneath shelving held the wrack of Chas' external affairs. Marketing shots and academic periodicals, all unopened. Phone bills and bank statements and an old benefits claim letter, all open.

The benefits claim gave me Chas' National Insurance number. The bank statements gave me nothing that Susan hadn't already mentioned. A mostly inactive account with a slowly-declining balance until the journal subscription ran out then just steady debits against his phone account. Current balance two hundred and seventeen pounds. The last sign of life in the statements was two years ago, August 2010, when Chas' card had been used to withdraw two hundred and fifty in cash from Barclays in Swiss Cottage.

I checked the phone bills. A standard contract, minutes and texts. No out-of-plan charges to indicate continued use in the last two years. If Chas had used his phone within its plan there was no way of telling. And getting hold of any detail, maybe picking up location data, would be tricky. We'd no contacts with Chas' provider.

I found a charger and powered up the boy's laptop. The machine asked for a password and I shut it down. Set it aside. Harry would take a look.

I riffled through the junk and journals on the off-chance, expecting nothing. But found something.

A plain white envelope with a handwritten address had got lost in the stack. I held it up for Chas' sister. She looked surprised.

I opened the envelope and pulled out a short letter on two sides of a single sheet, written in scrappy handwriting.

The letter was addressed to "Chazza" and was dated six months after his disappearance. An address in Harrow followed by a few short paragraphs of inane student-speak, references to past high jinks, questions about when they were going to get together. A sign-off by someone called Eli. A student friend from Exeter, it looked like, keeping in touch. But the content suggested that Eli and Chas had not been in contact since university. And by the time the letter arrived Chas was long gone.

Susan read the letter and shook her head. Just another person she and her mother knew nothing about.

I continued to rummage but found nothing except the fact that Chas had left his passport here. So we could rule out a trip abroad.

And that was it.

So I'd be looking for the boy armed with three names – one with an address – and whatever Harry might pull off the laptop.

Susan closed the door behind us and we went down.

Bottom line: Chas had walked out of this house and left nothing to point his family in any direction. A compass with no needle.

I asked for a photo and Patricia handed me a snap of a slightly chubby, scruffy-haired youth with pale skin and blue-grey eyes. Chas, two years before his disappearance. A little out of date but it was all they had. I laid it down and snapped it with my phone camera.

Chas didn't wear body jewellery or glasses, sported no tattoos, had no disabilities, injuries or scars. No obvious mannerisms or distinct speech. The boy wasn't loud or brash. Didn't smoke. Wasn't known to take drugs and had no health problems. Had no political or religious affiliations and kept his circle of friends to himself. Not in a relationship at the time. And the cash balance in his account said he wasn't in hock to anyone. No debts being paid or extorted.

In short, someone who didn't stand out.

All I had was a lost boy with an interest in the outdoors, wildlife, geography and ecology, history, farming and artisan stuff, a kid who saw his life outside the urban universe.

He'd gone of with a few clothes and his smartphone which had been dead for two years. Maybe he was using it with a new sim, a new number. Untraceable.

We finished and Susan signed the contract with a cursory glance that would not likely draw solicitor Leach's approval. Then I left my card with them and took Chas' computer. Promised to stay in touch.

~~~~~

As I drove back down the hill Herbie stirred and sat. Grinned over.

'Yeah,' I said. 'Lunchtime.'

We turned towards the centre and rolled under a railway bridge just as a black steam locomotive trundled across in a blast of smoke and soot.

Herbie growled and ducked.

'You're right,' I said. 'We're way out in the sticks. Maybe we'll see a horse and cart if we're lucky.'

But the sight of the train prodded me. I swung into the station and left Herbie to fend off wardens. Walked through onto the platform. Away to my right the vintage train was disappearing under a volcano of smoke and ash. Steam and smoke were dissipating beneath the bridge. I turned to look the other way to where the electric lines ran away towards London.

The day he disappeared, Chas had walked onto this platform with his rucksack slung over his back. And unless he was a steam buff his ticket had put him on the service to Waterloo.

The platform was empty right now. Between services. The tracks gleamed in the sun and swung away behind the trees towards the Metropolis. At the platform end a red light blocked the way.

The stats say there are about ten thousand miles of railways in the UK, most of them accessible from this platform.

If Chas' ticket had taken him to Waterloo he could have been anywhere in the country within twenty-four hours.

Ten thousand miles of steel. Two years of silence. Red lights standing guard.

I sensed a long slog.

Then I pushed the poetry aside and headed back to the car. When

Chas reached Waterloo, if that's where he'd gone, he could have gone anywhere or nowhere. By train or by bus or on foot or riding along with a travelling circus. Ten thousand miles just didn't begin to describe it.

I fired up the Frogeye and scratched around for another statistic. A hazy schooldays memory told me that the UK is around a hundred thousand square miles. Or was it a million? Maybe a million. That sounded more likely. And did it matter? A hundred thou. or a million was a lot of space to look for a guy with a rucksack.

But it's what we do.

I'd start by getting to the people who were with Chas two years ago. Fish for facts and guesses, hints, impressions. Build a first picture and look for the trail out through the haze, a sense of how fast and far Chas might have travelled.

Maybe he was still in London. The city's a big place. His drifting might have stalled right there. If not, then I'd have the hundred thousand or million square miles ahead of me.

Look at things a certain way and you'd see Mission Impossible. That's why the contract Susan Abbott had just signed was going to give Rupert Leach the shakes. The contract had been pretty clear.

For a fee we'll look.

And if Chas was findable we'd find him.

But if he wasn't then the money would be gone. No refunds.

Leaving the risk that Chas' sister and mother were paying to lose the last thing they had.

Hope.

CHAPTER FOUR
Just people

The address on Chas' unread letter from his pal Eli brought me to a terraced house near the centre of Harrow. The property had been divided into three flats. Eli's address was "B", the middle floor, but no one answered the bell. I stood back and looked up. Nothing. Mid-afternoon quiet. I tried the ground floor bell. Same result. Hit the top one. A good long push. Frustration.

Frustration worked. The tenant came down. A retired woman in her seventies. The location marked her as neither wealthy nor badly off. Medium sized flats cost a bob or two even in Harrow. I gave her my most harmless smile and confirmed her suspicion that the doorbell wasn't for her. Asked if she knew Eli.

She tensed her eyebrows. Annoyed at the wasted trip. Replied in the negative. The door started to close.

'Do you have a name for the middle flat?' I said. 'The address I have is pretty clear.'

And maybe eighteen months out of date. Maybe Eli had upped and gone.

The door stopped, halfway closed.

'Connors,' she said. 'And if he doesn't answer then he's out.'

I logged the reprimand.

'Has Mr Connors lived here a while?'

'Long enough.'

I thanked her. Said I'd try later. The door closed.

Chas' pen pal was looking less promising than even the letter had suggested. Was Connors Eli by another name? Or was Eli just someone who'd crashed here, used the address on his letter?

We'd come a fair way out of Town and the weather had brightened. Made it worth hanging around to see if the Flat B tenant turned up. We drove over to the Rec. and took a turn round the park. Herbie trotted ahead, diverting back and forth, checking things out. We gave it an hour then drove back and parked near the building.

Five-thirty. People were coming in from work. We waited and

watched. It took a while but a little after seven a chubby guy in a suit with an affected rolling gait came up the street and entered the building.

I hopped out and walked over. Ground or middle floor: a fifty-fifty chance. I pressed bell B again. Got a result. The guy came back down minus the suit jacket.

Answered to the name of Eli, in a manner of speaking.

What he actually did was draw his shoulders back and give me a double-take laced with incredulity, as if I'd just asked to see Beelzebub's mother.

Then he snapped back to the City up-and-coming his black shirt and snow-white braces advertised him as and shook his head.

I smiled patiently. Waited. Chubbs finished the head shaking and jabbed his hands into his pockets.

'And you're looking for Eli *because?*'

I grinned.

'Actually, it's a pal of yours I'm after.'

His turn to wait.

'Chas. Your friend from Alton.'

At the mention of that name his face dropped its pretence. He knew Chas all right. But a stranger asking questions on his doorstep was triggering alarms.

'How about we go in?' I suggested.

Chubbs thought about it. Smelled police, debt-collectors, insurance investigators. Whilst he hesitated I stepped past him.

'Up here?' I said.

I led the way and Chubbs huffed up behind me. Finally beat me to his door as if to block the way but then invited me in. We stood face-to-face in a minimalist lounge, all shiny floor and mood lighting, big screen, speakers up on stands.

Territory invaded, Chubbs struggled to get the whip hand. Stood back and glared at me.

'Why're you looking for Chas?'

'He's missing. Why do you sign your name "Eli"?'

He folded his arms to make it clear that was not my business.

I waited. Chubbs-Eli broke first.

'A nickname from uni,' he said. 'No one calls me that. What do you mean, missing?'

'He's vanished. His family want to find him.'

'And you are...?'

'A private investigator.' I pulled out a card. 'We're following up on known contacts. His family had an unopened letter from you so here I am.'

'You're reading his letters?'

'Just the one. It's been on his desk for eighteen months. Maybe he was never going to read it.'

Eli's face switched to concern.

'Sheeeit,' he said. 'Disappeared. I can't believe it.'

'It's true, unfortunately. He walked out one day and hasn't been heard from. Now I'd already figured from your letter that you didn't know much about the disappearance but if there's anything you know might give us a pointer to his whereabouts it would help.'

Eli backed up then turned to sit on a chrome recliner opposite his speakers. Planted his forearms on his legs. I walked across to look out of the window. Less threatening.

'How long have you known Chas?' I asked.

'Right through uni. We were in the same graduation class.'

'Close friends?'

'So-so. There's a bunch of us knocked about together. We figured we'd stay in touch after we left but I got kinda tied up with my job and Chas stopped replying to texts after a couple of months. I wrote the letter one night in the pub. Just to stay in touch.'

'No social media contact?'

'Chas wasn't into that stuff.'

'Got it. When did you last see him?'

'Graduation. He said he'd look me up over the summer but he never called.'

'I hear he was a little disappointed with his grade. His father was, at least. Did he say anything to you?'

Eli relaxed a little. Stretched back in the seat. Planted his palms behind his head to think about it. A la City. I turned and watched.

'He was fine. He'd given up on Business I.T. Completed his finals just on the chance of scraping through, putting credentials to his name. But he was never going to work in some corporate tower or insurance office. He regretted being pushed into Business.'

'That was his father?'

'Yeah. Chas didn't want any of it. Realised too late that he'd messed up by letting himself be pushed in that direction. He was interested in outdoor stuff. Earth sciences. Exploring. Ecology. All that shit.'

'So what were his plans?'

'He wanted time to think things through. That was about it. He was looking to spot an opportunity.'

'He never gave you anything more specific?'

'Hell no: it was just texts after we graduated. How you doin'? What's happened to So-And-So? Been to any good parties? We didn't have any actual conversations.'

'Got it.'

I turned back to the view. Terraced roofs and bay windows, parked cars. Down in the street I could make out brindle markings behind the Frogeye's perspex. Herbie, checking thing out.

'What's his family saying?' Eli said. 'Was he trying to cut ties?'

'They didn't pick up anything to point that way. Just his issues with his father. No reason to vanish or stay vanished.'

'Wow,' Eli said. 'They've gotta be worried. Sheeeiit! What the hell's the boy doing?'

'Can you think of anyone who might know? Anyone he might have talked to?'

He thought about it.

'Maybe a coupla guys from uni. But I don't know for sure. We all just split and went our separate ways.'

'If you had a few names and contact details that would help,' I said.

Eli pushed himself off the chair and went to fire up a laptop, root out a note pad.

'There's three or four guys he might have talked to. Couple of addresses. The others are just emails.'

He scrolled. Scribbled. Handed me the paper.

'Obliged,' I said. I checked the sheet. 'There's one name here with no detail.'

'Bart. London friend. He and Chas knocked around here in Town off and on.'

'No details?'

'Never really knew him. Not on my course. He's over in Southwark.' He thought about it. 'There's a geezer I know might have something – he was on Bart's course.'

'Appreciated if you could check.'

Eli scrolled his phone and called a number. Spoke to someone and gave them a résumé. Answered questions then scribbled on the pad. Tore off another sheet.

'Guy remembers Chas staying with Bart. This is Bart's number.' He handed the sheet over.

I pocketed both sheets and we walked back down. Eli held the door open.

'Tell Chas to call,' he said. 'Tell me where he's been hiding.'

'I'll do that,' I said. 'There's probably a few calls Chas needs to make.'

I went out.

~~~~~

I gave Bart a call. The line picked up a background of conversation, the chink of glasses, sudden hiss of a soda gun that drowned both our words. I repeated myself. When Chas's name registered Bart told me to hold a sec and walked out to find somewhere quieter. When he spoke again I caught the hint of a West Indian accent.

He asked the expected questions about who the hell I was and why I was asking about Chas and I gave him answers. The two-year absence made him pause before he swore in a voice that didn't have as much surprise as it might have. I said we needed to talk and he gave me the name of a cafe bar on St Katharine Docks. Told me to look for him by the bridge. I estimated an hour and told him to sit tight.

An hour was pushing it but Bart would hang on. I fired up the engine and drove down the road to where a mini roundabout let me spin round to head back out. As I completed the turn I had to slam on the brakes to avoid a car coming fast up the street between the parked vehicles. It braked, swerved past me and was gone. An Audi TT quattro Sport. My thoughts jumped to Harry and his quattro. After I'd talked to Bart I'd drop by and leave Chas's notebook. The detour would be barely ten minutes and Harry wouldn't be able to resist taking a peek at the hard drive overnight. He's the fidgety type: not likely to sleep whilst there's a challenge sitting on his kitchen table. My guess was I'd have the disk contents first thing.

Evening traffic was light and I made the docks by eight, parked under the hotel and walked Herbie round the marina. Bart was leaning on the gate by the West Dock bridge. He was a black guy in his twenties with a long handsome face topped by short neat hair. He wore a trendy goatee and a trendy tee-shirt and knee-length denim shorts, red trainers. He pushed himself off the gate and shook hands without enthusiasm. An hour's thinking had led him to the conclusion that he wasn't going to hear good news about his friend. I repeated my story of Chas' disappearance.

'You and he good friends?' I asked.

'Pretty much. We mucked about. Chas used to come stay with me.'

'When did you last see him?'

'Two years ago. He crashed for a week after graduation.'

'You recall exactly when?'

He thought about it.

'Middle of July, maybe.'

Which would be right after Chas walked out on his family. I'd taken my first step forward from that station platform in Alton.

'Any special reason he came to Town?'

'Just chilling. Getting away from his parents. His old man was giving him grief. They'd had a fight and Chas decided he'd had enough.'

Which tied in with what Susan and her mother had described.

'What were his plans?'

'He was taking a year out. Dude wasn't cut out for the nine-to-five. Needed to find something different. He planned to hike around, see the country, deal with the employment situation when he got back.'

'So why'd he stop off with you?'

'He needed dosh. Save flatlining his bank account. He grabbed a pot washing gig on Telegraph Hill and worked ten nights. He'd have given it another week or two but he didn't want to get comfortable in the wage-slave routine. Maybe never start on his trip.'

'He mention the restaurant name? Other people he was in contact with?'

Bart gave me a restaurant plus one contact.

'He'd talked about calling on a mate over in Belsize Park. The guy has a business in Camden selling that goth shit. Chas said he'd call by on his way out.'

'Was this a friend from university?'

'Nah. Just someone Chas got to know in Town.'

'You got a name? Business name? Address?'

'His first name's Ralphie. That's it. I only met the dude once.'

'Anyone else he might have called on?'

He turned to look out over the water. Thought about it.

'A girl named Carol, maybe. Lives on a houseboat up in Camden. Some kinda graphic designer. Chas knew her from back home. But all his talk was about getting out of Town. Heading up north. Scotland, maybe. He knew people there.'

'Any names there?'

'Just people.'

Bart leaned back on the gate, watched the hardware bobbing on the water. Herbie snuffled at the netting, eyeing a couple of seabirds that had taken a berth down below.

'Did Chas have any problems? Drink? Drugs?'

Bart focused back on me and shook his head. Emphatically. A raucous group of Japanese tourists burst into view across the marina, cameras and umbrellas waving.

'No, mate. Chas liked a drink like we all do. But it wasn't a thing. And he never touched drugs.'

'Was he okay? Emotionally? No personal problems? Relationships?'

'Nah. It was just himself, worrying about his future. Keen to get on.'

'Do you have a contact number for Ralphie?'

'Sorry mate. Don't know the dude.'

'Carol?'

He shrugged. Went back to watching the water. 'She lived on the Regent's Canal. That's it.'

'Got it. But I need to be clear here: Chas didn't have any specific destination in mind when he left you? Just that idea of travelling north?'

'Only that. He was just hitting the road. But I've wondered why I've never heard from him. It's kinda worrying.'

'For you and a few others. Thanks for your time.'

I tugged at Herbie.

Bart continued studying the water as we walked away.

CHAPTER FIVE
Diavolo

I drove out from under the hotel and spotted an oddity.

As I climbed the ramps I caught sight of a red Audi sports following me out, which had me recalling the TT that had nearly sideswiped me in Harrow. Red Audis aren't uncommon in London but this one stayed with me as I headed over Tower Bridge and down through Bermondsey, holding fifty yards back in the evening traffic. And it was still there at Lambeth. Then next time I glanced back my mirror was finally clear.

We get followed from time to time but the agency had nothing on right then to attract outside attention. When the car didn't reappear I put it down to imagination.

Chas' Telegraph Hill pot wash job was at an Italian restaurant on New Cross Road. The place was busy when I went in but a waiter invited me through the door with a flourish. It would have been tempting if I didn't have a hungry Staffie in the car. I asked to speak to the proprietor, which strained the smile on the waiter's face. He told me to wait and disappeared into the back. Came back ten seconds later to tell me 'Is busy.'

I grinned and stepped round him and strode through to the kitchen.

A blast of steam hit me, shouts, crashing utensils, roaring burners. Someone's dinner almost died as a waiter pirouetted out of my path with loaded plates, yelling profusely. The yells were in Italian and were answered by a stocky guy with a moustache and chef's hat working at the range. When the commotion continued he turned to see and his eyes opened like he'd been goosed by the pope. He started his own yelling and raised his spatula. Rushed over, waving it dangerously.

'No-no-no! No in here! Is private. Dangerous. Out-out-out!'

I stood my ground, planted my hand in the waiter's back and propelled him towards the door to get the blazing shrimp diavolo out of my face. Some risks are not worth taking.

Chef was still coming at me though and his spatula was still slicing air.

'Getta hell outta here! Who you bloody think you are?'

I held up my palms.

'I'm going ,' I said. 'Just a quick question.'

I figured this had to be the proprietor. A good chef. The shrimp smelled delicious.

Though his spatula work verged on the deranged.

'Outside!' he yelled. 'I no talk to customers in my kitchen. Can' you see is dangerous?'

He gestured at the door. A couple of assistants watched, frozen.

'I need to ask about a guy worked here. Then I'm gone. No more danger.'

'What guy? What the hell you questions? I'm busy, man! You not see?'

'I heard this guy worked for you.'

'I got a hundred people work for me. They don't come chargin' in my kitchen causin' accident!'

'His name's Chas Abbott. Washed dishes.'

'Name who? I donna' know Chas Abbot. When he here?'

'Two years ago. Just for a week or so. University graduate.'

Chef's eye's popped. The spatula speared forward, aimed at my jugular.

'He work a *week*, two flamin' *year* ago? You *crazy* man? I got ten new pot wash every damn week and none of them is good for shit. So how I gonna remember a guy two year ago? Get the hell outta here! Nex' time you open that door you get *mannaia* greetin' you.'

He reached sideways and pulled a twelve inch cleaver off its hook.

Mannaia.

The thing was massive. The kind of thing you dig roads with. He hefted the cleaver like Norman Bates and stepped forward.

'Getta hell out! I don' know damn pot washer from two year, I don' know what customer order two hour ago! You think I'm crazy?'

The thought had crossed my mind. As the cleaver lifted I pushed backwards through the door and exited to the genteel calm and bubbling conversation of the restaurant, wine glasses chinking. The shrimps had landed with a flourish on a corner table and still smelled good, and the faint yelling that continued behind the kitchen door was barely noticeable. Then a crash shook the place that almost

33

brought the ceiling down and got everyone's attention. The cleaver, coming down on a block.

Passion!

It's what fine cuisine is all about.

The waiter who'd greeted me in stepped up to wave me out. I threw him a salute and walked out into fresh air and back to the Sprite. Jammed my phone to my ear and talked to Susan Abbot.

Her voice sounded breathless. Like she was expecting news. And I had something, at least.

'Chas came to London. We've got him for the first week or so, building up cash for his travels.'

'Oh my god!'

The exclamation was harsh with emotion. For the first time in two years she had evidence of her brother's continued existence. Only ten days' existence but I guess it was a start.

'Who did you talked to? Was he okay?'

I filled her in.

'Did this friend say where he went?'

'All he had was a couple of contacts. One's the guy you named: Ralph. IT graduate. Runs a business selling goth gear. The second was a girl called Carol. You ever heard of her? She was from Alton, apparently.'

Susan thought about it.

'Now I recall, he had a friend with that name. Not particularly close. Just one of the mates he knocked about with. If Chas stayed in touch we never knew about it.'

'Any last name? Old address?'

'Sorry Eddie. It may not even be the same Carol. When it came down to it we weren't such a close family. Chas never told us much about his friends, girls he'd met, life at Exeter. I was the same. We both had our separate lives.'

'Okay.'

'But at least we've got a start. You've picked up his footsteps.'

'That's right. A start.'

Though knowing that Chas was alive and kicking, ten days after he left home wasn't much. We'd just pushed forward his vanishing by a few days.

I reached the car. Told Susan I'd stay in touch and drove towards

Croydon.

The drive took thirty minutes. I was checking my rear-view most of the time, watching the lights coming and going in the deepening dusk. It didn't take me long to spot the high vehicle, some kind of four-by-four, holding two hundred yards back. I watched it for a while and then it was gone, leaving me with my imagination. But as I cut through Croydon and turned towards Harry's the red Audi pulled out of a side road behind me and I knew the thing was real. People were following me.

I had multiple vehicles back there, taking turns. Out in the dark radio calls were going out. Positioning information. Handover countdowns. If I hadn't got jammed up with the Audi back in Harrow I'd not have spotted it for a while. A couple of days maybe. These people were good.

But certainty didn't bring any comfort. There was no way the Chas Abbott job warranted attention from a professional tailing operation, which left a mystery. Why were they here?

P.I.s don't like mysteries. You'd think that spending our lives trying to unravel them would give us an appetite, and if that's sometimes true it's also true that we've no appetite for things that threaten to get in the way of the next wage packet. Threaten to become a fixation that distracts us from the job in hand.

Fixation and indigestion.

You'll find them top of the list in the P.I.'s career information pack.

~~~~~

Harry was out but I handed the notebook to Kathleen who promised to hand it over the moment he got in. I gave her the usual reassurance that I didn't expect Harry to take a look tonight but we both knew the game. Both knew that Harry had his own fixations. Give him a tech problem and he'll not sleep whilst it's sitting downstairs. Kathleen smiled patiently and told me to look after myself and I headed back out.

I flicked on a Peterson album and cruised through Brixton with his *Night Time* intro easing me into the late evening. My phone rang. I muted the music and connected.

'Hello stranger,' my speakers said.

'Margot, how are we tonight?'

'*How we are* is wondering whether I'll recognise you should we ever meet again. Maybe you can wear a red carnation or something.'

I grinned. Flicked my sound system gizmo and brought Peterson back in as *Night Time* kicked into its jazz riff. The gizmo is a feature Harry wired in so I can take calls and listen to music at the same time. The rotary gives you volume control too. I flicked it up until my caller was shouting.

'What the hell, Eddie? Are you in a club?'

I pushed the volume further.

'Speak up! Can't hear a thing.'

'Speak up hell. You're gonna blow my phone Eddie. Don't tell me you're still driving round. Don't tell me it's work.'

'Just clocked off. Had to drop a little homework at Harry's'

'Harry! Next time I see him I'm gonna tell him to take that kit back out of your car. Why does a person need to hear music whilst they're talking?'

I flicked the rotary. Volume increased. Peterson's fingers danced wild.

'Hell, Eddie. C'mon. I'm going deaf.'

'Same here. But what a way to go.'

Lights changed to green and my foot stamped the floor. The Frogeye sprang forwards. On the seat beside me Herbie opened an eye then sat upright and fought for balance. I could still hear shouting above the music.

'Am I going to see you this week or not, Eddie?'

'Going to *what?*'

'*See* you!'

'Why are you shouting?'

Something profane came through. Then an order.

'Hand the damn phone to Herbie. I'm gonna tell him to chew up your audio.'

'You're on speaker. He can hear you. But he knows not to touch the equipment.'

'Answer the question. Are you avoiding me?'

I thought about it.

'Does Herbie avoid pigs' ears?' I asked.

'Oh, Eddie. Always the flattery. So how about a date with this pig's ear? Tonight. My place.'

I thought about it further. Thought about those shrimps. Thought of the Diavolo.

'You got anything in?'

'Do you need to ask?'

Good point.

'I guess we're both past our feeding times, Margot. Not that food could ever be the main consideration in my desire to see you.'

'Sure it isn't. Tell Herbie I've got tripe sticks.'

'In that case, answering for the two of us, I'd have to say that we've nothing on tonight.'

'How long?'

Brixton to Hackney Wick. Ninety minutes with a quick stop-off at my place. I gave her the estimate.

'I'll be waiting.'

'It won't seem but a moment.'

She cut the line and I boosted the music. Herbie flopped back down on the seat.

'You got lucky,' I said. 'Dinner whilst I shower then tripe supper.'

My canine assistant grinned up at me.

'Sure,' I said. 'Me too. I'm looking for supper myself. Then maybe a little dessert, know what I mean?'

Herbie's grin widened.

We hit Battersea and jogged into the apartment. Got ourselves sorted inside ten then headed back out for the drive east.

Margot Catch was the woman whose life I was currently disrupting with my unreliable schedules. She rented a penthouse apartment in an eighties' block over in Hackney Wick by the Olympic Park and made a living drawing strip cartoons behind her panoramic glass. Living off the products of an artist's drawing board is a minority sport unless your output happens to be syndicated world-wide, which Margot's was. Her strip character *Edgar* had been broadcasting his jaded view of the world from the back of a national broadsheet for eight years, and his evolving notoriety had pulled in impressive syndication and book deals as well as impressive remuneration on each contract renewal. When a Conservative peer sued Margot's paper in 2007 after one of Edgar's more savage transgressions the proprietor paid the fine and Margot doubled her fee. Rumour had it nowadays that there were three of her framed originals up in the House of Lords.

I can't say I liked Edgar but I admired him. Edgar was a supposed chartered accountant but there were too many similarities to the private investigator archetype to leave me feeling easy. I'd mentioned this point to Margot when we'd first bumped into each other two months ago at an arts do on the South Bank and she'd robustly disputed my assertion until she couldn't take any more of my grin. She dropped her own pretence of amusement and asked me what kind of big-shot P.I. expert was I anyway?

I had to tell her to lower her voice since the guy I was there to watch had turned to check out our exchange, and if he or his fancy woman realised who I was I'd have a substantial client fee to return. Margot had tensed like a steel spring when I grabbed her arm and steered her away to explain my need for discretion but when the situation become clear she'd gone along with the play and kept her glee under wraps to check out the guy herself. Then she left me standing and marched over to flirt with him just to stir the pot. I growled and faded into an alcove of avant-garde sculptures, cursing my stupidity and wondering whether I could legitimately hang on to the commissioning fee – which had delivered a preliminary report confirming the wife's suspicions – even if my chances of completing the job with a portfolio of snaps was looking limited.

I'd come to no particular conclusion when the guy and his girlfriend walked right past me without a glance, and when I poked my nose out Margot was scanning the hall to see where I'd gone. When she clocked me she scuttled over. Seemed her pointedly misinformed teasing of the guy and his plaything had drawn out a few useful snippets between the litany of lies they'd been forced to contrive to shield their situation. First among which was that the lady in question was the spouse of the lawyer who was acting for my client. With that little gem delivered she hijacked my evening and guided me through the less puerile of the exhibits before suggesting a bar that served immaculate cocktails.

The rest was history.

Herbie clawed at the stairs in her building, hoisting me to the top floor like we were fleeing the Titanic's hold. Those tripe sticks.

Margot appeared in blue camouflage lounge pants and a plain tank top, feet bare. Late night gear, comfortable for settling in, though it was also the gear she worked in. Like all her rags they fitted her shockingly well.

'I *do* recall you!' she said. 'You're the guy with the dog.'

I leaned to plant a kiss. Herbie was up between us with his paws on her thighs. Tripe! She tickled his ear.

'It's been four or five days,' I said. 'That Thai banquet, remember? I was the guy sitting across from you.'

We'd eaten at the Camden Thai that had me on free meals for life on the back of an old job. I wasn't one to scrounge but their food was too good to pass by and I took up their offer on a regular basis, re-categorising an estimated bill as gratuities. The place had the happiest waiters in London. Win-win. And if you can't impress a new girlfriend with wall-to-wall smiles and more fresh seafood than she can handle then she's not impressible. I knew damn well that Margot remembered my face.

'The banquet was last Friday,' she said. 'Which makes it a week.'

'So long? No wonder I'm hungry.'

'If it's gonna take food to get you round here just say so Eddie. I'll get some ready meals in.'

I grinned. Cooking was only one of Margot's talents. If I didn't show constraint I'd be round here every night.

She served Herbie his tripe and planted a spicy stir-fry in front of me. Royal Umbrella rice. The real stuff with the DNA certificate right there on the sack. The tastiest rice in the world according to Margot. I cracked a beer and we touched bottles.

'The contract signed?' I said.

Margot sat back and sipped. Looked at me.

'So you *were* paying attention last Friday.'

'Detail is everything to a detective.'

She grinned.

'It's signed. Fifty-two weekly panels for the Sunday edition. Bias towards the left according to the small writing.' She grinned wider.

'Sure I'll bias that way. Until the left wing harlots cross the line. Then it's going to be down to subjective opinion. I made that clear: no one gets a pass.'

'Just stay focused on politicians. Leave the rest of us alone.'

'No can do. There's no corner of life isn't mired in sleaze. You know better than any.'

I did. But I was wondering what might come out when my own profession took the spotlight in her corner-less world. With Margot I always had a half sense of being under a magnifying glass. I kept that to myself. Tucked in to eat. The stir-fry was heavenly. Herbie had wolfed his treats and now regretted it. That's dogs for you. He sat watching the two of us with an envious grin.

'Chillies aren't good for you,' I told him.

He growled. Licked his chops. Widened his grin.

Margot was still focused on me.

'So what's new in the investigation world? What's kept you away all week?'

There you go. The magnifying glass.

'I'm looking for a missing boy,' I said. I explained the job.

'That's sad,' she concluded. 'So many go missing. Cut ties and the families never know why.'

'This family has admitted to a certain friction. The boy's father was a tyrant. Pushing the kid into a degree course that didn't interest him. But if the boy had mutinied a little earlier maybe there'd have been a better outcome.'

'I bet his father regretted it when he realised he was dying and his son nowhere to be found.'

'Not for me to speculate. Right now I'm concerned only about the boy.'

'What do you think's happened to him?'

'Anything. Or nothing. Maybe he's just holed up somewhere enjoying the life *he* wants.'

'But why would he not use his bank account or his phone?'

'That's the puzzle. Though if he was set on disappearing off the grid then he might ditch those things. Work cash in hand for a year or two, phone off.'

'If he's off the grid how long will it take you to find him?'

'Hard to say. The next person we speak to might take us straight there or the trail might run dry, leaving us scratching.'

'Two years is a long way behind.'

I didn't disagree.

'What about the other job?'

That snapped me back. Seemed I'd talked a little too much last week over that Thai beer. Sensed the magnifying glass of the radical cartoonist hovering. If you wanted to satirise the P.I. business you didn't need to look much further than casket-bugging activities.

'That job's ongoing,' I said. 'We've got the sound and vision in.'

She gave me incredulous. Maybe she didn't think we'd go through with it. I guess Margot was learning all the time.

'The coffin's wired,' I summarised.

That's when she threw her back head and laughed. When she got it out of her system she shook her head.

'I really thought you were shining me on last week,' she said.

'No shine. Just a job.'

'So what happens next?'

'We wait for the audio to trigger and transmit out. When we get the voice from beyond we go in.'

'Poor old guy. Bugged in his grave. Is it actually legal?'

'The guy's solicitor's on board so I guess that makes it legal. I can't speak for any higher authorities.'

She was chuckling still, shaking her head. I looked at her.

'The thing's in a good cause, remember?'

The head shake continued.

'There can't be any cause makes it worthwhile putting wires on a dead guy. A moment's sanity would tell you that.'

'Sanity isn't part of our remit. That's up to the client.'

'The guy's lawyer really went along with it?'

'It was his call. If the dead guy has complaints he'll go through him.'

I finished my prawns bar a couple that dropped to the floor. Herbie smacked his lips. I smacked mine and sat back.

Margo was sitting back too. She looked good. Had a way of making any pose provocative. But right now the weight of rice had killed any inclination in that area.

'Let's have music.' I said.

'Check it out.'

Margot was a jazz freak. The one thing we had in common. The checking was easy. I walked over and pulled out Mason's *Hot Five* to ease us into the weekend.

When I turned back Margot had migrated to the couch and shed

her outer layers.
  I went over.
  The night chilled.

CHAPTER SIX
Legally there's no issue

My digestion, and what came later, took longer to recover from than anticipated. It was near eight a.m. when I tripped out of Margot's and drove out into the rush hour traffic. The sign was already "Open" when we got to Chase Street and the sound of industry came from inside. We went in. The sounds amplified into the cough of the coffee machine and Lucy arguing with the utilities people. I heard her demand that someone in authority talk to her. Then she held the phone away like it had gone dead. Herbie and I waited at the refreshments table.

'Can you believe it?' Lucy said. 'The line went, right in the middle of the call.'

It was a problem we'd been having.

'Pay them,' I said.

'We've a direct debit. We're up to date.'

'Then sue them. Better still, let downstairs sue them. It's their line too.'

Though I wasn't so sure. We shared the line in but I suspected it was just our number dropping out.

Lucy got busy with the drinks and I went through to my room. Lifted the sash to let in the West London air. When I went back out Harry was handing a memory stick to Lucy.

'The hard drive,' he told me. 'Lucy's gonna sift through it, though it looks mostly like course work and academic papers. There's no email password so we're locked out of that.'

Access to email would have been good. It might have put us in touch with people who knew Chas. Might even have shown that he was still *writing* emails. People leave their passwords on their computers all the time. Seemed Chas Abbott wasn't one of them.

'Look for anything that might give a pointer to the kid's plans,' I told Lucy. 'Interests, places he's researched, any names.'

'I'm on it,' said Lucy. She handed down a biscuit. Herbie snarfled it then looked surprised by its disappearance. I spooned sugar and creamer into my mug and sipped. The cobwebs cleared. I gave Lucy another name.

Ralph. IT grad. Running a goth business. Lived up in Belsize Park.

Lucy looked at me. Waited.

I shrugged. That was it. Just how many Ralphs could there be? And not all of them would be running goth businesses.

I told Herbie to sit tight and gave Harry the nod.

We headed out.

We had a nine-thirty meeting down in Wandsworth. Took the Audi to save Harry's back and cruised the morning rush in retro style. I wore my shades with the window down and got looks. Eighty-five quattros are a rare sight. And you don't get more street-mean than Shaughnessy's specimen growling past cabs and buses, jet black with the Audi rings on the doors and a windscreen tint that would get Shaughnessy busted if cops didn't have a soft spot for vintage.

Traffic was heavy but you can't hurry style. Harry feigned nonchalance but worked the pedals at each standstill and got noises to turn heads. I kept my elbow out and looked cool. Regular gangsta. Not that the drugs fraternity went for vintage. Merc S Class and Range Rovers Sports are more their thing unless they're undercover. Then it's Polos and Fiats.

We hit Wandsworth and drove in under the Town Hall buildings. Left the car in a visitors' spot at the back. I unhooked the shades and we went in and up to the same meeting room as last time, where the same three people were waiting.

Basir Jamali was the senior Trading Standards guy. He stood to shake hands and offered us seats right beside him. He was the high-up overseeing the shenanigans, which explained his worry lines. Trading Standards tend to run their own investigations. Working with an outside agency is not their thing. For affairs of *this* world, at least. But when you went beyond you called in the P.I.s. Our actual case worker was Karen Foster, a bouncy woman in her mid-thirties sitting on the far side of the table. She leaned across with a bright smile to exchange handshakes. I returned the smile. No worry lines in her face. She just saw the ridiculous side of this. She'd go far.

The third person also had a smile but it was kind of wary. He saw this thing for what it was, which was marginally legal. He was a short, mid-sixties guy in a grey wool suit by the name of James Diamond.

He was too far away for the handshake but he nodded across in lieu, holding his tight smile. This was the sort of activity any sane lawyer would run a mile from but Jimmy was in as deep as the rest of us.

Jimmy Diamond. The late Tom Gallagher's solicitor.

Executor of his estate.

Diamond had picked up the job of disposing of Tom's assets in line with a last will and testament that was pretty simple in light of Tom's dearth of relatives. Confidentiality considerations prohibited Diamond from disclosing details but we understood that substantial sums were heading for various charities and local community initiatives. Jimmy and Tom had been business associates for decades and the two, Jimmy told me, had been friends of a kind. In the end, Jimmy had been Tom's only confidante.

It was unlikely that the business being discussed in this room had featured in Tom's plans for the afterlife, but the key thing, according to Jimmy, was that what we were up to didn't conflict with either his character or ethics. Nor with Jimmy Diamond's, who'd been the decision-maker when Trading Standards approached him. For Standards this was simple opportunism. The stars had aligned over Tom Gallagher's deathbed and Karen Foster had moved in to take advantage, courtesy of a professional link between herself and Diamond's firm. And right after Karen dialled Jimmy's number she'd called ours, courtesy of a social link with Lucy.

Basir sat forward and looked at me.

'We're go,' I said.

'The monitoring's in place?'

'Whatever happens in that casket, we're on it,' I said. I turned to Harry.

'The mike's transmitting fives,' he confirmed. 'And the camera's set to trip at the first action. The vids are flash storage. No transmit, as we mentioned. When the mike picks up something we'll need to go back in.'

Basir nodded. 'A pity about that,' he said. 'I'd have been more comfortable without the need to return.'

Harry grinned. 'Us too. But the other stuff in there: that would be more than you'd want to write off. So the lid was always coming back off.'

'You'll know immediately anything happens?'

'Right after,' Harry said. 'The audio receiver's out in our vehicle. I'm checking it two or three times a day. When something comes through we'll go straight back in for the videos.'

'How long have we got?' Basir looked at Diamond.

'Five days,' the lawyer said.

'And if we get nothing?' Basir turned back to me.

'We'll have to recover everything and cut our losses,' I said.

Basir worked his strained smile.

'Let's be optimistic,' he suggested. 'Harry will get his signal.'

Harry concurred. He was the only one without nerves. A bugging job's a bugging job. 'With the bait you've got in there,' he opined, 'we'll get a bite. There's no reason the thing won't work.'

Basir smiled at him.

'Sod's law,' he said. 'That's one reason.'

Harry shrugged. He couldn't argue with that. Sod's law works right alongside us in most jobs. And Tom Gallagher was in the hands of forces beyond ours. I grinned across at Karen. Stayed positive.

'We'll be back in and out before you know it,' I told her.

But her own smile had gone.

CHAPTER SEVEN
Scary people, man

Back at Chase Street Lucy was packing to head off to her afternoon gig in Bethnal Green. She checked her watch and decided there was time for a quick bite, meaning she was desperate for the update on our assignment in the beyond. I turned the sign we went down and grabbed a table in the sun outside Connie's.

Connie's wife Anastasia came out to serve us personally. I raised my eyebrows.

'You not cooking today, Annie?'

'It's my day off, sweetheart.'

I picked up my cue from her broad smile.

'It's your day off from kitchen duties so you're out front serving?'

'Only you Eddie. I'll take your order right in since you're our special customer.'

My own smile wavered. Was Annie after money?

She looked harmless and she seemed in good humour but I always imagined those Elizabethan executioners had a grin behind their masks as they dropped the axe.

And my suspicions deepened. Annie exchanged a look with Lucy.

'Eddie represents all my hopes and dreams,' she confided.

Lucy planted her hand over her mouth. Looked shocked.

The shock was uncalled for. Certain women *are* attracted to me. Or would be if they weren't married with a husband who'd just thrown us a wave from the counter. I waited for clarification.

Annie planted her hand on Lucy's shoulder. Stooped to confide.

'Constantine tells me that as soon as Eddie clear his arrears he's taking me on a cruise. First class. Round the world. It's something I've dreamed of since I was a little *paidí*. And get this, dear: he says he'll give me diamonds if Eddie clears the whole tab.'

Lucy choked.

I held my grin.

'Everyone should have dreams,' I said.

Anastasia had been runner up in the Miss Greece competition a decade and a half ago as she completed her chef's training and

Connie, twenty years older, no great looker and without a pot to piss in had pulled off the romancing stunt of the century when he persuaded her not only to marry him but to finance his culinary investment in London.

The rest was history. And the great thing about Annie was that she had a heart of gold and would sooner spin a story about a world cruise than offend me. Though I threw a worried glance Connie's way. I'd cleared the firm's tab barely a year back in a fit of exuberance following the conclusion of a celebrity case. If it had built back to *world cruise* levels so soon that was worrying. Maybe we'd have to cut back on the deli lunches. I made a note to review the situation in a couple of months when the weather broke.

Our drinks came out. Lucy sipped diet Coke and pulled a sheet of paper from her bag.

'I'm still not through the hard drive,' she said, 'but I've probably got everything there is. Which is just five names that might be linked to Exeter. I'll get onto them tomorrow if I can dig out contact details but I'm thinking they'll be long shots. But here's your Ralph guy.'

I sipped water, read an address in Belsize Park.

'I found stuff on social media and LinkedIn that sounded like him – he runs a business under Camden arches called Planet Goth. Social media hinted at a Belsize Park home so I checked Directory Enquiries and got a number and address. No reply on his landline. Probably at work.'

'Good work, Luce. I'll talk to him.'

I asked about the other name: Carol, the graphic designer living on a boat on the Regent's Canal two years ago.

'Nothing yet,' Lucy said. 'There's a million graphic design businesses round here and none of them may be hers. Or she may be an employee. Might not be in the directories. And I can't get a telephone number without a second name. Do houseboats have telephones?'

'Beats me. Though my bet would be that she uses modern technology.'

'I'll continue tomorrow,' Lucy promised. 'Top priority.'

The food arrived. We sat back to let Connie's assistant plant the plates. When it came to bill time Connie would attend personally. I'd need to watch for movement, be ready to move.

Connie's face looked our way occasionally as he attended his paying customers. Choosing his moment.

But we knew the routine.

When he did come out from serving in the back twenty minutes later our table was empty. Anastasia's cruise would need to wait another month or two. Winter in the Bahamas sounded just the ticket. As we stepped smartish along the pavement I told Lucy I'd see her tomorrow and we split up.

~~~~~

Euston Road was all racket and fumes. I cancelled the din with my ANC buds and Terry St Clair's itinerant voice. The music was from a quieter time where thoughts had space to echo, squeeze out a few tears maybe. The only thing I had to counter the fumes was speed. I flicked the gears, floored the pedal, cut left and right and lanced towards Euston Square. Herbie sat rigid, jowls in the wind as speed limits blew. Traffic hurled past us going backwards. Herbie lifted his head and worked his jaws but nothing came through above St Clair's lyrics. For sixty seconds it felt like we were getting somewhere. Then we hit the underpass too fast to grab the exit lane. I held the wheel rigid and plunged into the black, came up into bright sunshine and a traffic choke in front of the station. I bit down on impatience. Crawled out and took the left to get us back on track to Camden where we parked on Primrose Hill. If anyone was on my tail back there they'd have a few speeding tickets to add to their collection.

Planet Goth was a garishly lit cavern under Camden arches, stretching away towards a distant scarlet glow that might have been the gates to Hades. We walked in between two seven-foot skeletal reapers, scythes poised for shoplifters. Fill your pockets here, pal, and prosecution will be the least of your problems. Beyond security, surround sound Eldritch ricocheted off the brickwork. We cruised Detonation Boulevard. A deep growl resonated below the beat. I looked down. Herbie. Teeth bared. The music or the people. Hard to say which.

'Easy,' I said.

The growl intensified. Eldritch sounded hesitant.

We hit a makeshift counter fronting a rail of black coats and parkas, a rack of Doc Martens. Further back, wooden tables were stacked high with skulls and cauldrons, crescents and candles. A half dozen customers browsed, dressed for the part. I stood amongst them like an albatross in a penguin colony until big woman in a black jacquard and lace dress cinched with chains and zips came over. She had black lips and hair that was a shade of white I couldn't quite place. The effect was scary. I grinned. Made a note to send Lucy here next time. They could scare each other. Herbie racked up the growl as the big girl leaned over but then her voice broke into a squeaky croon as she spotted the midget customer. She rooted behind the counter and handed down a dog treat and Herbie cut short his speech and took it. Crunched. Swallowed. Switched the anger back on.

Simple extortion. Herbie's savvy that way.

I tugged the lead.

'Easy,' I said. I suspected I'd already said that but I keep communications simple. I got back to smiling at Morticia. When her black lips parted she was pleasant looking behind the impasto makeup.

'Is Ralph around?' I said.

Shouted.

Eldritch was progressing down the Boulevard, courage regained. The Sisters' beat was cracking bricks.

'He's out. Back in ten minutes.'

Ten minutes. I considered browsing. But absent my ANC buds ten minutes wasn't survivable.

'I'll call back...'

'Yeah, mate. Wassa name?'

'Flynn. I'm a private investigator.'

I was still shouting but Morticia's voice kind of carried. And either her hearing was sharp or she'd got good at lip-reading because when the P.I. bit registered her face straightened. Her mouth became a black slash.

'Whadda ya want? Ralph doesn't need trouble.'

'No trouble. It's a personal matter. I'm looking for a friend of his.'

'The friend's in trouble?'

'He's missing. I'm hoping Ralph can help me find him.'

'Whassa name?'

'Tell him I'm looking for Chas.'

Morticia's face changed. Her eyes pinned me. Her black lips made an "O".

'Chas?'

She knew the name. Maybe Chas was a regular.

'He been in lately?' I was still yelling.

Morticia came round the counter and beckoned me out. We exited into the yard and turned a corner, got brickwork between us and the music. I repeated my question.

'No, he's not been round.'

'Do you have a name?'

'Janine. Ralph's me fella.'

'Got it. Why's Chas not been round?

'How would I know? He's not here.'

'Since when?'

She pulled out a fag and lit up. Gave it some thought.

'Coupla years. Whassamatter?'

'We don't know. But his family are looking for him.'

Janine took a drag. Blew clouds. Her eyes were on her shop, waiting for anyone to come out with more than they went in.

'That's bad. Has something happened to him?'

'Haven't a clue. Did you know Chas well?'

'So-so. Just a mate of Ralphie's. I met him a coupla times. He crashed at ours a coupla summers ago. We had a few chats. Then he took off.'

'That was July, two years back?'

'July and August. He stayed a month.'

Bingo! My timeline moved forward. He was with these people in Belsize Park after he left Bart. A month would take us to the end of August 2010, give or take. And a month with Janine and Ralph was ample time for them to pick up a sense of his plans.

'Any particular reason he came to stay?'

'He was just a mate. Passing through.'

'A month is quite a stay. What was he doing?'

'Working shifts at a Spar. Building cash for his travels.'

Which all sounded pretty similar to what he'd been doing when he crashed with Bart over in Southwark. But when he'd moved on he'd not hit the road like Bart thought. Instead he'd drifted down to

Belsize Park and stalled there. Maybe struggling to make that decision, cut himself adrift.

'Any reason he stayed so long with you?'

Janine took another drag. Shrugged. Her black lips were turned down. The recollection seemed to bring sadness to her eyes.

'No reason,' she said. 'He just kinda let things drift. He had a job and cash coming in. Didn't seem in a hurry.'

'Second thoughts?'

'Nah. All he talked about was hitting the road. See where it took him. He had all kinds of crazy ideas. But he wasn't in a hurry. Seemed almost lost. Full of urgency to do all these things but a bit slow on the first step. He had all these ideas but I think he was lost.'

Her eye caught someone coming out of the crowd. Her face brightened again and she held her fag down to clear a kiss from one of the biggest guys I've ever seen. Big in every direction, a mix of genetics and calorie intake. Leather pants and sleeveless jacket sprouting arms like draft-excluders. Tattooed pale skin. Up top a heavy brow and buzz cut, eyes that turned to me. He was wearing enough chains and ironmongery to scare Marley's Ghost.

Ralphie.

Janine introduced us. I repeated my story.

'Holy cow,' he said. 'How long you been looking?'

'Just getting started. But I'm two years behind. I was hoping you could give me a few pointers. Right now you're my last contact with your friend.'

'Shit,' Ralph said. He shook his massive head. Looked at Janine.

'Is Chas a good friend of yours?' I said.

'Yeah. We met two or three years before. He crashed with me a few times outside term time, worked here on and off. You saying there's a problem?'

'It's possible.'

'Shit,' Ralph repeated. 'Poor old Chazza.'

'Anything you can give me would be appreciated.'

Ralph thought about it. Shook his head. Nothing.

'Was he okay? Any problems?'

The same thing I'd asked Bart. Same answer. No alcohol or drug abuse. No emotional issues. Nothing that caught Ralph's attention.

'What were his immediate plans once he left Town?'

Ralph shook his head again. Still nothing. Chas had left them with only vague stories of travelling the highways and byways, seeing Scotland and the north, trying his hand at farming and environmental technology, wildlife and wardening. Just a guy smothered by choices who couldn't figure which way to go.

'He bought a new rucksack and camping stuff,' Ralph said. 'Then he was off.'

'Any friends he might have visited?'

'He mentioned a girl called Carol,' Janine said.

This was the old friend from Alton. Living on a houseboat on the Regent's Canal. The same details I'd already picked up. Then Janine pulled up a memory.

'The boat's name was the *Lucky Lay,'* she said.

'Where Chas and Carol just friends?'

'Yeah. Nothing romantic,' Ralph said.

'Got it. So he left late August and that was it?'

'He sent a message a few days later,' Ralph said. 'A pic.'

'To your phone?'

'Yeah.'

'Mind if I take a look?'

Ralph pulled out his phone and brought up a picture and a short, message: "On my way. This is Riley and Sam"

The picture was a selfie of Chas goofing around with two companions on a bench by a seafront somewhere. Riley and Sam were a couple, from the way they were leaning in towards each other. Boy and girl. Early twenties. The girl wore a tee-shirt with a logo crossed by the words "Paris Match". The bottom corner of the picture caught the shaft of the monopod pole Chas had used to get the snap without badgering a passer-by.

'You know where this is?'

'No. He didn't say. I didn't ask. Just somewhere up the coast I guess.'

I looked again. There was a sliver of sea to the right but the rest could have been anywhere. Some kind of scrubby garden area stretching away behind the kids and on the landward side of that a line of tall residential buildings, red brick and white stucco. Nothing to raise the place out of anonymity. But we'd work it.

I asked for a copy. Handed Ralph a card with my number.

Then Janine recalled something. She flicked her cigarette down and trod it absentmindedly into the pavement.

'There was that funny thing,' she said. She looked at Ralph. He looked back at her and picked up on it.

'Yeah,' he said. 'That was weird.'

I waited. Funny things and weirdities. The stepping stones guiding the P.I.s feet.

'Tell me,' I said.

'It was just before he left. Chas was out on a late shift and a couple of geezers showed up at the house.'

'Geezers?'

'People. Tough guys. They had questions.'

'About Chas?'

'Nah. They were looking for someone called Alfie. I told them I didn't know no Alfie. But the geezers just pushed right in and looked like they were ready to kick off. Make an issue of it.'

'And *did* they make an issue?'

'No. They took a look around the place and asked if I was telling porkies and asked who was the other guy with Alfie. But I didn't know no Alfie.'

'So they were looking for two guys?'

Ralph shrugged. 'Dunno. Alfie was the only name they gave me. I was shittin' myself, truth be told. These looked like serious people, man. But I didn't know nothing. Told them they were mistaken and said to get the hell outta my door, and they just walked away. But they were scary people, man.'

Coming from the man-mountain in front of me the statement put the mystery guys way up on the scary scale. The level usually held by criminal types. This was something out of the blue. And it was hard to see how it was anything to do with Chas. But when strangers barge into your home without asking, that's a little unusual. And when they barge in at a time and place that puts them right on the trail I'm following then I'm not going to ignore it.

'What did they look like?'

'They were white guys. Muscled. One o' them was six foot plus and mean. Long messy hair.

'And you don't know anyone called Alfie?'

'No. These guys came to the wrong door.'

'Ralphie threw them out,' Janine said, 'but they said they'd be back. I was shitting myself for months. But they never did show up.'

Ralph shrugged. 'I'd have forgotten about them if Janine hadn't mentioned it.'

'Did you mention them to Chas?'

'Yeah. He didn't know anything. Didn't know no Alfie.'

'Think he was telling the truth?'

Ralph looked at me. 'Why would he lie, man?'

'And this was just before he left?'

'Day before. He already had his travelling gear ready and he decided to split next day. Couldn't face another shift at the Spar. Decided it was time.'

Interesting. Maybe the tough guys' visit was a coincidence, an error, but maybe not. But if the guys *were* looking for Chas it would be a puzzle. Everything I'd heard said that Chas was just an ordinary kid, up to nothing and into nothing. It was hard to imagine anyone who'd be less likely to show up on the radars of dodgy types. Maybe his friend Alfie was the one with the questionable background. But could that have brought some kind of a threat Chas' way?

I filed the thing away in my drawer called "Thought So" to be opened after the event. Thanked Ralph and Janine. Tugged the lead and walked back across the bridge.

I gave Herbie a turn on Primrose Hill and forwarded Ralph's seaside pic to Lucy. Then we drove on up to Belsize Park and located the Spar where Chas had worked his shifts. Two years is a long time to remember an itinerant employee. I'd learned that lesson yesterday. And after talking to the Spar duty manager I realised that two days would be a long time. Staff came and went continually. Typical employment duration three to four weeks. The guy told me to get serious. I showed him Chas' picture. He looked at it then told me again, louder. I grinned. Snapped the photo away and drove back into the city. Passed a Barclays branch as I turned towards Euston. The cash machine in its wall was Chas' last electronic location. He'd withdrawn cash that August. Probably purchased his rucksack and camping gear then replenished his wallet with his Spar earnings. Then he'd quit, sent a final selfie to Ralph and Janine and was gone.

When I got my eyes back on the traffic I saw that my other oddity was back. I had a tail again. The red Audi was with me, holding a hundred yards back. Then as I turned in towards Paddington a black BMW pulled onto the road behind me and took over. When you're looking for these things, handovers are easy to spot. Looked like there were three, maybe four, vehicles on me.

I'd have put the tail down as a police operation but the class of vehicles was a little high. Cops drive ordinary cars. No bright colours or add-ons. And they have a crew of two in each. The BMW and Audi were personal vehicles and solo drivers.

I turned over our current caseload again and still found nothing that would interest an outside agency. So who the hell were these guys? A connection to my search for Chas Abbott wasn't credible. Not only was a missing boy of no interest to anyone but I'd only been on the job a couple of hours when I first spotted the Audi, and there's no way a tail could have been put together in that time. But whatever their business, following me round as I searched for Chas Abbott was going to be costly. This was a professional tail with professional costs. Someone would be haemorrhaging cash as we followed that long and winding trail.

A couple of minutes later the BMW figured out my destination and dropped back. No point fighting for a parking space on Chase Street. They'd pick me up when I drove out.

I mulled over the two oddities: the mysterious tail and the mysterious callers who'd turned up at Ralph's door two years back just before Chas took his walk into the blue.

Maybe they were not connected to him.

No reason for them to be.

They didn't fit.

But the oddities had sprouted as soon as I started looking for the boy.

So either I was imagining things or my simple missing person job had complications I didn't know about.

CHAPTER EIGHT
Weird guy

The sunshine slanting through Margot's Veluxes woke me at seven. I lay for a moment listening to her breathing over the background snore from across the room. Considered taking an hour. It was Saturday. Hell, why not. Margot's soft warmth was a temptation hard to walk away from. Then Herbie's snoring ceased. My silence had disturbed him. I sensed eyes watching. Then the patter of claws. I was up and out of the bed in the half second I had before he launched himself.

'Okay,' I said, 'let's go. Just keep it quiet.'

Herbie changed direction, skidded and scratched on the floorboards and sideswiped the bed, ran his morning growl by me. The growl crescendoed and rattled the Velux and I grabbed the door to get him out onto carpet. Margot stirred behind me.

'Up so soon, Eddie?'

Disappointment purposely emphatic in her voice.

I grinned stoically and said I'd be back in forty-five. Went to grab my running gear. Fitness is important just like an hour snuggled with Margot is important. The decider is a dog. Something was off kilter there.

Margot's place was next to the Olympic Park but only the athletes were allowed in so we made do with Mabley Green which didn't quite match my Battersea circuit but was fine for the job. I covered five miles of sprint-jog with Herbie tagging along as if the thing was nothing. It was not nothing. Summer had drifted back in and I sweated cobs beneath unbroken blue sky, drops stinging my eyes. Beyond my blurred vision early morning walkers enjoyed the park's tranquillity, good humour on their faces as Herbie worked his act, nipping my ankles periodically to relive boredom.

When we got back Margot had breakfast on the table. She had her own fitness routine that was a little tougher then mine, wasn't the jog-buddy type. She exercised alone and hard, ran ten fast miles every day and attacked her multi gym like it was a demolition challenge, working off her many and varied frustrations as she ground out ideas for her strip cartoons. If you read the strips you knew that all that political venom had been worked up in some kind of furnace of rage.

She'd a heavy day's work lined up so I was on off the hook, which was good. I was restless to keep moving on the Abbott boy. Would have been lousy company. Itchy feet: the P.I.'s affliction. The need to sustain momentum, peer round the next corner, snap at the heels of your quarry. But today's itch was different, because no route to the boy had yet emerged from the mist. The tenuous leads I was following might peter out and leave me with nothing. All I had was a couple of names and a maybe location from two years ago. And if the boy's habit of packing his bag and walking out into the unknown persisted then somewhere up ahead, maybe just two or three names on, I might be looking at a blank.

I was itchy to know that that wasn't going to happen.

And added to the mix was the oddity of people crossing the trail who shouldn't have been there. The duo who'd turned up at Chas' last known address, even if they were asking for someone else. The vehicles following me round which I was linking to Chas even if no one could have known I was looking for him when they appeared two days ago. They'd come into the picture at a funny point and there was nothing else I could think of to explain their interest in me.

Itchy feet.

'What's your plan?' Margot interrupted.

'I want to find the girl friend. If she's living on a houseboat called *Lucky Lay* how hard can that be?'

'There's a lot of miles of waterway running through this town,' Margot pointed out.

'I'm going with my source. The boat's on the Regent's Canal.'

'That's still a lot of water. So if you don't get your *Lucky Lay* just come right back here,' she said.

I grinned. Finished my coffee.

I'd be back either way. The only difference might be my mood. But Margot would handle that. She had ways all her own. So even if I got lucky with my search I might have to pretend that things had gone to shit just to see what she could come up with.

~~~~~

Herbie moves fast but not in straight lines. I left him with Margot and headed across to Camden to start my search for Carol. Known address two years ago a houseboat on the Regent's Canal. The canal is shortish – a little under ten miles – but I was looking at a full day's hike, and if the boat was moored further out, beyond Paddington or down past Limehouse, I'd need a chopper.

I drove sedately in the early traffic, watching my rear-view. Spotted the red Audi moving into position five or six cars back. My tail was still with me. Which meant they'd been sitting outside Margot's waiting for me and that fact annoyed me. As someone who spends his life with his eye to the magnifying glass it's not uncommon to find myself squinting from the wrong side but what I had with Margot was new and fragile and special. And the thought that it was all just part of a fishbowl of interest to some unknown party threatened to sully things.

What the hell they were up to I couldn't imagine but whoever was doing the watching was spending big money. I countered annoyance by looking at the positive side: if my search for the boy hit a dead end then the party watching – assuming they *were* linked to this job – might be my way on. If they were still watching when I hit the dead end I'd be turning the glass.

But right now I didn't need these people.

I pulled into a tight spot at the bottom of Primrose Hill where the kerbs were lined bumper-to-bumper and the Audi would have its work cut out to find a place. I hopped out and jogged across the road as it rolled up behind me. Left it to its futile quest. Dodged round the back streets at a snappy pace and crossed the bridge. Five minutes later I was amongst the crowds at Camden Lock and my tail was history. The Audi guy could clock his hours watching the Frogeye.

On the canal bridge I flipped a mental coin and hopped down the steps to the towpath east.

The path was busy with walkers and cyclists, tourists following leaflet routes. I dodged them, moved fast, wondering how many boats there might be on this stretch of water. Two minutes later I hit the Kentish Town bridge, came out into a buzz of chatter and music and had a number: zero. Not a damn mooring in sight. I pressed on through the locks, wondering whether I'd chosen the wrong direction. Resisted the urge to turn back and walk west. Sensed madness in that tactic. Better to stick with it, though if I got nothing by Limehouse it would be a long slog back.

I finally hit moorings on the far side of St Pancras Way, and beyond the station the first basin opened up. I hopped up to street level to cross the canal and check out the vessels. Mooring technique was to plant the boats side by side and the only way to clock their names was to get close up, ask questions about any vessels with no visible names. On the plus side the summer weather had brought people onto the decks and questions were easily answered. Though the one that mattered drew a blank all round. No one knew the *Lucky Lay*.

I climbed between street and canal, navigated mazes, repeated my questions, got the same answer.

The canal crossed the King's Cross lines and came out under York Way. Ahead was a solid line of moored boats alongside the towpath and a basin on the far side jammed with brightly painted vessels below a vista of New Century office blocks and multi-million pound apartments. I covered the towpath vessels first and got nothing. Retraced my steps to cross the bridge and follow the streets round to the basin.

Which played coy. Street access wasn't the thing.

I searched ginnels and crevices for access between the buildings and got nothing. Wondered whether I'd have to swim across from the far side. Then I spotted a keypad-guarded gate between two buildings that had to lead somewhere. I waited for opportunity. It came ten minutes later when a woman came out towing a pair of Pomeranians. I moved fast, held the gate for her and went in. Rounded the corner and came out onto a private wharf with narrowboats packed like sardines. Decks alive with tenants enjoying the sun. I walked down and checked names, asked about the *Lucky Lay*. Finally got lucky. A weather-beaten guy up on the wharf in a canvas chair waved me towards the canal end.

I walked down and spotted the name on the second last boat moored end-on.

Lucky Lay.

I'd been trekking for two hours and it felt like ten but fact is I was lucky. I'd not seen a hundredth of the vessels moored along the waterway. I could have been hiking all week without a result.

The *Lucky Lay* was a seventy-foot widebeam with a cabin decorated in a burst of green, white and gold and a spectacular multicoloured bow bedecked in planters. The front doors were open and a thirtyish woman in dark crew pants and headscarf had a table set out at which she was scraping and rubbing at some kind of old lamp. Antique restoration. I stopped to watch. When she registered me she gave me a polite smile. I guess she got audiences. I asked if she was Carol.

She wasn't. She turned and called into the cabin and a younger woman appeared. Blonde, broad boyish face with freckles. Denim shorts and tank top displaying the tanned skin of the outdoor lifestyle. I grinned and said "hi".

She smiled back, waiting to see what I wanted.

I told her I was looking for Chas and the smile turned puzzled.

She said she didn't know where he was. Threw me a look that asked who the hell I was.

I held my own grin.

'Damn,' I said.

She angled her head. Still waiting.

I explained who I was. Reached a card out to her. Carol stepped forward and read it then handed it to her companion. The other woman raised her eyebrows.

'A real P.I.! Holy shit.' She looked at me. 'Are we being investigated?'

Her eyes had a look. If I wasn't thick skinned I'd have sensed mockery in lieu of the respect – or plain hostility – you see in the old movies. Maybe I needed a gun and a hat.

'Don't worry lady,' I said. 'I'm not here for trouble.'

I've seen all those movies.

The woman smiled sweetly, hamming right back. I guess they didn't get many P.I.s on the Regent's Canal.

'Thank god for that,' she said. 'A girl's gonna worry when a tough guy comes snooping.'

Carol didn't join in the play acting.

'Why do you want to see Chas?' she said.

'I'm working for his family. They're looking for him.'

She watched me, searching for meaning.

'Why's that?'

I shrugged. The answer was obvious, I guess.

'Has something happened?' she said.

'That's what I'm trying to find out. I heard you and he were friends. Thought you might help.'

Carol thought about it a little more and decided I was legit, or at least that she needed to know more about what I was up to. She told me to come on board and I hopped on and squeezed past her friend into the cabin. The friend followed. We were in a kitchenette opening onto a bright, spacious living area with fitted units and wide sofas that presented the comfortable opulence you usually only get on dry land. Doors at the far end looked like they gave onto decent bath- and bedrooms. The advantage of a thirteen foot beam. The boat was a nice place to live. Luxury at a discount price.

Carol pushed her curiosity aside for a moment to offer me a beer and I said that would be nice. Walking the canal had been kind of hot. She cracked two cans, offered me one. The beer was cool. I took a swig whilst Carol perched herself on a stool at the breakfast bar and introduced her friend as Angela. Angela leaned back against the wall, watching me with a twinkle in her eyes.

Carol's eyes weren't twinkling. She retrieved my card from Angela and gave it a little more attention.

I explained about Chas' two-year absence. His family's concerns. Then asked about her friendship with him.

'We go back,' she told me. 'Alton. His school was next to mine and we kinda hung out. Stayed friends after we both split the place. When Angie bought this boat I moved in with her and Chas came up for odd weekends.'

'Cool guy,' said Angela. 'I like him.'

'Have you seen him since university?'

'Couple of times after graduation,' Carol said. 'He dropped in overnight one time, stayed two or three days another. He liked living on the water. He loved the idea of the bohemian lifestyle right here in the city.'

'Bohemian lifestyle sans bohemian prices,' Angela clarified. 'Chas wasn't going to be living anywhere like this until he'd made his stash.'

Angela was speaking like she'd made her stash. I guess restoring brassware was lucrative. She picked up on my thoughts.

'Think about it,' she said. 'The same cash gets you a one-room basement apartment or a beautiful canal boat. So who wants to live in a cellar?'

'Location and lifestyle at a discount,' I said.

Carol shook her head. Flapped her hand in a dismissive gesture.

'The discount's gone. The price of boats is still favourable but mooring fees have gone crazy. Everyone wants to move onto the water and the boats are becoming second and third leisure homes, somewhere to sink spare cash. So mooring charges are going through the roof.'

Angela concurred.

'We won't be here in five years,' she said. 'We'll be bohemian for sure.'

'Best option,' Carol said, 'is we sell up and find a smaller boat, way out of Town.'

'Yeah,' Angela said. 'Way out in the sticks. Chas would approve of that.'

'So what's happened to Chas?' Carol said. 'You're scaring us.'

'His family too. So I'm following his trail. See where it leads. I've got him here in Town until August two years back, kicking his heels and packing his bags. Then nothing.'

'Then you know as much as we. We've had no contact. I assumed he was off the grid for a while. Why are his family suddenly looking.'

'I guess two years is a long time. And his father died six months ago. They think he should know about it.'

Carol looked sombre but something firmer was in Angela's eyes. She pushed herself off the wall. Kicked around the kitchenette.

'I don't know if Chas would care so much. He didn't have much time for the old guy.'

'So I heard. But I guess he'd want to know that he'd died.'

'Maybe,' Angela said.

The boat rocked. People coming aboard next door. A few shouts and yells. Kids voices. Weekenders. I looked at Carol.

'The story I heard,' I told her, 'is that Chas was high and dry with a degree he had no use for and pressure to conform, get a nine-to-five. But my feeling is he'd be over that by now. Would have contacted his family. I'm told he'd given no hint that he planned to disappear permanently.'

'To us neither,' Carol said. 'We expected to see him.'

'How was he, the last time you saw him?' I asked.

'Just chilling. Taking time to figure things out. He was sure something would come up.'

'Was he specific on any plans?'

'He was going to hit the road. That's all he knew.'

'No worries? Problems?'

Angela quit drifting and joined Carol at the breakfast bar.

'He seemed okay,' she said. 'Lots of ideas but cool. Waiting to see which way the wind blew. He didn't mention problems.'

Carol concurred.

'Chas didn't have debts or enemies or issues. He enjoyed a spliff or two in college days, and here if Angie was feeling generous. Liked few beers. But he'd no addictions. Nothing to take him down a wrong path.'

'He mention other friends? Places?'

Carol pushed her beer around.

'Only friends around Town. And no particular destination. Just the idea of travelling.'

'How about Scotland?'

'Yeah, now I recall. He had a friend up there. But he mentioned most places. He wanted to see the whole country, wait for things to come together.'

'Do you have the names of any friends here in Town?'

'He mentioned a couple,' Carol said, 'but I don't recall. Just first names. They meant nothing to us.'

Probably the people I'd already spoken to.

'There *was* one guy,' Angela said. 'He brought him here once. We had a night in the Lion.'

Carol searched the sky beyond the open doors. Dug into her memory.

'The weird guy,' she said. 'Alfie.'

My ears pricked up.

Maybe this was the guy the people who'd barged into Ralph's place were looking for. So if Chas had told Ralph he didn't know anyone by that name he was lying. Which might make Chas the "other guy" who'd been seen with Alfie. Maybe connecting him to people you wouldn't want to mix with. I asked the two what they knew about

Alfie.

'He was just a friend,' Carol said. 'Chas didn't tell us much. He was with us that one night, drinking too much, getting too loud and we never saw him again.'

'No second name?'

'None.'

'You recall what he looked like?'

Angela went to grab her phone. Pulled up a snap she'd taken the night they'd been drinking together. In the picture Chas was standing with Carol out on the deck and beside him was a tall guy in his early twenties, all acne and black straggly hair. I asked for a copy and Angela sent it through.

Carol searched her memory. 'You couldn't have any kind of conversation with Alfie. He didn't make sense. Spent half the time coming on to me and Angie and half the time telling stupid stories about scrapes with the law. But when the conversation moved on to anything interesting he had no response.'

'The guy was not all there,' Angela agreed. 'What Chas saw in him I don't know.'

'Any idea where he lived? What he did?'

'He worked for a health equipment company in Streatham,' Carol said. 'Gym stuff.'

'Back room staff for sure,' Angela said. 'Alfie wasn't exactly a walking advertisement for health gear.'

'You know the company name?'

They thought some more.

'*Physical* or something,' Carol said.

'That a shop? Supplier? Club?'

'Alfie mentioned gym equipment sales but he never gave any detail and we didn't ask.'

'Got it. Anything else?'

They shook their heads.

I leaned back against a worktop and tipped the last of the beer down my throat. Complemented them on their place, stalling for a few seconds in case anything else surfaced. Nothing did so I planted the can and asked them to give me a call if they heard anything new.

Carol's face dropped again. Back to worrying about the boy.

I went back out into the heat and stepped up onto the wharf. The boat rocked a little as I made dry land. I turned to nod goodbye.

'Let us know when you find him,' Carol said.

I promised I'd do that. Walked back out.

CHAPTER NINE
That's confidential

I drove down to Streatham and parked on Tooting Common. Hiked up the avenue to the cafe and ate a sandwich whilst I worked my phone, searching for *Physical* under gym equipment suppliers or shops. Got nothing. If the business where Chas' friend claimed he worked actually existed I was going to have to find it the hard way.

I walked the mile into the centre and checked two small gyms I'd seen listed on the High Road. Neither knew of a supplies business called *Physical*. So it was going to be footwork. I started north towards Streatham Hill, walked the length of the street, scrutinising doorways as I dodged weekend traffic and shoppers in tee-shirts and shorts. If the *Physical* business was trade-only I might be looking for just a nameplate, no public presence. The street was mixed commerce and residential. Ground floor retail windows and apartments up top. Newer developments wedged in between. But no sign of the business I was looking for. I checked each side street but there was no commerce beyond the first fifty steps. By my twentieth street I sensed futility. If the business was based in Streatham at all it might be a couple of miles out, might take a week to find.

The afternoon was hot. I slung my jacket over my shoulder and moved steadily. Reached the station. Crossed against the lights and took a near hit from a bike doing double the traffic speed. The guy yelled profanities into his slipstream then a bus horn threatened far worse as I sprinted for the kerb. I waved them both away and headed up the intersection.

It was a busy road with traffic backed up from the lights. Low shack-style shop fronts ran up one side housing taxi firms and kebab takeaways, shoe repairs. The other side was more retail units beneath five and six floors of apartments. And thirty yards up the street I got a hit. Sometimes you get lucky like that. I was looking at a shop front across the road sandwiched between a charity shop and an off-licence.

Carol had heard *Physical*.

Which was almost right.

The name was *Fizikun* according to bold white lettering displayed on a flaking black fascia. Window decals announced the firm's business as *Fitness Equipment Specialists* and I could see the shapes of gym machines inside. The place was in need of a serious re-paint but I guess you could say that of half of Streatham. Certainly whoever owned the apartments up top was holding back on the cosmetics budget. The woodwork was peeling all along the block, dropping paint flakes onto the pavement.

I stayed across the street and watched.

Hints of movement behind the window decals suggested that the business was operating but in twenty minutes the door didn't open once. We were fifty yards too far from the High Road for casual footfall. Maybe the place was trade only.

I gave it another ten, wondering if I was looking at nothing, then the shop door finally opened and discharged two men. Both wore black jeans and tee-shirts, wrap-around sunglasses. I couldn't say whether they glanced at me behind the lenses as they turned up the road but they didn't lock on. I was just a guy across the street waiting to cross. They were big, short haired, muscled. I watched them as they headed off down to the main road.

Ten minutes later I walked across and went in.

The shop was brighter and better equipped than you'd guess from outside. I made my way through a maze of physical fitness machinery and asked the guy standing behind the back counter if Alfie was around.

He looked at me a moment then shook his head. The barest of movements. Dismissive. Words unnecessary.

The guy was the same type as the pair who'd left, minus the shades. Same black jeans and tee-shirt, muscles, frizzy blond hair. The guy's broad face was shadowed by a prominent brow, and a swastika hung from his left lobe. I hadn't noticed whether the other two had earrings.

I tried to interpret the head shake. Perhaps Swastika didn't know Alfie or perhaps he *did* know him but Alfie wasn't around right now or maybe he just didn't give a damn about my question. Hard to say. I repeated my question. Shuffled words around to give the guy a different angle, but it added up to the same query. To which his answer was the same. But with vocals.

'Sorry mate.'

He gave me a shrug to emphasise his disinterest.

I grinned. Kept at it.

'Alfie does work here, right?'

The guy suddenly sensed potential nuisance. He drew himself up and folded his arms.

'No,' he said. 'He no work here.'

His Eastern European accent matched his faintly Slavic face. I couldn't say whether his face was just disinterested or outright hostile but his demeanour wasn't your typical sales person's.

'But he used to, right?'

'No.'

"No" is a short word but this guy shortened it to vanishing point, putting an emphatic full stop on the conversation. He threw in a black scowl to embellish his message, like he was seeing me as a time-waster as opposed to a pal of Alfie's who'd come in on the chance of a discount. A customer perhaps.

I gave him puzzled.

'*Alfie,*' I said. Emphatic myself. Like there was a misunderstanding.

He returned nothing. Shifted slightly on his feet.

'He definitely worked here,' I said with the P.I.'s confidence substituting hard facts. 'Might be a couple of years ago,' I conceded.

Which got me a lifted lip.

'You mistaken. No Alfie. Sorry.'

He finished with a cold smile conjured by the concept of me getting the hell out of his face.

But his assurances were a little too firm, too quick. He hadn't needed to tug at memory. He knew the instant I asked that he didn't know Alfie, like it was some kind of official line.

I turned to take a gander at the equipment and gain thinking time. The machine beside me was the size of a small building. Steel frames reached almost to the ceiling, wrapped in hoists and pads, pull-down bars, pulleys and screens. The thing looked like a medieval torture device. What doesn't kill you makes you stronger I guess, though this contraption looked like it might do the former. If I had a room the size of Shaughnessy's gym I'd put in something like this, even if only for show, though all Shaughnessy had in his gym was a twenty-foot floor mat and a punchbag, a few weights. I guess he'd never visited this place. The rest of the showroom was jammed with similar stuff but on a smaller scale. I stepped forward to tap the screen on the monster. My touch brought up something called *Power Megathon Workout* which looked like a routine that would see you through a hard couple of days before they carted you off. A nice bit of kit for just eight grand. When I turned back Swastika was still watching me but he wasn't bothering with the sales patter so I continued the gab.

'Nice shop,' I said. 'You the owner?'

'No,' Swastika said. 'He.'

He nodded at a guy who'd come out of the back. This one was big. Six-five at least, lean with natural muscle. His long face and sleepy eyes, prominent nose, suggested Italian or Eastern European, maybe matching the counter guy. He wore a stubble beard and straggly black hair that touched the shoulders of his summer jacket. Swastika's gaze caught his attention. He threw a question in a foreign language that wasn't Italian. Eastern European, I guess.

Then he stepped over.

'You look for who?'

Swastika repeated the information on my behalf while the long-haired guy stared into my face.

'Who's Alfie?' he said.

I stood back to avoid cricking my neck.

'Just a kid I know. He used to work here. Thought he might be good for a discount.'

Longhair pursed his lips and pushed out a "No".

I waited.

The guy's eyes were drilling right through me. Cold. Searching. Shielding something. 'I've no Alfie work for me. What your business?'

'I'm trying to catch up with him,' I said. 'This is the last place I heard he worked.'

'You heard wrong. Why you want find him?'

I grinned. The question was nonsensical since he didn't know Alfie. The guy was talking instead of thinking.

I repeated my assertion about catching up.

'Well,' Longhair said, 'sorry. There's no Alfie. So...'

He glanced over at the door to close the issue. I stayed put.

'Okay,' I said. 'I guess I picked up some wrong information.'

'Yes.'

'Got it.'

'So...' he rolled a hand now in a different invitation: 'Who are you, my friend? What your business?'

I held my grin as the nonsensical questions continued. It was getting harder by the second to believe that these people didn't know Alfie. And to avoid connecting this shop to the dodgy people who'd come looking for the boy at Ralph's place two years ago, one of whose description would fit the guy in front of me.

My turn to be coy. I repeated that it was nothing. Clearly just misinformation.

'No,' Longhair said. 'I need to know. Who the hell are you?'

His hand had stayed out, frozen in a slice through the air, the universal gesture of invitation, and we suddenly had a tension thick enough to cut.

I watered down my grin. Took half a step back.

'Considering you don't know Alfie,' I said, 'why does it matter who I am?'

'Because I say.'

His eyes drilled me from behind a frozen mask. Something had started to rattle the guy's cage and he was reacting from instinct instead of sense. Sense would have been to let this go and I'd have walked out none the wiser. But his instinct was to have questions answered. To know everything. When Swastika started moving round the counter I started to plot a way through the machinery with my peripheral vision. It would take a little agility but the door was well within reach.

But I held fast a few more seconds. Sometimes you go with the flow, and right now something was flowing that I couldn't quite explain. Maybe this was just a wild goose chase, a wasted Saturday afternoon, but any day now I could be facing a dead end in my search for Chas so if the boy was linked even indirectly to the people running this shop it had to be worth lighting a fuse. Maybe leave something smouldering that would blast apart that dead end.

The guy wanted to know who I was.

So.

I pulled out a card and handed it over.

Longhair scanned it and his eyes narrowed. When he looked at me again he had a dangerous smile on his lips.

'Private *investigator?*' he said. 'You bloody serious?'

Swastika was beside him now, standing legs akimbo, arms loose, waiting for the signal.

'That's my job,' I said.

'Is your job. Okaaaay. So who you working for? Who want Alfie?'

I shook my head.

'That's confidential,' I said.

He thought about it and things teetered on the edge for a second or two. Then he shook his head.

'Okay,' he said. 'I just asking. We like to know who in an' out.' He gestured with his free hand. 'High value stock.'

'Got it. I'm not here to pinch your stock.'

'Of course.'

I brought up my grin again.

'And if you don't know Alfie then I'm on the wrong track.'

He took a moment again. Turned my card in his fingers. Nodded.

'I think so. Wrong track.'

'Then thanks for your time.'

Longhair nodded but didn't look like he was about to shift to let me get clear so I turned to find my way out through the machinery. No one stopped me.

I turned at the door. Longhair was watching me, still turning the card in his fingers.

'Actually,' I said, 'it's not Alfie I'm looking for. It's a friend of his. A kid called Chas Abbott. Do you know *that* name?'

Longhair kept quiet for a full five seconds.

'No,' he said finally. 'I can't help you. Sorry.'

I told him thanks and pulled open the door. Walked out.

~~~~~

Back at the main road the sun turned the traffic to silhouettes. I pulled out my shades and crossed and walked back towards the Common.

I turned things over. After that little scene the *Fizikun* people would be top priority if I was looking for Alfie and not Chas. Something more than the fitness business was going on at that shop.

Maybe Alfie had been involved in something dodgy there. Was Longhair the big guy who'd come searching for him two years ago?

Maybe. But the people visiting Ralph had only asked about Alfie, even if they were also interested in a guy seen with him. So whatever these people were up to, and whoever Alfie was, the significance for my search for Chas Abbott wasn't clear. Chas had stayed with his plan: left Town. That selfie snap had him well on his way somewhere out on the coast soon after the incident and with no Alfie in sight. And whatever the link between him and Alfie and the *Fizikun* business I doubted that I'd find Chas in Streatham.

I reached the Common and walked a circuitous route under the shade of trees back to the car. As I crossed Bedford Hill my phone rang.

Harry.

'We got contact from beyond,' he said.

He was calling from Balham where he'd just checked the Mondeo gadget for sign of transmissions from Tom Gallagher's casket. They talk about the eternal silence of the coffin but in Tom's case the quiet hadn't lasted. Seemed Harry's audio link had been triggered late yesterday, and unless Tom had a snoring problem something was going on.

'How'd it sound?'

'Like what we're looking for.'

'Okay. The vids?'

'Time to dig them out.'

I returned the smiles of two women pushing strollers as I thought of Burke and Hare. *They* were probably just regular guys *sans* spades. Good for a few stories down the pub. I bet the girls were all over them.

'We're locked out tomorrow,' I noted. 'Sounds like a Monday morning job.'

Harry laughed.

'This business,' he said. 'We got Monday mornings to beat any. My advice, Eddie: go in before lunch. You might be more comfortable.'

I killed the line.

Harry.

This business.

But he was right. Some Monday mornings are special.

Logic said that Tom Gallagher couldn't be much worse for wear after three days but logic also said that there might be special circumstances. As I continued across the Common it was hard to get the image of those feet out of my head.

Then my phone rang again.

'Luce!'

'I got it,' she said.

She was talking about the selfie Chas had sent his friend after he'd left London. Seemed Lucy had been putting in a little overtime as she kept shop at her uncle's music showroom.

'Where?'

'Lowestoft.'

The name was a surprise. The place didn't immediately come to mind when you thought of seaside resorts.

'They're on the prom. Right by the pier.'

'Got it,' I said. 'Good work, Luce.'

So Chas had travelled a little over a hundred miles in the couple of days since he'd left Ralph two years ago. His planned trip was well under way.

Lucy echoed my thoughts.

'We're on his heels,' she said, 'though two years is a long time.'

'Look at the positive. We're two days nearer to him than we were yesterday. At that pace we'll have caught up in a year.'

'To where he is right now. But by then he'll be another year ahead.'

Lucy.

Always the pragmatist.

'He can't be moving continuously,' I said. 'Every week or month he's stationary we'll be closing the gap, assuming the trail stays live.'

'Big assumption, Eddie.'

'We work on big assumptions.'

'Well let's hope this one pans out. You might reach the boy sooner than you think. Just a simple missing person case.'

I grinned as I came out from the trees. Didn't mention the simple situation I'd just stumbled onto in Streatham.

But with Chas confirmed a hundred miles away two years ago maybe the Streatham thing really was irrelevant.

Maybe I'd find out in Lowestoft. I'd something on with Margot tomorrow so it was going to be Monday before I got there. Then I remembered the Tom Gallagher job. We needed to go in for the videos Monday morning. That couldn't be postponed.

I thought it through and saw only one solution that allowed me to hit the road first thing. And one that had a certain attraction. Sometimes inspiration flowers under pressure of the moment.

'What time are you in Monday?' I asked.

'What time do you want me in?'

'Nice and early,' I said. 'I need cover on a job.'

'Okay. Any real detective stuff?'

I grinned. Reached the car.

'This is as real as it gets, Luce.'

'Wow, Eddie, count me in. Is it dangerous?'

I killed the line to cover my laugh. Hopped the door and pressed the button. The Frogeye coughed and roared and I drove out with a renewed eagerness for the week ahead.

CHAPTER TEN
Technically, we're not robbing anything

I followed the A12 out into Essex early Monday morning against the flow. Coordinated activities back in Paddington hands-free as I skirted Chelmsford. By Ipswich I was clear for the day, phone muted, watching my mirror for signs of company. Saw nothing.

I made Lowestoft by ten and drove round the wasteland north of the river searching without success for the seaside of Chas' picture. Found only the remnants of the fishing industry, dilapidated sheds, car dealers and ugly residential blocks sprouting from repurposed land. The residential balconies looked out over concrete onto the empty vista of the North Sea. A view to depress. All it needed was wind turbines. I was beginning to doubt Lucy's research when the road took me round and back across the bridge to a turning into the old seaside area. A promenade backed by car parks and mixed Edwardian and modern terraces. I hopped out and fed a machine and walked across straggly gardens onto the prom, pulling up Chas' snap on my phone. I reached the pier and turned to look back at the terraces. Saw that the view was right. And the bench in front of me was right. Two years ago Chas was sitting here with his two friends.

That was August 2010, Chas two days out of Town, a hundred miles along his journey into the unknown. No sign of his friend Alfie in the snap. The goings-on at a Streatham gym equipment shop were a million miles away. And probably unconnected.

Did Chas spend time in Lowestoft, maybe with his two friends? Earn a little more cash? There'd be seasonal work. Maybe someone would remember him.

I went to see.

It turned out that casual jobs were not so plentiful. This wasn't Brighton. The pier presented the only kiosk jobs on the seafront and I covered it in less than thirty minutes. No one recalled hiring or working with Chas two years back. The street behind the residential terrace delivered nothing more. A pale imitation of a seaside thoroughfare but with a sufficient number of cafes, pubs and chippies to demand three hours' footwork. When I came up blank I headed back over the bridge into the town proper and took a break at a tiny pizza place by the station. Showed Chas' picture in there and asked fruitless questions then ordered a Neapolitan and sat down to wait with that sense all P.I.s know: the threat of futility that can drag your feet. Chas had been sitting right there on the seafront bench two years ago but just by walking across the bridge I'd left behind any ethereal remnants of his presence, maybe walked away from any chance of picking up the thread. But the seafront hadn't pointed the way. Chas wasn't there.

The pizza was surprisingly good, washed down with a glass of fizzy water. Half way through my phone vibrated. I picked up.

'Luce! How's it going?'

'I think it's going as you planned, Eddie.'

I grinned. Planted my fork and sat back. The roar obscuring her words said she was out with Harry in the quattro.

'We're just on our way,' she said. 'We couldn't arrange it this morning.'

'Understandable,' I said. 'The dead can't be hurried.'

'Hold the quips, Eddie. I don't even work afternoons.'

'Emergency exception, Luce. You wanted to try your hand at the detective stuff.'

'Detective stuff like this I can do without.'

I grinned wider. Kept my voice steady.

'We take the good with the bad. There's no Sherlock Holmes stuff without the other side.'

'Sherlock Holmes never went grave robbing.'

That was true. But if necessity had pressed then assuredly Holmes would have been good for it, though I guess Watson would have done the digging.

'Technically,' I said, 'we're not robbing anything. It's our gear in there. Expensive gear. Ask Harry.'

'Harry already briefed me. He also told me there's other expensive gear that can transmit video right out. No need to go frisking the dead.'

'That's a good point. Put it on your list Luce. We'll take a look at the budget.'

'That doesn't help me right now, Eddie.'

'Guess not. But the job's not so bad, Luce. Two minutes tops. And it would have been me going in but for eventualities.'

'I know that, Eddie. And I wasn't going to watch.'

'Sure you would. Watch and learn. You can treat this as a learning experience. Field stuff.'

'I know what you do in the field, Eddie. That's why I stick to my desk job.'

'But you're always yearning for the action. You told me a million times.'

'Well I guess this is gonna be my cure. My desk looked pretty comfortable when I came out.'

'You'll handle things, Luce.'

'Sure, I will. And maybe I'll be on PTSD for the next twelve months.'

'PTSD's in our blood, Luce. You'll know you're a real detective when the dreams come.'

'Dreams?'

'The funny ones. I've had them for years. Never understood them.'

'That helps so much, Eddie.'

'Don't mention it. But I'm guessing you're calling me on something else.'

There was a short silence whilst she reset, waited for the roar to subside as the quattro leapt away from a stop. Lead-foot Harry!

'Yeah,' she confirmed. 'I've got something to help ease your own day.'

Harry's foot was still heavy on the pedal. I couldn't say whether there was an undertone in her voice. I waited.

'That girl's tee-shirt,' she said, 'with the name "Paris Match". I assumed it was the magazine but the logo isn't theirs. I checked it out and found that it's the name of a fashion boutique in King's Lynn. I don't see a small boutique selling their own brand so I think the tee's a special. Those two could be the owners.'

Attagirl! How many businesses have front desk staff who can not only pick corpses' pockets but are ready with the next lead when the detective is staring at a dead end?

If the couple in Chas' selfie were linked to a shop then they were reachable. Might tell me something about that day two years ago that would give me direction, save a week chasing shadows in Lowestoft.

'Luce,' I said, 'you're a miracle worker.'

'That's not true. Because if I was then you'd be back here and I'd be at my desk and not sitting in this car heading towards yuck.'

I grinned. Still on that thing.

'Luce,' I said, 'my life is a litany of regrets. But you're right: my afternoon will be eased by the knowledge that you've got things covered back there.'

Lucy replied just as Harry gassed the engine. Her words were drowned out. I killed the line and swigged water then picked up my fork. The Neapolitan tasted astonishingly good.

~~~~~

It took me two hours to drive to King's Lynn and locate the boutique on a commercial street just up from the river front. It was late afternoon when I pushed open its door and walked in.

The shop was as tiny inside as out. Just five or six rails of expensive fashion in limited sizes. A particular clientele: twenties, early thirties. The doorbell brought a young woman out from the back who had the face from Chas' photo.

She gave me the bright smile elicited by a lone guy walking in at the end of the working day. Here for his girlfriend's birthday present, whose size would be exactly known and whose taste would run to the expensive.

I smiled back and reached into my jacket to disillusion her. Held out my phone with Chas' Lowestoft selfie. Her own face on my screen.

Her reaction was surprise tinged with momentary pleasure before reality snapped in to ask what a stranger was doing with the picture. I rooted again and pulled out my card and explained.

When I finished her face had changed to dismay.

'A pal of Chas' gave me the pic,' I said. 'Along with a couple of names. I'm guessing you're Sam.'

'Samantha.'

'Would you happen to know where Chas is, Samantha? His family would like to find him.'

But the dismay stayed. Even if the Lowestoft meeting was just a brief hook up there's no downer like a private investigator showing up to ask about someone you once knew.

'We don't really know him,' Samantha said. 'It was just that week in Lowestoft.'

'How did you get together?'

'We were on holiday. Met Chas at a camp site. He was hitching. Touring the country. We kind of got on so we hung out.'

'In good spirits? Enjoying life?'

She thought about it and her fears deepened.

'I don't know. He was good company and had all these ideas that excited him but it was like they were a burden. All kinds of plans for the future but he didn't know which way he was going. I don't quite know whether he was okay.'

'Any immediate concerns? Anything on his mind?'

'Only his finances. He wasn't sure how far they'd stretch so he was stuck searching for casual work. A few days minimum wage only takes you so far.'

'Was he keen to move on? Stay on the road?'

'He didn't exactly say it but I think he was impatient to progress. As if his trip was all laid out and he just had to do the miles and he'd find whatever he was looking for. But I think he was kind of scared he'd complete the trip and still not find it.'

'Did he leave Lowestoft with you?'

'No. Our week was up three days after we met. We came home but Chas stayed on to work on a market stall job in Lowestoft.'

'Did you see him again?'

'Yes. The job fell through two weeks later and he came on up the coast. Called in here. Riley had invited him if he was ever passing and he took us up on it.'

'When was that?'

'Early September.'

Another bulb lit up on my map. The trail extended forwards. I was a step nearer the kid, seven weeks along from that station platform in Alton and two hundred miles up the road.

'He came here straight from Lowestoft?'

'He was a couple of days on the road. Stalham. Cromer. Camping out.'

'How long did he stay here?'

'Just the night. We've not much room upstairs and we didn't really know Chas. I guess Riley shouldn't have made the invitation. That was the beer talking. We made an excuse so Chas wouldn't get any ideas about staying longer but he was fine. Happy to crash the night and catch up.'

'Anything specific in his travel plans? Did he say where he was going next?'

'Just continuing on up the coast. Nothing specific. He talked about Scotland, maybe the islands. Maybe a month or two in the Lakes over winter. He was playing it by ear.'

But she thought about it and pulled up another recollection.

'He was thinking of checking out a cafe up in the Wolds, near Spilsby. He'd worked there as a student and thought they might have something for him – cafe work, odd-jobbing – before he continued north.'

'Did the cafe have a name?'

'He never said.'

'And he left next day?'

'He hitched out of town first thing. Said he'd hang out along the A47. Wait for a lift up through Lincolnshire.'

'And did you hear from him again?'

She shook her head. Concern bright in her eyes.

Lincolnshire and the Lakes. Scotland. Direction of sorts, sufficient to cancel my planned drive back to Lowestoft in favour of moving on north, though I couldn't help feeling the trail ahead was becoming indistinct in the mist. I'd made good ground, gained seven weeks on the boy, but the next stepping stone might not be there.

I asked Samantha if Chas had mentioned anything else. Ideas. Hints or stories. But she shook her head.

'We hardly knew him,' she said. 'Told him to call back on his way home but he never did. Do you think he's okay?'

My turn to shake my head.

'We're trying to find out. His family are keen to know.'

'So am I. Two years. Shit! He was okay, you know?'

I nodded. I knew. An okay guy. Everyone was telling me that. But Chas was also a guy who'd been mostly forgotten.

I thanked Samantha and left. The street was busy with businesses locking up, pick-ups waiting, late shoppers drifting back to the main drag. I hit a blockage where an open car door and waste skip blocked my path and skipped across the road just as my phone connected. I dodged sideways to avoid a tubby guy as I jogged between parked cars to gain the far pavement. The guy gave me a curse and an "idiot" quote but I waved him off. Kept moving. Lucy's voice came on the line.

'Mission complete,' she said. 'We've knocked the nails back in and cleaned the shovels. Dodged the thunderbolts. We're home free.'

I sensed a certain cockiness now the deed was done. Ammunition to trump her friends when they were swapping scandal stories.

'No trouble with the Reaper?' I quipped.

'Easy peasy, Eddie. How hard could it be?'

I let it go.

'Has Harry checked the vids?'

'Yeah. They're good. Full colour coverage. Wait till you see it, Eddie. You're just not going to believe.'

See?

Cocky.

I didn't ask her about the PTSD and she didn't mention it.

But the dreams would come.

I thought of my own dreams. Decided they could play out here tonight. Save the trip back into London. I could be in Lincolnshire first thing tomorrow.

The signal went bad and I cut the line. Drove out of the town and took the road west for a quick gander. If Chas had followed his plan he'd walked this road, thumb out.

I crossed the Great Ouse and pulled onto the verge. Walked back to check the view from the bridge. Upstream a flat vista of open fields was cut by the Ouse like a ship canal. A sterile landscape. The other way, across the road traffic, I could see two old bridges, one of them wrecked, that blocked the view of where the river curved towards the Wash. Travellers stop instinctively on bridges and peaks. Maybe Chas had taken ten minutes two years ago to check out the same view before he walked on, thumbing traffic. I went back to stand at the car. Immediately ahead the routes diverged at a roundabout. I read the signs and thought it through.

Which way had Chas gone? If he'd got lucky with a lift his plans might have adapted to the direction of his pick-up. If he'd reached the roundabout and continued on foot he'd most likely stick to his planned route, take the road to Boston.

Evening traffic raced by making it hard to think. An HGV blatted past and took the main road towards the A1 and all routes out. If Chas was up in a cab by the time he hit the roundabout then the trail might end right here.

But I stayed positive. Maybe he'd returned to that cafe near Spilsby. And that's where I'd go.

I swung the car round the roundabout and re-crossed the bridge. Drove back to a Travelodge I'd spotted. I'd spin the roulette wheel tomorrow.

I ate in a Portuguese restaurant in King's Lynn and called Margot. Some kind of foolishness over the weekend had spawned suggestions of a night out this week. Maybe catch some theatre. Supper and live midnight jazz. The theatre in question was closed tonight but tomorrow was looking unlikely too and I needed to keep options open on Wednesday in case I needed to rush back out of Town. Fact is, the whole week wasn't a safe bet. I opted for the politicians' promise: everything soon. Distract from the fact that the table's empty right now. Margot wasn't fooled.

'You want me to book the tickets for the weekend?' she said.

'Might be safer,' I said. 'Though maybe we should wait until Friday.'

'You're going to be chasing this boy all week?'

'He's not been seen for two years, Margot.'

'And that's too long for London's smartest detective?'

'Is that flattery or cynicism?'

'I'm quoting you, Eddie.'

I grinned.

The beer again.

'Where are you?' she asked.

I told her. Described my progress.

'Seven weeks is good,' she commented. 'Before the family hired you they couldn't be sure the boy wasn't dead from day one.'

'Minus his cash withdrawal a while later.'

'Even that could have been someone else. This is the first proof he actually existed after July. It's rather like you're disinterring the dead, moment by moment.'

I forked my cod and onions. Grinned. If the Chas Abbott case was resurrecting the dead I wasn't sure how Margot would characterise our other job. But her words brought me back to what I'd thought a hundred times since we took the case: that after two years the search was just as likely to end with bad news as good.

'So when can I expect you back to chase our night-out mirage?' Margot asked.

'I'll be in Town on Wednesday. That's when we're closing off our grave-robbing assignment. Just a quick in and out but maybe we'll get together and plan something.'

'Should I hold my breath?'

'Better not. I'm not confident about my resuscitation skills.'

'It's lucky I'm a patient woman, Eddie.'

'I know it.'

'You say you're closing the other case?'

'I'll give you the gory detail when I see you.'

'I look forward to being shocked.'

I grinned. Told her take care.

Made another call.

'Luce, how's things?'

'You mean have the shakes gone yet?'

The cockiness was still there. Seemed things were fine. The girls'-nights-out were probably arranged.

'You're fine, Luce. I'm more worried about Tom Gallagher.'

'Tom's fine. If not, he'll be back to let you know.'

'You're giving me goosebumps. But that's not why I'm calling.'

'I know. So, booting my welfare aside Eddie I'd say we've got good news and we've got bad news.'

'That's good. It's usually all bad.'

'Well the bad news more or less cancels the good. So maybe it amounts to the same.'

I planted my fork. Sipped beer.

'I've finished the hard drive,' Lucy said. 'There's nothing else on there.'

'Okay, how about the names and emails I picked up off Chas' pal Eli?'

'That's the good news. We've talked to them. Harry's just back in now and I've got responses to emails. We've covered them faster than we could have hoped.'

Which was the good news. Leaving only one possibility for bad.

'None of them has seen Chas since he finished uni,' Lucy confirmed. 'Those contacts are colder than the ones you've been chasing. There's nothing for us, Eddie.'

Which left the trail that ended up on the bridge back there as the only one. I'd go with that. Maybe the Lincolnshire cafe was findable. And maybe Chas had called in there two years ago.

I double-checked the arrangements for our final sit down with Trading Standards on the Tom Gallagher thing and told Lucy I'd be back in tomorrow evening, ready for the kick-off.

By Wednesday we'd have Tom laid to rest.

I wondered if Chas Abbott's trail would still be alive by then.

CHAPTER ELEVEN
Cobwebs

I drove out early and took the Boston road. If he'd gone with his stated intentions then Chas Abbott had travelled this road two years ago looking for casual employment at a cafe he'd worked at as a student. There had to be a thousand or ten thousand cafes in Lincolnshire which made quite a haystack but you go with what you've got. A call to Susan Abbott gave me nothing to help point the way. Seemed the family had known little about what Chas got up to in his university holidays. I brought her up to date with my incremental progress which seemed to strike her as positive. More evidence of her brother's continued existence. We were six weeks on from the day he disappeared. I stayed cautious. Six weeks out of two years is a toe in the ocean. I promised to keep in touch and left her to her hopes.

Morning haze lifted as I crossed the Fens. Vistas of summer wheat and beet opened up. Distant tree lines. The mist and sun limited my rear-view but a tailing vehicle was there again, holding three hundred yards back. I got onto the dual carriageway that sliced through Boston and my escort closed the gap sufficiently to get ID. It was the red TT. Someone still wanted to know where I was and what I was doing. Someone prepared to pay these people to stay with me twenty-four hours, bivouacking at King's Lynn ready for my drive out. What I still couldn't fathom was why. If the tail was linked to my Chas Abbott search how did anyone even know I'd started working for the family? The cars were there before the ink was dry on the contract. But I'd sifted through our recent jobs a dozen times and nothing there could possibly attract outside interest. This had to be about the boy.

For the moment I decided to live with it. I'd a tight schedule that had me back in London tomorrow morning. If my tail was still with me in a couple of days I'd find out why. For now the TT kept me company as Boston faded and the sun warmed my neck. I ignored the rear view and let Terry St Clair's rumbling vocals ease me towards Spilsby, a town I'd never heard of before yesterday.

Twenty minutes later I realised why the place was unknown. It was a town in hiding. The unbroken flat countryside was still stretching away in carpets of wheat and barley even as I drove past the town's boundary sign. All I had were fields, trees and a deserted road. Then I hit a crossroads and the place sprang into view in a cluster of fifties' bungalows with the air of sheltered accommodation. I turned down past them. Coasted through to where older buildings led onto a market square. A tiny space, understated, the mish-mash of shop fronts and drinking places I associated with small Yorkshire towns. I rolled through and two hundred yards later a dogleg spat me out on the far side of the town. I spun the wheel and drove back in.

As I regained the centre I passed a side road where a white Mazda had diverted as I made my turn. The vehicle had taken over from the TT five miles out. I looked for it now but saw nothing. No sign of the TT either, though both had to be within spitting distance. Professionals. Skilful. If they were any better they'd have known I was onto them.

I parked up and found a bookstore selling Ordnance Survey maps. Sat back on the Sprite to mark a rough circle, two miles in radius. My search area for Chas' cafe. There were cafes in the town but Samantha recalled Chas saying *near* Spilsby which meant near and not in. I'd give it a couple of hours, come back in for lunch if I drew a blank.

And a blank was a possibility. The area was open country, B roads and small lanes. I'd not spotted a single hospitality business on my drive in. We weren't in transport caf. country.

I drove round for an hour and spotted only a single shabby service station and Spar. I fuelled up and showed Chas' picture to the guy behind the counter. He shook his head. If Chas had worked a few shifts here two years ago it was lost to history. I drove back out and continued my search pattern.

Leafy roads and my fisherman's cap gave me cover from the sun as I toured the area looking for anywhere an itinerant kid might find casual work. A two mile radius is a big area to cover, even when the map looks empty. A spider's web of winding lanes that never end but just split into two to draw you on, left or right, another mile then another turn. By mid day I'd covered the northern sector, learned ten new hamlet names but spotted only one village cafe and a handful of pubs. All checked. No one recalled a scruffy youth. No one could suggest alternatives. No one cared.

Maybe it was anxiety, the sense of a trail going nowhere, but I was beginning to hear the word *desolate* echoing through the silence between St Clair's songs as I crossed endless flat fields. The landscape wasn't desolate; it was a summer vista of greens and gold, somewhere you could wander for hours on lost tracks, but I didn't have hours to spare and I didn't have a clue whether there was anything to find down those tracks, or whether Chas had even come here.

Desolate stuck.

Then as I coasted back in along a lane from the west I crossed a tiny river and spotted something. I hit the brakes at a stand of trees butting up to the road like a giant caterpillar. A narrow track ran off alongside them and there was a sign pointing to a garden centre and cafe.

I turned and drove down at a dead crawl, watching the Sprite's springs, and arrived in a gravelled parking area by a brick and wood building. The building housed a small shop and a second entrance whose sign identified the place as the *Out On A Lymn Cafe*.

It was cool and dark inside. Ten tables, six occupied. The aroma of home cooking wafted over the counter. I checked the board. Lasagne, oven fresh. Fizzy water in the chiller. I decided to grab my lunch out here.

A thin black woman with blue bifocals was tending the counter and recognised neither Chas' name nor his picture. But she'd only worked here eighteen months. Suggested I talk to the proprietor who was next door in the shop. I put in my order and went round and showed Chas' photo to a burly sixtyish woman with sun-browned skin and a shock of white hair.

She looked at the photo briefly then at me.

'Why do you ask?' she said. Not friendly, not unfriendly.

I smiled at her and stashed the photo.

'Chas Abbott,' I said. 'I'm looking for him. Heard he worked here a couple of years back.'

'I realised you're looking for him,' she said. 'I asked why. And you heard wrong.'

'He *didn't* work here?'

'I'm still waiting to know why you're asking.'

She crossed her arms to make it clear that we were going nowhere until I'd cleared customs.

I handed her my card. She pursed her lips as she handed it back. Looked at me with a new suspicion.

'His family have asked me to find him,' I explained.

'Oh?' A spark of interest now.

'He's missing. They've not seen him for two years.'

Interest deepened to concern. The concern of someone who knows the person we're talking about. Of someone who's suddenly worried. I'd exchanged barely a handful of words but I already knew that this woman could tell me about Chas. And that she cared.

She asked for details and I told her what I knew, which amounted to a repeat of my last two sentences: missing; not seen for two years.

Not seen, not heard.

Gone.

'...and his trail brought me here,' I said.

'Oh, my. That's bad,' she said.

'So why am I wrong? About Chas working here.'

'He did work here but not two years ago. It was the summer previous. He was here for six weeks. I took him on as pot-washer and ended up moving him to the greenhouses. He had a talent for horticultural work. A quick learner.'

'Sounds like you remember him well. Mind if I ask your name?'

'Jessica Long.'

She relaxed a little. Dropped her arms, though she didn't offer a handshake. The detective thing. We're like traffic wardens in that respect.

I smiled but wondered if I was following Chas' trail *back* in time instead of forward. His whereabouts and activities a year before his disappearance weren't much help. I explained the tip-off that brought me here, Chas' declaration that he was planning to call by on the off-chance of work.

'Yes. He came back two years ago. He'd hiked out from Spilsby to ask about a job. But it was the end of the season, mid September, and the two people we had were working out their last week. We had nothing for him.'

'Did he say what his plans were when you told him that?'

'He didn't need to. I found him alternative employment. With a friend of mine in Spilsby. Chas worked for him for a fortnight.'

She grabbed a notepad and scribbled down a name and address.

'John runs a removals company back in town. It's a two-man business and his partner had injured his back. John needed help with the lifting. Chas was ideal.'

I took the note. Asked about her impressions of Chas when he called in.

'Pretty much his usual self. We only had a short chat but he was full of plans. Travelling round. Twelve months off. Getting himself sorted out. He asked about a job here the *next* summer and I told him to call me by Easter and we'd arrange something.'

'*Did* he call?'

'No. I assumed he'd decided not to come back this way.'

'So you never heard from him again?'

'No. But I never imagined he'd gone missing. His poor family. Do you think he's okay?'

To which I had no answer.

'Did he ever mention his family? His relationship with them?'

'No. He was quite a private person.'

'And that last time you saw him there were definitely no problems?'

'He was fine. Excited about his trip. Keen to earn a little cash and move on. He was pleased as punch when John told me to send him over, especially with the chance of accommodation thrown in. He had his backpack but free lodging in the town made things much easier.'

'Will John talk to me?'

In reply she grabbed a phone and made a call. Hung up.

'You're in luck. John's in the garage. He'll expect you.'

'Much obliged, Jessica, you've been a big help.'

She thought about it. Her worried look hadn't shifted. 'I'm just happy to assist,' she said. 'But if Chas has been out of touch for two years then you're nowhere near him Mr Flynn.'

I smiled. Asked how their lasagne was. She told me their lasagnes were spectacular.

I thanked her again and went to see if my order was on the counter.

~~~~~

Back in Spilsby I followed the main street again but turned off at the dogleg then took a second turn into road running out east. Fifty yards down a high brick wall concealed an old workshop with the name Mason Removals on the gate. Two small lorries decorated with the company's name were parked in the yard. I eased in next to them and a short guy in his seventies wearing overalls came out.

He wiped his hand on an oily rag then shook mine. Introduced himself as John.

'What's up with the lad?' he said.

I explained. He shook his head and told me that was concerning.

'I heard he was a stand-in for your partner.'

'Aye. Covered for an injury. It was a lucky break for us having the boy here. We'd have been cancelling jobs otherwise.'

'He helped with the shifting?'

'He did. He couldn't drive the wagons so we still had to make two journeys instead of one but we got by. My partner kept the office and Chas came out on the wagon.'

'How long did he stay?'

'Two weeks. Alan was able to lift by then.'

'How was Chas? Any sign of problems?'

'None I noticed. He just mucked in and got the job done. Kept himself to himself.'

'And he moved on at the end of September?'

'Yes. He packed his rucksack and headed off up north. This gap year thing.'

'Did he say where he was headed?'

'No. He just had a notion of hitching round the country.'

Which gave me Chas at this location at the end of September, still with no evidence of problems, keeping himself to himself, then packing his rucksack and hiking out for destinations unknown.

'Do you know where he stayed whilst he was here?'

'He stayed wi' me. I've a caravan out back. Gave him free lodging for the duration. It was a bit basic but he was happy with it. Saved him having to camp around or spend on B&Bs.'

'Has the caravan been used since?'

'No. It just stays locked up.'

'Mind if I take a look?'

'If it helps. No problem.'

He went back into the shop and yelled to a guy working in the back. Came back out and walked me down the lane between brick cottages to turn at the road and cross to a semi-detached building with one side converted to a tiny shop front.

'Firm's office,' John said. 'I live next door.'

He took me round to the yard to show me an ancient Elddis caravan with rusting metalwork and flat tyres. The thing hadn't seen the open road for a decade or two. He brought out a key and opened it up and I climbed in and took a look round.

The interior was the size of a shoe box. A mess. Cleaning bottles and rags blocked the sink and coat hangers were strewn on the bench seats. Discarded plastic sacking littered the floor. But it was dry. With a bit of a clean up you might live here. Had to be as comfortable as a farmer's field. Mould-flecked net curtains filtered the light.

I lifted the bench seats and checked the storage areas underneath. They were empty bar a few bits and pieces. I brushed aside cobwebs and pulled out a copy of the Daily Mail dated 1998. A remnant of John Mason's last towing holiday. Beneath the paper was a domino travel set with nothing of interest inside the box. A second seat concealed a few angle brackets and bag of screws from an old makeshift repair plus two empty Coke bottles and a broken food timer.

I dropped the seats back down and checked the kitchen area. Tiny units, a few pots and pans in the top cupboards, cutlery and cups and saucers. I pictured Chas in here, cooking rudimentary meals or bringing in takeaways, lifting up the table to set out his meals. Wondered what his thoughts were. Impatience to move on? Or temptation to stay longer, settle into the comforts even a spartan lifestyle brings. Was the caravan an adventure to him or a shit-hole?

Or just somewhere to stay whilst he accrued some cash?

I opened side drawers. The first two had nothing except old newspapers lining the bottom. The third held three discarded leaflets: bus timetables dated 2010.

Chas.

My guess was that I was the first to open the drawer since he'd left.

I checked the timetables. They detailed local routes covering Spilsby, Lincoln, Grimsby and Saltfleet. Maybe Chas had taken the bus a couple of times or maybe he'd planned on taking public transport out of here. I popped my head out and showed John but he shook his head. The timetables meant nothing.

I flicked through them and found something: on the Grimsby to Grainthorpe route Chas had circled a rural stop towards the end of the journey. And the routes in the other leaflets connected to this one. Grainthorpe was just thirty miles away, up towards the coast, but it seemed there was no direct public transport. If you wanted to get to Chas' marked stop you'd need to make a four hour circuit from Spilsby and connect the routes. But what was Chas' interest in a country stop miles from anywhere? I went out and showed the marking to John and he went to grab a map. He came across again with a fifty thou' and we checked the road north from Grainthorpe and the location of Chas' marked stop. The only place nearby was a hamlet called Low Rasen. A fifteen minute hike from the stop, towards the coast. I asked John but the place meant nothing.

I went back into the caravan and finished my search. Pulled open the last few doors and drawers and discovered nothing. Apart from the timetables there was no sign anyone had been living here two years ago.

Then as I squatted to check the tiny cleaning space below the sink I spotted a crumpled scrap of paper behind the empty waste bin. Something thrown that had missed its target. The scrap was a hand-written receipt from a place called Torley's Bookshop which had an address back in the town. September 2010. A single book purchase. The receipt was pierced, as if it had been stacked whilst an order came through. The seller had written an ISBN but no book title.

Maybe Chas had made the purchase to stock his rucksack before heading out. Maybe the shop could tell me something.

But John shook his head.

'They closed down,' he said. 'We've an Indian takeaway there now.'

I wondered if the bookshop's proprietor would recall Chas but John shook his head again.

'That's Ronald Torley. He died.'

Leaving me with the receipt. Maybe the ISBN would tell me something, though it wasn't clear how Chas' reading matter would move me forwards. But I needed every scrap.

And the scrap I liked most was the bus timetable, the marked destination.

What had put that destination into Chas' head? And had he gone there once this job finished?

I took a last look round and felt for a moment like I was right in Chas' footsteps. But I knew that was pure deception. The footsteps were two years old and Chas had walked away forever from this place. It was just an overheated empty caravan with dust motes floating. I went out, and John locked up.

I walked with him back to the workshop, dropping a call to Lucy to give her the book ISBN. Then I thanked John again and fired up the Frogeye. He wished me luck and stood watching, still wiping his hands, as I drove out.

CHAPTER TWELVE
Vodka

I drove slow roads across never ending Lincolnshire flatlands. Hedgerows disappeared to yield vistas of beet and barley, distant woody outcrops and country power lines. I hit the main road and turned towards Grimsby, then turned again and drove towards Grainthorpe. I pictured Chas Abbot two years ago riding the back of a local bus under the same hot sun. He was two hundred miles from home and two months along his trail and I needed to find something at the end of his ride, if he ever took it. I stopped and checked the map then drove slowly on and spotted an isolated bus shelter by a crossroads. The mark on Chas' timetable. His possible disembarkation point.

A signpost next to the stop located Low Rasen a quarter of a mile down a tiny lane. The hamlet wasn't important enough to have the bus turn off the main road and take you right in. If you were set on reaching the place you walked. I eased the Frogeye into the lane and drove down. Found nothing much. Just a terrace of three cottages alongside the road, summer crops washing round them, then a little further another scatter of cottages and a monument opposite a shabby pub. Beyond the pub, open road. I pulled onto the pub's tiny parking area and killed the engine. If Low Rasen existed this was it.

I hopped out. The pub was called The Thistle in honour of its tiny beer garden which had adopted the vegetation. Its three bench tables were besieged by the weeds and needed urgent repair. One was occupied by a backpacking couple. The others were empty.

I went in. Adjusted my eyes. The only thing moving in the place was the landlord, busy behind the pumps.

My cafe lunch turned out to be a fortuitous decision because this place didn't open its kitchen until six p.m. and the advertised cuisine would have presented some hard choices. I ordered a fizzy water to cool me down. The guy threw me a sour look and reached for a glass. I thanked him and planted a fiver. Told him to keep the change. If the windfall impressed him he didn't show it. It took all of his willpower just to lean across and check out the photo on my screen.

'I'm looking for this guy,' I said.

He showed no recognition. I told him the boy had perhaps been in the area a couple of years back, might have called in or asked about work. Which finally got the guy into a conversational mood.

'You're bloody joking,' he said. 'You think I'm Memory Man?'

'The kid was travelling. Taking on casual jobs. If he stayed over in the area and popped in a few times you might recall.'

'Which I don't.'

Certain. No second look required.

I hadn't been optimistic. If Chas did ever get here he'd have full pockets from his two weeks' work with John Mason. And if he'd taken that long bus route it was for a specific reason. And socialising or casual work at the Thistle would not have been part of it.

'You get many customers in?'

'A handful in season.'

'And you wouldn't remember a kid if he came in one time?'

'Two years ago? I wouldn't remember the bleeding Pope if he'd been in.'

At which point he walked off to clean glasses. I picked up my water and shifted down the bar. Re-planted the glass. I was sitting by him again.

'The boy's missing,' I said. 'I'm just looking for any clues to his whereabouts.'

The guy kept his back to me.

'You'd better look somewhere else. You'll not find him here.'

'It was just a long shot,' I said. 'I'm still not clear why he came here in the first place. Is there anything round here?'

'We're farming country. Just the fields and the birds.'

'Any farms take on seasonal labour?'

'I've not heard of it.'

'And nowhere to attract a visitor?'

'As I said.'

He shifted to polish the spirit bottles. His back was still towards me.

'Are there any campsites round here?'

'None I know of. This isn't Bournemouth.'

'Do you have rooms here?'

'There's no call for it.'

'So no one would stay in the area?'

'We get a few walkers passing through and that's it.'

I grinned. 'I guess word's not got out about the hospitality.'

The guy finally turned. I shrugged. Looked round his empty room. There were a thousand pubs a year closing and this one was well into the relegation zone. I turned back. Raised my glass to his prospects and polished the water off then left the guy to his losing battle.

I drove round for two hours. Covered every lane within a mile, checking for anything that might have induced Chas to mark that bus stop on his timetable. But whatever it was it eluded me. The landscape was an emptiness of isolated farms, drainage channels, dykes and sluice gates, pumping stations and the odd deserted chapel. Occasional scattered cottages. As Mine Host had said: nothing to pull the tourists in. I spiralled back in towards the hamlet and checked out the farm I'd spotted close by. It was a sizeable concern called Low Farm but no camping facilities were advertised. And there was no sign of activity to entice me along the dusty drive up to the buildings.

Then as I rolled back through Low Rasen I spotted the first activity of the afternoon. A group of four youths disembarking from the back of a rusting grey Transit outside the cottage terrace. Three boys and a girl. Late teens, early twenties. I slowed as I passed, saw them push through a tiny iron gate that serviced the end cottage's front door. I drifted on, slowed to watch the Transit in my rear view as it turned back towards the pub.

The youths were out of place in this empty landscape, a bustle of activity that didn't fit. I thought of casual farm work but they didn't look right. I turned and drove back. Parked outside the cottages. Youth and casual work were part of the circle Chas moved in, making the kids who'd just gone into the house the nearest thing to any kind of life that might have drawn the boy here.

I knocked on the door.

It was opened by a gangly boy with messed up hair. He blinked at me but stayed back as if he was used to people barging in. I picked up the cue and brushed past. Found myself in a tiny front parlour. Chatter and the sound of cooking utensils came from a back room. I went that way.

I came into a kitchen with a wooden table at its centre, an ancient electric cooker and small fridge-freezer. A boy and girl had just sat down with freshly opened beers. The fourth boy was opening tins on the counter. They all looked at me as Gangly bumbled in behind and asked belatedly what I wanted.

I grinned. Jabbed my hands in my pockets. Leaned on the work surface next to the chef.

'Sorry to intrude,' I said.

Which didn't ease the tension. The kids looked at Gangly for a clue as to whether I had a right to barge in. Which was interesting. I'd assumed they were tenants, but even tenants expect privacy. Seemed this cottage was a more open establishment, which had me wondering who their landlord – or employer – was.

'I spotted you guys coming in,' I explained, 'and wondered if you might help. I'm looking for someone.'

I pulled out my phone with Chas' picture on the screen and handed it to Cookie. He planted his can opener and scanned it without recognition. I took the phone back but before I could hand it to the girl she spoke.

'Are you looking for Alfie?' she said.

~~~~~

I *wasn't* looking for Alfie, but the people who'd barged into Chas' Belsize Park crash pad a couple of years ago *were* looking for someone of that name. Right before Chas left Town, and just a few weeks before he did or did not get off the bus a quarter of a mile from here. And if the *Alfie* the girl was talking about was the kid knocking about with Chas then things were moving.

Finally we had keys turning, cogs rotating, machinery chattering. The SALE flag popped up and went "ping".

I grinned and brought up another pic, this one with Alfie alongside Chas. Handed the phone to the girl.

Who came up with a blank.

But the wrong type of blank.

It was a blank that comprised a widening of the eyes and a look that was coloured by fear. And even though it only lasted a moment before she got control and handed the phone to the next kid it was enough. The kid beside her looked at the screen without recognition but I was still watching the girl. I put her around twenty years old, nice looking though her face was gaunt from certain angles and her thin blonde hair needed attention.

'You recognise either of them?' I said.

'No.'

The kid at her side handed the phone to Gangly and he looked at it and handed it back. No recognition. But I was still talking to the girl.

'The one on the left is Chas Abbott,' I said. 'The other is Alfie.'

When I continued watching she turned to the others for backup. They looked at her then me.

'You don't recognise either boy?'

I waited until she looked at me again. When she did she shook her head.

'Okay,' I said. 'Different Alfie, I guess. Who's yours?'

The others looked at her.

I saw her struggling to right wrongs. She'd let something out of the bag and wanted to get it back in.

'Sorry,' she said again. 'It was just a misunderstanding. I used to know someone called Alfie. I thought you were looking for him.'

'Petra,' Cookie said, 'be quiet.'

She looked at him and clamped her lips.

I stashed my phone.

'Used to know?'

She gave me perplexed. Her eyes flicked back and forth.

'You said you *used* to know someone called Alfie.'

She pushed out a little laugh. Shrugged. Shook her head.

'Just a guy. We lost touch.'

'Got it. And why would anyone be looking for him?'

To which there was no answer. Then Cookie stepped in.

'Mister,' he said, 'I don't think you should be here. It's not our property.'

'But you live here?'

'Yes.'

'So you can invite guests in?'

Cookie was either running out of patience or getting nervous. He got assertive.

'Man, we don't know you. You'd better leave.'

I stayed leaning on the counter. Pulled out a card and tossed it down beside him. He picked it up and checked it out and shook his head again. Flicked it back down. The others strained but couldn't read it.

'That's who I am,' I said. 'I'm here looking for Chas Abbott who's missing from home. But if any of you can point me towards Alfie that would probably help.'

'Not gonna happen, mate,' Cookie said. 'We already said. We don't know the dude. Can't help.'

'I heard you,' I said. I pulled out a chair. Sat and leaned forwards on my elbows.

'I need a break here,' I said. 'The boy I mentioned is missing and it's my information that he called in here a couple of years ago. Now I realise that's a while back but with all the teeming life round here it's not beyond reason that he was spotted. And I'd say you people are the sort he might have mixed with, especially if he was looking for Alfie. And truth be told, from the smell of things I'd say there's something you're all not telling me. Have I got that right?'

'No, mister,' Cookie said. 'We've never heard of anyone called Chas. Most of us weren't even here two years ago. You're barking up the wrong tree.'

A P.I.'s habit. But it's amazing what comes down sometimes.

'I'm trying to help the boy,' I said. 'Just looking for pointers.'

I was looking at Petra again.

Because she knew something.

'Okay, man,' Cookie said. 'You gotta leave.'

I looked up at him. Stared him out then rapped my knuckles on the wood. Stood up.

'Okay,' I said. 'Thanks anyway.'

But I didn't rush out. Looked round the room again.

'You people work round here?'

'No,' Cookie said. 'Holiday park at Mablethorpe. Pontins.'

'Okay. That's quite a distance they bring you. Is a house in the country a staff perk?'

'There's no perks. And the wages are lousy. They've no choice but to put us up out here.'

'This a seasonal gig?'

'Yeah. On and off.'

I smiled round the room.

'Okay. Well thanks for your time. One last question: is there anywhere to eat round here? I could do with refreshment before I drive back.'

'There's the Thistle,' Gangly said. 'That's it. Food sucks.'

I grinned.

'Basic will do. Just a pie and chips. Thanks for the recommendation.'

'Go to it, man,' Cookie said. 'The pleasure's entirely ours.'

For the first time there were smiles round the room.

I left them to it and drove back to the pub. It was after six now and four customers were inside plus a bar girl. Mine Host was absent for the moment. When I re-examined the board it looked no more appetising than before. The stars of the show were boiled gammon and pease pudding and a concoction of haggis and tatties. Decent beer non-existent. I settled on a half of Heineken and asked about pie of the day which turned out to be rabbit and game. I grinned and checked the food board again but it was still unchanged. Rabbit it was. I heard once you could starve to death eating rabbit – more calories out than in – but I guess the pastry and beer would balance things.

The food when it came was everything it promised to be, but beggars and choosers and so on. I sipped my Heineken and ate slowly. The other patrons left after fifty minutes and I had the place to myself bar the girl and the landlord who'd reappeared to throw dirty looks my way. I stopped once and checked out the juke box but didn't spot anything that would work and worried what the silence would be like after any music played out. I left the thing and went back to my table.

The pie was edible even if slow eating wasn't recommended. The chips I stayed clear of. I was just finishing up when the door opened and the girl Petra came in and walked over.

I grinned up at her. Invited her to sit. My hint at the cottage had worked, though if she'd turned up forty-five minutes earlier she could have saved me the culinary adventure. I offered a drink but she declined. I didn't press her. I knew why she was here. Which was to talk about Alfie and maybe Chas. I pushed my plate aside and opened my hands.

'Tell me,' I said.

She pushed back her hair. Took a surreptitious look at the bar and leaned in.

'Okay,' she said. 'That *is* Alfie in your picture. And I recognise Chas. And it's not true what Neil told you. The others have only been here since last summer but I was here two years ago.'

Which I'd assumed.

'So you know Chas Abbott?'

'Not really. It's Alfie I know. Chas called looking for him and we had a drink in here. I shouldn't have done it. I shouldn't be here now.'

'Why's that?'

'It's complicated.'

'I'm good with complicated.'

'No: I'm not talking about it. You were asking about Chas. Maybe I can help you with him.'

'But you're more interested in Alfie?'

She said nothing.

'Okay: Chas. What happened to him?'

'Nothing. He camped down the road for two nights then left.'

'Did he talk to Alfie?'

'Alfie wasn't here. He'd left a month or two earlier.'

'But Alfie had worked here?'

'Yes, he was at the farm.'

'What farm?'

She hesitated. Shrugged. 'Some local farm. I don't know where exactly.'

'How did you know Alfie?'

'He stayed with us at the cottage.'

'Who was at the cottage back then?'

'Me and three or four others. Plus Alfie.'

'Were you all working at the holiday park apart from him?'

Hesitation again.

'Sure...'

'Who owns the cottage?'

'I guess it's rented by the holiday park.'

'Pontins. Mablethorpe.'

'I guess.'

'Quite a long way out,' I noted again.

'I guess it's cheaper than renting in the town.'

'Sure. And Alfie was living in the property too, even though he didn't work for Pontins?'

She shrugged. 'There must have been some arrangement...'

'Got it. And the boy I'm looking for – Chas – did he tell you what he was up to?'

'He was just passing through. Called in on spec hoping to catch Alfie.'

'Did he say why?'

'No.'

'Did he tell you where he was going next?'

'He was heading to Scotland. He knew a girl called Heather who was farming up there. He planned to catch up with her before the weather turned. Maybe stay the winter, depending on how things worked out.'

'Did he say where the place was?'

'Just Scotland.'

'And when he realised that Alfie was no longer here at Low Rasen he moved on?'

'Yeah. We had a drink in here on his second night then he was gone first thing next morning.'

'You sure he left?'

'Yes. I spotted him on the way to work. The van passed him. Hiking out with his rucksack.'

'Okay. So why did you think I might be looking for Alfie earlier? Why would someone be looking for him?'

'You were looking for someone. I just thought...'

'Sure. But people only come looking for someone when they're missing.'

'...I suppose.'

'And if Alfie had simply quit his job and left there'd be no reason to think he was missing.'

She said nothing. Searched for a way out of the tangle. There was something she didn't want to talk about but she'd come in here because she was hoping to trade her info about Chas for news of Alfie. Something was off. She pushed at her hair again, a girl uncomfortable with herself. Up close her face was weary, a slight darkening round the eyes.

'Tell me about Alfie,' I said.

'Just a friend...'

'No. I mean who was he? Why was he here? What was the connection between him and Chas?'

'I don't know. I didn't know him that well.'

'Where was he from?'

'London.'

'Did he ever talk about Chas?'

'No.'

'You'd never heard of Chas until he showed up here?'

'That's right.'

I thought about it.

'Lincolnshire's a long way to come for casual farm work. Did Alfie ever talk about his job?'

'No. Like I said...'

'...you didn't know him that well. Got it. But you knew him well enough to be worried that he's not been in touch – a little like my boy Chas.'

'I just wondered. Alfie left kind of suddenly.'

I grinned. Over Petra's shoulder Mine Host was watching us. I leaned in, kept my voice low.

'Petra, there's something you're not telling me.'

'No.'

'You came in here because you're worried about Alfie.'

'I wanted to tell you about Chas coming here.'

'Which you could have told me back at the cottage.'

Her lips parted. Said nothing.

'Do the others know Alfie or Chas?'

'No.'

'So why did they want you to keep quiet?'

She was still looking for ways out of the tangle. Her eyes darted around for ideas. None came.

'Your stories about working in Mablethorpe, and of Alfie temping as a farm labourer. They kind of puzzle me.'

She stared at me.

'Because,' I said, 'Alfie doesn't look the farming type.'

She said nothing.

'And the thing is,' I said, 'I've done a quick check and there's no Pontins in Mablethorpe.'

She looked at me.

'The holiday park where you say you work – it doesn't exist.'

I gave her a moment.

'Low Farm,' I said, 'the one up the road. Is that where Alfie worked?'

'I don't know. Just some local farm.' She was getting nervous as hell.

'And did you work there too?' I said. 'Since you didn't work at Pontins.'

She dropped her eyes. Watched the table as she decided whether this was the moment to cut and run.

Then the door opened and two guys walked in. Both were tall with hints of muscle under navy tracksuits. Both wore the same close-cropped hairstyle and had faces that had been around. One wore a navy trilby with a grey band, which wasn't farm-labourer fashion any more than the tracksuits. They walked casually towards the bar trying to hide the fact that they were looking for me. When they got to the bar Mine Host greeted them with what might have been relief.

Petra caught the vibes. She tensed and stood.

'I'd better go,' she said.

I started to say something but she'd turned away and was gone. She didn't look at the two guys.

I hadn't expected her to solve my Chas Abbott mystery but there were things she knew that would have been useful if I'd had time to coax them out. All she'd given me was that Chas had been here and had left, without friend Alfie. He'd moved on, hiked out with his backpack heading for Scotland.

Which was a long jump from Low Rasen, leaving this place as the end of my solid leads. I was nearly seven weeks along Chas' trail but it felt like I was standing at the end of the pier after the ship has sailed.

I watched the two men at the bar. They were side on, still trying to hide the fact that they were watching me. Then their lagers arrived and the guy with the hat noticed me. Turned to raise a glass.

I nodded back, lifted the dregs of my Heineken. As a prop to delay my departure it was marginal so I jumped up and walked over to order another. Mine Host did the dirty, worked the tap sharpish, businesslike, like this was part of a scripted act.

The guy with the hat turned so that his back wasn't to me. He watched me sip my drink.

'We no see you in here,' he said.

A faint Eastern European accent. Not uncommon in the UK but it was hard to make the guys fit here. If the two had been wearing crusty jeans and tee-shirts I'd have put them down as migrant farm labourers. But the tracksuits said otherwise.

'Just passing through,' I said.

The far guy emitted a laugh-like cough and Hat nodded and grinned. Teeth gleaming like a Merc's grille.

'Okay,' he said. 'Watering hole. Good food here. Nice beer.'

'First class,' I said, making no more effort than he to hide my sentiment. Nor the fact that our exchange was pure phoney. But phoney I could do. I suddenly had the time and inclination. I wanted to know where this was heading.

'You holiday?' Hat said.

'Just passing through.'

'In little car?'

'That's the one.'

Hat turned and exchanged grins with Cough.

'Neat,' Hat said, turning back. 'Like kiddie car.'

'Vintage.'

'Vintage I bet. But go like flaming hell, hey? Vrooooom.' His hand made a jet takeoff from the counter.

'It's fast enough,' I said.

He chuckled and his pal Cough sipped his beer and leaned round him to smile at me.

'You guys work here?' I said.

Hat turned to consult with his partner again. Mine Host stood quietly. Then Hat turned back to me.

'Round about. You know. Agriculture.'

'Nice place to live,' I said.

'Nice place?' Hat and Cough consulted again and they were both smiling. Cough leaned further.

'Shit-hole,' he said. 'Back end of arse.'

That got them laughing. I raised my glass.

'At least you've got the pub,' I said. 'Nice for a drink. Good food.'

More jollity. The men's shoulders shook.

'Worst shit-hole in UK,' Cough said. He was still leaning to communicate. 'In our country, landlord get told to clean up fucking place or you get arms broken. And get good beer.'

Mine Host moved away and busied himself at the far end of the bar.

I leaned in. Lowered my voice.

'You're right,' I said. 'The place is a disgrace. Have you tried their food?'

More laughter.

'You bloody joke? You think we wan' end hospital.'

I grinned and shot a pistol finger at them then reached into my jacket and brought out my phone.

'While you're here,' I said, 'did you ever see this guy around?'

They leaned. Looked. Smiled and shook their heads. No, they didn't recognise Chas.

I'd known it.

'How about this one?' I pulled up the photo with Alfie and they both looked again.

When they checked back this time Hat's smile had faded a little. He looked at me.

'No,' he said. 'Sorry. We no know these people.'

'Damn,' I said. 'I heard they were here a while back but I just can't find any sign.'

'They not here for sure,' Hat said. 'Never have. Nothing here for anyone to come. Mind me ask: why you looking?'

'Just work stuff. I'm trying to find these guys.'

I pushed back the phone and planted a card in front of them. Hat took it and read it and turned it over to check the back, which was blank. He planted it back on the bar.

'Okay,' he said. 'Let be clear: these boys never here. Sorry we can't help. But better you look otherplace else. There's people round here no like strangers. No like private investigations. Better I say you that.'

I gave it some thought.

'Any reason they not like strangers? Or private investigators?'

But Hat was just looking at me. The smile had gone.

'We clear?' he said.

I thought some more. Then pushed my half empty glass aside and made to head off.

'Very clear,' I said. 'Have a nice evening.'

Hat pulled a faint smile back up.

'Have nice day,' he said.

They watched me go out.

I stepped out just in time to catch another puzzle. This one was a face. One that shouldn't have been here. I caught just a glimpse before it disappeared behind the foliage backing the monument across the road. Someone had been watching the building. It took a moment but then I got it. The tubby guy I'd almost crashed into yesterday outside the King's Lynn boutique.

Seemed my tail was still with me.

Which was a puzzle.

I knew these people were good but who is that good? I'd watched my rear-view half the afternoon and hadn't spotted anything behind me. But here they were and I wondered how.

I hopped into the Sprite and drove out to where the Low Farm track went off. Coasted slowly past. If Alfie had been working a local farm this one would fit.

Two hundred yards up the track a cluster of buildings was highlighted in the setting sun. A brick farmhouse under a stand of trees, concrete and corrugated iron barns behind. Still no sign of life.

I found a gate down the lane and pulled the Sprite off the road. Waited.

Nothing.

If the King's Lynn guy was following me he was holding well back. I hopped out and walked back to where the cover of a bushy verge gave me a sight of the farm entrance. Settled in to watch.

It wasn't the King's Lynn guy I was waiting for.

The ones I was interested in appeared ten minutes later in the black 4x4 I'd spotted outside the Thistle. Seemed Hat and his pal were not heavy drinkers. Twenty minutes in and out. Their lights were on in the dusk and they drove fast towards me then braked hard and swung up the farm track.

I was tempted to take a look but getting near the farm buildings would take longer than I had. I was still a long way out of Town. I watched for another few minutes then headed back to the car. Drove out fast with an eye still in the mirror. At the main road I kept my foot down for thirty minutes then turned off just before Boston and parked in a quiet lane.

Hopped out and discarded my jacket and shades. Grabbed my torch and squatted to check the Frogeye's wheel arches and bumpers. It took less than a minute to find the small package taped up behind the chrome of the rear bumper. A tracking device. That explained why I'd not seen my tail today.

The device allowed my watchers to hold well back, catch up at their leisure. But it was following someone the lazy way. The moment I found the transmitter they'd lose me.

I gave it some thought and decided that now was not the time. Better to keep these people close and choose the moment. Which would maybe be after I'd figured out why they were following me. I was still connecting these people to my search for Chas but damned if I could imagine a reason. When I figured it out maybe I'd know more about the boy.

And how did Low Rasen make sense? Why had a farm out in the sticks and a physical equipment shop back in Streatham both drawn an Eastern European crowd? A crowd that didn't take to strangers. I might have convinced myself that I was imagining the link between the two places if it wasn't for the fact that Chas' friend Alfie was connected to both. Even if that didn't mean that Chas himself was connected. Chas had left both London and Low Rasen behind. He'd hiked out to continue his road trip without giving anyone the detail of his plans. Probably because he had no detail other than the vague intention of continuing north, seeing a girl in Scotland.

I hopped back into the car and drove back to the main road.

For a boy who'd just walked off into the sunset to seek a life elsewhere Chas Abbott had pulled a hell of a circus around him.

Question was: how was I going to get ahead of the circus, cut through the remaining twenty-two months and get on Chas' heels? Low Rasen was an oddity but it had given me nothing more than continuing vague direction.

I drove back to London with my tracker pinging my location into the ether, keeping the circus rolling around me.

Just before the Orbital my phone rang.

Lucy. Still hot on the trail.

'I ID'd the book,' she said.

This was the book Chas had supposedly bought in the shop back in Spilsby. Lucy had checked the ISBN.

'It's a book about crofting in Scotland,' she said.

Interesting. I asked about location.

'The author was living at a crofting settlement on the west coast. A place called Smirisary.'

Smirisary. For a second I had that same feeling I'd had an hour ago, the feeling of almost recognising something – like the face outside The Thistle. I searched around. Dug deep.

Got it.

Chas' mother had recalled the boy talking about Scotland. About farming or crofting and a girl called Heather. And he'd mentioned a place name that his mother couldn't recall but sounded like vodka.

Vodka.

Smirisary.

That would fit.

CHAPTER THIRTEEN
We had sound, too

We assembled in the late Tom's drawing room. Me, Lucy, Jimmy Diamond and his wife Jackie. Lucy had reverted to black hair and matching skirt suit, sad eyes shaded behind Prada gradients. She looked kind of fetching. Back when we were a pair I'd never seen this monochrome side.

Diamond thanked us for coming. His wife looked at us and shared a moment then we all went quiet because there wasn't much to say. No whispered commiserations or memories. Just four strangers feigning interest in Tom's display cabinets and framed oils, his small bookcase. It was one of those silences.

Then movement outside. A hearse and limo swung in through the gates and we all filed out. The hearse rolled past, leaving space for the limo whose shotgun door opened to dispense the old guy, Edward, looking even older and dustier than before. His professional sorrow almost dimmed the daylight as he came round. He pulled open the middle door and invited Lucy in with a weariness that reminded us that we've all got tickets to this picnic. Best enjoy the spectator seats whilst you can. I sensed sincerity in his message: the guy was nearer to riding in the front car than any of us.

Proprietor Unwin had climbed out of the hearse to stand guard as we embarked. I guess his father had taught him etiquette, though junior's stance didn't quite work. His edgy movements and outgrown suit coat looked every bit an act. The worry across his balloon face though was real, explainable by the message he'd received at nine this morning, which was that burying Tom Gallagher was going to involve a little more ceremony than planned. Trading Standards had been keen to shut things down right then but Jimmy Diamond had asked one favour: get Tom into the ground with dignity. Loose off the fireworks after.

I ducked into the limo behind Lucy, and Edward opened the rear door for Jimmy and his wife. Then he shut us up tight and climbed into the front. Steve Unwin bowed briefly and walked back to the hearse and we rolled out.

I sat back in the cracked leather and relaxed. The limo's heavy tints blocked the sun, and the double glazing killed sound as we floated through silent streets across to Earlsfield. We were riding between two worlds, part of neither.

Lucy sat upright beside me and wouldn't catch my eye. Probably pondering the investigation business. And if you were in a pondering mood this was as good an example as you'd get. Four actors in a car following a dead guy.

I gave up with Lucy. Went back to watching the grey street. A job's a job, but I guess what Lucy was thinking was it was too damn bad that Tom Gallagher's last journey was a sham. Maybe not for Jimmy Diamond. Jimmy was an old acquaintance at the least, maybe almost a friend. But the rest of us were out and out phoneys.

But without us there'd have been no one.

That's why Jimmy's handshake had sincerity back there. Tom had been a good guy, had just outlived everyone he cared about. Which left just the handful of strangers whose business crossed his at the finale. But maybe we could claim to be looking after his final interests. So maybe not quite phoney, but riding in the funeral car of someone you don't know was not on Lucy's list of feel-good activities. I checked again and saw it on her face: sadness tinged with a bursting need to call her friends and get a night out arranged.

We pulled in through the cemetery gates and rolled to a stop by the top buildings. Edward released us then went to help with the lifting. When they were ready we followed as they hefted Tom across to the freshly dug hole by his family monument. The guys at three corners of the coffin sweated as they compensated for Edward's lack of lift. The old guy was way past it, but the only other option was their boss, and Steve Unwin didn't look like a guy who got his hands dirty.

A solitary cleric was waiting. Tom had dispensed with religion decades back but this last little rite was from respect for his wife who was watching from somewhere up above.

The cemetery was almost deserted, just a handful of visitors tending graves and a few figures waiting up by the houses. I'd spotted Karen, the Trading Standards officer, holding back discreetly with two uniformed constables.

This was the finale of Karen's show. A case about to be closed. She'd picked up the investigation when insider rumours of substandard embalming and casket construction first surfaced. Seemed Unwin was picking up cheap flat-pack caskets with veneering and passing them off as solid mahogany and oak. Cutting costs on the embalming side whilst charging the earth. Rumours unsupported by customer evidence. Who brings a tape measure to their loved ones last party?

But Karen dug around and found herself building different suspicions concerning the deceased's valuables. Seems around one in fifty of us are despatched wearing favourite jewellery, and whilst much of it hasn't value beyond the sentimental a sharp undertaker might spot the occasional nugget. Which someone in Steve Unwin's firm had done. Problem is, they were careless: Trading Standard's first hard evidence of shenanigans appeared when relatives of two recently deceased people spotted family heirlooms. One in a pawnshop display and one on eBay. And the factor in common was Unwin's firm.

Karen reviewed the growing list of rumour and evidence and decided that the firm needed checking out. The question was how to arrange a sting? It's hard to get cooperation from the bereaved, even harder to find a family kccn to bury valuables along with their beloved.

Then Tom Gallagher died and Trading Standards were gifted a once-in-a-lifetime opportunity.

Because Tom was rich and alone and because his executor happened to work with Trading Standards and proved amenable to assisting their cause. Seemed Tom had never been too fond of crooks and scammers and had left his estate to charities and... here was an opportunity for a final service to society. All endorsed by the guy with the executive powers. Jimmy Diamond agreed to contract the funeral to Unwins and arrange that Tom be buried with his Rolex Daytona and a 24 carat wrist chain his wife had gifted him on their golden wedding.

All Trading Standards had to do was find players with the technical skills to get the casket bugged and pick up the light-fingered party in action. So Karen talked to her pal Lucy and Lucy talked to me and we signed the contract.

And the bugs went in.

And got a bite when the casket was opened a few days back. The camera triggered and snapped pics at 1 frame per second of Tom's Rolex and chain disappearing.

We got the pics out by dint of Lucy's late-late request for a last viewing. When she walked out of Unwin's yesterday the cam and flash were in her bag along with Tom's valuables which she'd asked to retrieve after a change of heart. Tom would rather, she'd decided, see the stuff converted to cash and his favourite charities gifted. Which had the light-fingered party thanking his stars that he still had the goods in his possession. When the casket was re-opened Tom's watch and chain were both where we'd left them.

Mission complete.

Bar this one last favour to Jimmy Diamond.

For the eyes of the world Lucy would stay Tom's grieving niece until he was in the ground. Just a couple of hours none-billable. The agency doesn't penny-pinch that way. We do what we have to do. And I'd had no problem persuading Lucy to play out this last act. She'd have put her own money down for a ticket on this ride.

The cleric opened his book and spoke a few words of fond affection for the guy he'd never met and Tom's casket was lowered to join his wife then Unwin's people pulled up the straps and went back to the cars.

Lucy thanked the priest and dabbed her eyes and looked anxiously after them. We needed to give it a few moments for decency's sake but when we crossed back over Lucy was out in front.

Up by the buildings the action was under way.

Karen Foster was standing by the Hearse with the uniformed officers beside her. Unwin's people had been guided clear apart from Steve and Edward, and Karen was talking quietly and firmly to Edward. But it was Unwin whose mouth was open, even if he'd known this was coming. Edward's face showed nothing, the same blank sorrow he'd shown to us the last week. As we came up, Karen was confirming that Edward understood the charges and then cops confirmed that he understood his rights and invited him to go with them.

But the old guy stiffened up and found his voice and it wasn't the one his customers heard. He faced Unwin whose skin was tight across his face like one of his own cheap embalming results.

'This is on you, you bastard,' he said.

Unwin said nothing. Just shook his head.

'If your father was alive he'd roast you, you cheapskate, ungrateful, bloodsucking tub of lard,' Edward said.

He was set to say more but his breath ran out. Age. Lung capacity just isn't what it used to be.

'Dear mother,' Unwin said. 'What have you done, Edward?'

Edward took another few moment but once he'd replenished his oxygen level he came back into it.

'Cheapskate! Bloodsucker! Fifty years I worked for your father. Never let him down, never once shirked a job or took it easy, didn't take a single sick day. Fifty years! For what? So I could work at seventy-three at below minimum wage just to put food in my mouth.'

'What on earth's got into you?' Unwin said. 'Your wage is the statutory level.'

The policewoman took Edward's arm gently but the old guy shook her off. Lucy's eyes were popping. Beside her music degree she's a couple of secretarial courses under her belt. Prides herself in getting down my occasional dictation as fast as I can speak, even when I'm trying to trip her up. She once told me she stores it all in her head, bangs it out later. Audiographic memory, she calls it. Right now the record button was jammed hard down.

'This is a misunderstanding,' Unwin was saying. 'They've got it wrong.'

'How long was I due to continue you tub of lard? Eighty? Ninety? Your father told me a hundred times, that he'd see me right. He had a pot set aside. The firm would pay an annuity at least equal to the state pension. A hundred times he promised me that.'

'We pay an annuity,' Unwin said. His face was a mess of confusion. 'An annuity and your wage.'

'Fourteen pound a week?' Edward was vibrating like a demented gearstick now. His hands were clenched on the end of rigid arms. The policewoman stepped back. 'What on earth am I meant to do with fourteen pound a week you little toerag? That doesn't even cover your underpayments on my basic salary!'

'I pay statutory wages! Why are you saying this?'

'I'll tell you why, you little weasel. You squeeze twenty hours a week out of me *gratis* as the price for me keeping the job. Do you think I can't do the arithmetic? Your father would skin you alive if he was here.'

The policeman stepped in. 'Sir,' he said. His colleague reached for Edwards arm again. They both looked like they were considering calling for backup.

Unwin finally went on the attack. 'I can't believe you've been stealing from the clients,' he said. 'Dear god, what have you done to us?'

Edward knew exactly what his filching had done to them but his breathing stopped him again. It took five or six raspy breaths to get him back in.

'I'll tell you what I've done,' he said. 'And I'll tell you what I'm going to do. I'm going to buy a bloody big whistle and *blow* it. How about that? All your little frauds with the caskets and the preparation. I'm giving them everything. So you can go home and shut up shop. You're out of the business, *Junior!* That's what I've done.'

It was as if a firecracker had exploded under Unwin's backside. He launched himself at the old guy and would probably have knocked his head off if the policeman had been slower. Unwin's pasty face had found colour and he fought against the cop's grip, arms flailing until the buttons on his wesk't finally blew and scattered shrapnel. I stayed well clear as the uniformed guy finally got tough and manhandled Stevie away from the old guy.

Edward was already moving, steered by the woman officer, but he kept his head turned back to continue the debate.

To his credit, Unwin calmed down and snapped back into something resembling the dignity the occasion demanded. He stepped away from the policeman and opened his arms in supplication to the four of us standing by the hearse. But he was in a quandary with his apologies because he didn't know if we were part of it.

I put him out of his uncertainty.

'Save it,' I said. 'We're none of us real. Tom Gallagher just got the saddest funeral of the year. If you care at all you'll throw in a couple of extra wreaths on the firm. Just in case his wife's watching.'

But Unwin promised nothing. The revelation just put his blood pressure back up. Complementary wreaths weren't part of it.

The old guy was right.

Cheapskate.

But the show had ended. Unwin waved his people over and got them back into the vehicles then cracked the whip and the wagons rolled out. We watched them go. When the silence and the birdsong returned Lucy was the first to react.

'Holy shit,' she said. She was talking to her pal Karen but Karen shrugged it off. They saw this stuff all the time. Behind her, Jimmy Diamond just looked glum.

He stepped forward and sighed. Shook Karen's hand and accepted her thanks. Then he shook mine and Lucy's and thanked us. I wasn't sure whether it was for the professional help or the turnout at the graveside. Maybe both. I shook Karen's hand and thanked her for the business and Lucy gave her a pop-eyed look that screamed *night out* and told her she'd be in touch and we walked back to the road behind the Diamond couple, looking for our lifts.

My and Lucy's lift was a green Mondeo. Harry pushed himself off the bodywork as we came up.

'That looked interesting,' he said.

I grinned. 'Fireworks at a funeral,' I said. 'It's been known.'

'That was one weird case,' Old-Hand Lucy said.

I turned to Harry. He grinned. You could see those nights out coming.

'At least you've got your wheels back,' I said.

Harry shrugged.

'Same old, same old,' he said. 'I'm not gonna miss that racket.'

Sure he wasn't.

I waited. Harry wasn't here just to drive us home. He tightened his grin and nodded out at the road.

'You were right,' he said. 'They're out there.'

I looked across to where shrubs and railings concealed the parked vehicles along Magdalen.

'We've got 'em,' Harry said. 'We know who they are.'

Bingo.

He was talking about the people who'd been following me this last week. They'd just been ID'd. So now we knew *who*. All we needed was the *why*.

How they were linked to Chas Abbott.

CHAPTER FOURTEEN
He had skill at something, though not enough to finish the job

I threw the sash up to get fresh air. Planted my palms on the sill. Checked the skyline. Dusty tower blocks, grey-blue skies, scattered cumulus hanging, the hiss of the Westway.

Harry was sprawled in one of my visitors' chairs behind me, and Herbie was snoring on my Herman Miller desk chair. This was a new thing. The trick was to beat me into the room and grab the executive seat. My own trick was to spin the thing until he was too dizzy to remember where he was or why. When he fell off I reacquired the top seat. For the moment I let him be. Breathed fresh North London air whilst I puzzled over what Harry had found out and tried to figure whether it moved me forwards or just sideways.

He'd picked up the vehicle tailing me as I came off the M25 yesterday. A black BMW that had followed me in from Lincolnshire and right back to my apartment where the Audi TT was waiting to take the night shift. A tight operation, though not tight enough to spot Harry as he tailed the BMW home. Harry grabbed a snap of a tall dark haired guy in his early fifties locking up the car outside an apartment building in Catford. He waited. Picked the guy up when he came out an hour later and followed him round the city through three watering holes and an unsteady midnight drive home. No notable contacts, no ID. But when the BMW drove out this morning Harry was still there. And that's when he got his result.

The car drove over to Merton where the guy parked outside a two storey terrace opposite the old hospital and pushed through a door serving offices above a ground floor beauticians. The glass over the door had an etched business name.

And it was one we knew.

Terry Tickner. Private Investigator.

Which was interesting.

I'd known Terry since I started in this game. Ex-army, veteran of the Bosnian and Gulf conflicts. Quit the forces and set up as a security consultant in the late nineties and diversified into private investigation after he discovered a certain talent in the field. Tickner had built himself a decent reputation even if his techniques were even more suspect than ours.

We'd met in 2007 when I was hired by a rich lady looking for a slam dunk divorce on the back of her belief that her three-year husband was a serial cheater. Seemed the guy was wandering despite the clarity of the savvy and prescient prenuptial agreement she'd made him sign. She took me through the agreement, line by line, which was unnecessary, but I agreed that she had a watertight case in the event that I could pull in hard evidence of her husband's philandering. Which didn't take long since her thirty-something toy boy was not only serial but multiple. In the two weeks I was on him he dated three women, all considerably younger than his sexagenarian spouse. Either the guy wasn't concentrating when he read that prenuptial or he was a daredevil of the first order. Because he was just begging to be sent packing with all his earthly goods in a bag on a stick.

When you're hired to catch a spouse with his paramour and come up with three of them then all that's left is to print the invoice, though you won't take three times the fee. But in this case my final night's socialising netted me more than another face for the report. What I got was a nice little firecracker. The fuse was lit when I spotted a third-party face twice that same evening and realised that someone else was watching the couple. And this guy clocked me as involved with them about ten minutes later which threw him into some kind of black mood. Apparently he didn't welcome intrusions into his own snooping. He jumped me as I leaned out of a doorway across from the Ritz to snap a portrait of the couple heading in for their evening's entrée. I'd just hefted my Leica when I became aware of a big guy at my shoulder. He was as tall as me but a little wider, with the same unfriendly face I'd seen an hour earlier. Someone had bust his nose one time and whoever had set it was lacking certain skills, though the party that engraved the scar under his cheek had skill at something, even if insufficient to finish the job. It was the same face but an hour angrier in the dusk street light.

The anger was detectable in the way he described what he was about to do with my camera. I sensed trouble and whipped off the telephoto, which was expensive kit, and pushed the gear back my shoulder bag. I asked the guy what was bugging him.

When he explained, things became clearer for both of us.

Firstly for him when I explained that he was barking up the wrong tree. I wasn't the press. And what if I was? Society philanderers grab the front pages from time to time. Who the hell should care?

Who should care, apparently, is the husband of the lady being philandered with, currently hanging on our boy's arm as they disappeared through the revolving door. Turned out the big guy who'd jumped me was out watching his lady wife. Had seen what I'd seen. And your wife having an affair is one thing. Reading about it in the tabloids is another.

I gave him my card and told him to cool down. My snaps were headed only for a solicitor's office, confidential eyes only, and the playboy currently impressing the big guy's wife with dinner at the Ritz had a lifestyle change in the offing. He'd soon be wooing his fancy stuff at McDonald's.

The prospect seemed to calm my assailant. He handed me a card of his own.

Terry Tickner. Security and Enquiries. I liked that. The title avoided the stigma of the P.I. trade. "Enquiries" sounded reputable, though I guess it added up to the same thing. And tonight the guy was doing exactly what I was, with the downside that his hours were pro bono and the subject closer to home than an investigator likes.

Confidentiality considerations prevented me from aiding his enquiries with the info I'd gathered but it wouldn't take Tickner long to finalise his own picture. What he did once he had it wasn't my affair and I didn't fancy being a prosecution witness in a murder trial so I didn't ask. But my hints that our lover boy was in for hard times seemed to lighten his mood as we watched the pair disappear into the glitzy foyer.

We stayed outside for a while exchanging head shakes and black chuckles then closed off the night with a couple of drinks at a Soho jazz club. Terry Tickner wasn't a jazz fiend and I can't say I liked him much but the guy seemed solid. Big, tough and holding in whatever he felt about the upcoming loss of his wife. We shared a few drinks and a few anecdotes and kept off the sensitive subject of matrimonials. Finished up with agreement that we'd see each other around but stayed carefully unspecific.

Our paths hadn't crossed since, and my only subsequent

knowledge of the guy came from the occasional snippets that came through the grapevine. Apparently Tickner was doing okay. Okay enough, it now seemed, to take on a twenty-four hour tailing gig. The guy had resources on call.

After fifteen minutes the BMW guy came back down and drove off. Harry let him go. Stayed put outside Tickner's building and was rewarded with a sight of the man himself coming out ten minutes later. Harry followed his Range Rover over to Battersea. Tickner taking his own shift. Harry had called me and I'd watched his Range Rover in my rear view as I drove over to Tom Gallagher's, though I didn't know then who was driving because Harry had held that detail back. That's Harry: likes to choose his moment.

Whilst I was over at the graveside ceremony Harry had snapped pics of Tickner out on the road chatting to his TT driver. The TT driver was another face I recognised: the tubby guy I'd spotted at King's Lynn and Low Rasen. So now we'd had a sight of the whole gang following us, Tickner and all, even if I still couldn't imagine what they were up to.

I should have felt offended that Tickner thought he could tail me without being noticed. And investigators are a little like lawyers: they don't go after their own. But like I said: we weren't pally. Just ships passing. I hadn't liked the guy much back then but I sensed he was someone to respect and neither of those things had changed.

And now we'd come full circle. Tickner had watched me watching his wife. Now I was watching him watching me.

Next job: find out who Tickner's client was. And why they were interested in my search for a missing kid.

CHAPTER FIFTEEN
I didn't mention the oddities

I took an early morning flight out of London City and was at the SIXT desk in Glasgow a little before nine picking up the keys to a Skoda hatchback. I'd told Lucy to go budget and she'd complied, though the wisdom of the economy was less clear with my teeth gritted and foot planted to the floor on the M8 down-ramp to match the traffic speed. Once I was cruising though things got easier. I fired up my MP3 and played loud jazz through my buds, crossed the Clyde and turned north under a grey sky. Drove two hours through the highlands to Glencoe and Fort William.

It was a solitary drive. Tickner's guy had been right behind me at London City and picked up a ticket for the same flight but we'd parted ways on touchdown. Tickner's first mistake. If you're planning to follow someone out through car hire you need to book ahead. Make reservations at three or four desks to give you the choice of the shortest queue. And if the desks are dispersed round the airport perimeter you need a team of two: one to pick up the wheels and one to watch the subject and guide you round, ready to follow him out. Any other way you're out of the game. My guess was that Tickner's guy was already boarding the flight back to London as I crossed the Clyde. Hopeless is hopeless.

Which had me wondering about my jaunt. Not exactly hopeless but maybe my expectations were a little heavy on speculation, a little dependent on the roll of a dice. Chas Abbott had hiked out of Lincolnshire leaving nothing more than a hint that he was still aiming for Scotland, hints of catching up with a girl friend living off the land, with a book in his backpack about a place called Smirisary. Which might take me straight to his next stop or to nothing. Did Heather live at the settlement? Was Chas aiming to catch up with her?

My fifty K map had the settlement marked far up on the west coast. A cluster of buildings by the sea, barely worth a name. No road in or out. Maybe you got there by boat: the map showed a *Port* on the nearby coast which I took to be the Scottish term for a rocky beach where you might or might not get ashore alive. My own route in would be a hike over the hills.

If Chas *had* reached Smirisary I'd be taking a giant leap, closing the gap by weeks or months. And the place made sense. If Chas was bent on dropping out where better than the Highlands? Where more off-grid than a remote crofting community? And since I was buying the long odds I might as well aim high: maybe I'd find Chas himself there, sitting tight and watching the world go by.

I dropped down through Glencoe drizzle and hit the coast in an interlude of blinding sunlight. Parked in Fort William just before mid day. First stop: lunch, then a tour of the local campsites and hostels. Smirisary was still a long way for the hiker. If Chas had passed through here he'd have probably stopped over for a couple of days, getting his bearings, maybe picking up more causal work.

I ate a fast sandwich then called at tourist information and they gave me seven campsites and hostels.

I covered three hostels in the town and a nearby campsite with no result. Then I headed out up Glen Nevis to check another hostel right under the mountain. This one was a bright, modern place with facilities a three star hotel would envy and the sort of staff a travelling youngster would want greeting him after a tough winter's day on the hills. The staff didn't recognise Chas' picture but pointed me to the visitors' book and invited me to take a look.

I looked.

And got a hit.

Late September, 2010. Below the entry of a couple from Freiburg who'd raved about the hostel despite weather they described as *schlekt* – which I took to be the German term for "Scottish" – was a scratchy and barely legible entry within which only the name *Chas Abbott* stood out. I took a moment to decipher his message. Squinted at it from every direction, applied context and de-encryption and came up with my best shot which was that Chas was dispensing the words of wisdom: "Keep walking to stay near home" which was either a sentiment I didn't quite grasp or just his lousy handwriting. But whatever the boy was saying there was an immediacy in his scrawl: the ballpoint ink was as clear as the day he'd passed through, giving the sense that he'd just walked out of the door. But the date was two years old, the immediacy an illusion. He'd checked in here less than a week after striking camp at Low Rasen. So the boy had either picked up some good rides or taken the train.

I stood over the book and snapped a picture. Something to fire off in my next report to Susan and Patricia. The first material evidence of Chas' continued existence. Something to reassure them that their money was pulling in results. I pictured them following my reports up in Chas' room in Alton, checking out his half-mill. map. Marking lines, places and dates.

I thanked the hostel staff, drank one of their coffees and drove back into town to fill the tank. Then took the Mallaig road west.

Forty minutes out from Fort William I spotted an inn close to where the road split towards Smirisary. It was late afternoon. I pulled over and grabbed a room. Donned my lightweight running gear and ran forty-five minutes along damp tarmac to work up an appetite. The rain kept me cool whilst I ran inland. Froze hell out of me when I turned back into the westerly. I gritted my teeth and upped the pace, stayed warm. Back in my tiny bathroom I took a long shower and went down to the bar. Lamb shank was up on the board. I put in my order and went with the waitress's recommendation for a good cask ale. Sat down and called Susan Abbott.

I brought her up to date and sent through the visitors' book snap. Heard a gasp as she checked it out. Hope building. I threw in a warning but the excitement stayed in her voice. She had the Proof of Existence she and her mother had been lacking for two years. I didn't mention the oddities accumulating round her brother. Time for that if they ever became relevant.

I told her I'd stay in touch and cut the line to return a missed call. Harry.

'They wasted those air tickets,' he told me.

'I figured that. My rear-view's been clear all day. You pick the guy up when he jetted back in?'

'Yeah. ID too. The guy's name is Luke Preston. Long associate of Terry's. He came back on the afternoon flight and headed straight home. I guess Tickner's crew are standing down.'

'No choice. They're not gong to pick me up in the Highlands in an un-bugged car. I'm off their radar till I get back.'

But they were on ours. Harry suggested I call Shaughnessy. He'd been following Tickner himself. Had a result. I made the call and caught Shaughnessy outside a house he was watching in Kingston.

'We've got the client,' he said.

He sent a photo through. My food arrived: lamb shank, mash and peas, mint sauce on the side. And at a price any Yorkshireman would appreciate. I held back my hunger for a second whilst I scanned Shaughnessy's pic.

The photo showed Tickner at a cafe table on the river front at Kingston, drinking a shot opposite a trim guy with curly black hair wearing an open neck shirt under a navy suit. The guy was early- or mid-thirties, handsome, privileged looking.

'Is this about us?'

'I'm seeing it that way. The two of them were gabbing for forty minutes, which is a big chunk of Tickner's day if he's been hired twenty-four seven on you.'

Twenty-four seven currently on hold, since I was in the wind. Maybe that's what he was explaining to the guy.

'We know who this guy is?'

'Lucy's working her society connections right now.'

'How do we know he's society-worthy?'

'I followed him home. Take a look.'

He sent through another pic. The new snap showed an ornate gate protecting a driveway off a leafy road that Shaughnessy identified as the A308 somewhere up near the university.

'The guy works for Holland International. They're just over the river from the first photo. I hung around until he came out this evening and followed him here. And the way his car activated the gates tells me it's his crash pad.'

Holland International. A merchant bank conglomerate with all kinds of billionaire-gestating offshoots. I didn't know anything about them apart from their name but if the suited guy lived at a place like this he must be one of their key people, which meant we were looking at an even bigger puzzle. The dodgy types I'd bumped into at the *Fizikun* shop and Low Rasen were an equal puzzle but at least they were a puzzle on the same stratum as our missing graduate. But what in hell could link a multi-billion pound financial enterprise to our boy?

'Tell Lucy to keep looking,' I said. 'I want to know who he is.'

'Will do. Any sign of the boy up there?'

'Still hoping. He was up here, heading towards the crofting settlement if I'm guessing right. If Chas wanted to drop out of sight it's as good a place as any.'

'You think he's there?'

'I'd give it a million to one. Does that sound over-optimistic?'

'Wildly,' Shaughnessy said. 'But we've gotta stay positive: this could be all over when you get there.'

'Yeah,' I agreed. 'A million to one's a little fanciful.'

I shut off the phone and tucked into my lamb. The shank was cooked to perfection, almost took my mind of the fact that every day I chased after Chas Abbot seemed to bring a whole new set of things that didn't fit.

Maybe I *would* catch up with Chas at Smirisary and he'd clear it all up.

Or maybe I wouldn't and this thing would just get denser.

P.I.'s are optimists by nature but we also go with probabilities. Which pointed to the latter.

CHAPTER SIXTEEN
Circus

I grabbed an early breakfast in the inn's deserted dining room then drove out fuelled by early morning optimism. The road took me along a sea loch into bright sunshine, a brief interlude between showers. I wound the window down but the fierce westerly breeze swirled and rumbled inside the Skoda and forced a re-think. I worked it back up and continued in hermetic silence. Ten minutes down the loch I caught sight of open sea and two minutes after that a signpost pointed down a lane cutting off towards the Sound and announced that Smirisary was that way. The signpost was a surprise, as was the tarmac covering the lane. Maybe the beach landing was no longer the only way in to the settlement.

Things clarified a mile on. The lane narrowed and climbed over rocky heathland with vistas of sea and distant grey mountains then petered out, tarmac and all. I parked in front of a gate and a much older signpost that confirmed the way on. The climb over the hill ahead would be by more traditional transport. I pulled my trainers on. Not good footwear for what might be a wet hike but I was travelling light. My sole concession to the elements was a lightweight cag clipped to my belt, and even that wasn't going to cut it if the weather turned nasty.

I pushed through the gate and climbed towards the ridge whilst the rain held off. Breathed fresh air and enjoyed the sun. I pictured the boy trudging this route two years ago. Wondered if he'd hiked all the way from Fort William or hitched the Mallaig road, hopped off where the roads split.

All speculation.

The walk would have been welcome if I wasn't endlessly dodging puddles and boggy patches to keep my trainers dry but when I hit the top of the ridge the view out over the Hebrides rewarded the inconvenience. I stopped for thirty seconds to take it in then continued, slid and skidded my way down the steepening path towards the settlement I still couldn't see. I was beginning to wonder about the signpost's fidelity when I rounded an outcrop of bushes and spotted slate roofs and solar panels down near the beach. The view opened to reveal half a dozen stone cottages scattered across the scrubby heathland below me. I'd speed-read a copy of Chas' book. Pictured crops and animals but saw only a few vegetable gardens bounded by low stone walls, a handful of sheep on the far rise. Maybe the place was no longer self-sufficient.

By the time I got down to the buildings my feet were sodden and my trouser legs were caked in mud. I zigzagged across the boggy land and rapped on the door of the first cottage. A guy in his eighties came out and pointed to a building nearer the rocks just before the land dropped to the shore. I zigzagged again and reached a tiny stone building with a water tank at its side and solar panels on the roof. Behind the cottage a shed housed a diesel generator that a guy in his thirties was tinkering with. He looked up as I opened the gate, and when I asked for Heather he came round to take me in.

The cottage was a surprise. Modern. Open-plan. A main living space with a bathroom and bedroom opening off one end. Bright wooden floor and furniture, Velux lights. I hung back at the door despite the guy's invitation, grinned at a woman sitting at a wooden table working a computer. She looked up surprised. I guess they didn't get many visitors.

She was fair-haired in her early twenties with a broad faced and a slight stockiness that looked genetic.

I guessed this was Heather.

A toddler was playing beneath the table with a scattering of home-made rag dolls and wooden play stuff that went out fifty years ago. A simple life.

I kept it simple: said I was looking for Chas.

When she heard the name Heather's face turned puzzled and I knew right then that I wasn't going to find Chas here. But the smartish way she stood and asked what was wrong told me that she knew things.

I grinned and gestured to my feet. I was bringing half of Moidart across the threshold. But the guy waved me in again. Told me no prob., man, mopping up's what they did. I compromised, walked part way across and stretched to hand Heather my card. When she'd read it I gave her the story of Chas' family losing touch.

She listened then looked at me and said 'Shit!'

Then got active. Asked if I drank coffee. I was able to confirm that fact and she headed over to a small filter machine with a half jug on the hot plate which was probably powered by the solar panels. She poured me a mug. I should have declined, seeing as how they had to bring everything in from Ireland or somewhere, but I was in need of a kick and in need of a prop to keep us on a talkative basis. So I took the brew and sipped whilst Heather asked me what had happened.

I'd just told her everything I knew, which amounted to the fact that no one knew anything, but it was interesting that she was assuming that something had happened. She stooped to pick up the child and paced the room to give it some thought.

'I knew it,' she said. 'He wasn't happy.'

Interesting.

Everyone else I'd talked to remembered how terrifically fine Chas was that summer. This was the first hint of anything amiss. I sensed movement in my search, even if the direction might not be a good one.

'I knew it,' Heather repeated, 'when he didn't get in touch.'

She glanced at the guy for his view, but he gave nothing. I sensed he was peripheral to whatever connected Heather and Chas. I looked at him and he smiled and came across to extend a hand.

'Luke,' he said. 'The crazywoman's husband. You've had a long trip for nothing, dude.'

I explained that most of the miles were courtesy of British Airways but his point remained apposite. We were a long way from Alton.

'When was he last seen?' Heather asked.

She bounced the question abruptly off me, as if she'd suddenly found the need to unravel things herself. I sensed a proprietary concern for the boy. Or maybe guilt. Something that had happened, perhaps.

I put her right.

'Chas had cut contact before he arrived here,' I said. 'His family know nothing after he left home in Alton. And right now you're my last contact with him. Assuming that he did come here. Maybe we can start there.'

'He was here early October two years ago,' she confirmed. 'He'd missed the good weather. Came in looking like a drowned rat.'

'Dude hitched to Glenfinnan,' Luke said. 'Hoofed it the rest of the way. He'd been on the road for two days and got caught by a storm as he topped the pass. Slipped twice on the way down. He was covered in mud. Luckily we've a decent bathroom and hot water.'

'We put him up in here the first night,' Heather said. 'After that he pitched his tent outside and just popped in for meals. He'd brought a stack of provisions, which was a nice thought, though I think he consumed more than he brought.'

'I heard you and he were friends at university.'

'Sort of. We had shared interests.' Heather bounced the child and pushed at her hair. 'We'd talked about living off the land, which was my big thing. I'd stayed here at Smirisary with my aunt as a child and caught the bug. When she died my parents inherited the lease. The croft was left to rot for five years but I decided take it on and get things up and running. Modernise. There's no internet but I can work remotely and connect up periodically in Fort William. Compared to sitting in a London office it's a no-brainer.'

'And you passed on the bug for remote living?'

'I guess so. Chas lapped up the idea of living somewhere he could breath. But I beat him to it when I ditched my degree and moved up here in '09.'

'But you kept in touch?'

'Off and on. We exchanged letters. And we got together briefly down in London just before his final term. He was still talking about the life and I urged him to call in if he ever came north.'

'And he did. Two years ago.'

'Yes.'

'Did he talk about his plans?'

'He was taking a gap year. Big decisions and all that.'

She stopped. Turned away to pace the room again. Give herself a moment to think.

'I think Chas had picked up the wrong idea,' she said. 'We were friends but not close-close. I'd no romantic plans linked to him. But when he turned up here I think he expected me to be alone. He'd maybe read more into my invitation than was intended. He was surprised to meet Luke.'

She put the child back down and looked at her husband.

'He tried to hide it,' Luke said, 'but I think Chas took a hit when he saw how things were.'

'Romantic assumptions dashed?'

'I think so,' Heather said. 'We both just went along with the pretence that it was just a flying visit, passing through, but I think he'd expected more. Maybe even to stay here.'

'How long did he stay?'

'A week,' Luke said. 'The weather was lousy and we had to relocate his tent twice after it flooded. But he worked about the place and made himself useful and was positive about everything but I think he was kinda lost once he realised that Heather and I were a thing.'

'Did he explain his plans when he moved on?'

'They weren't specific,' Heather said. 'I think they'd ended here. Once he realised he wouldn't be staying everything was vague. Just an idea of moving on, picking up work, living in his tent, which wasn't the most attractive idea in Scotland. Damn! I should have seen. I *did* see! And we let him walk out.'

'Couldn't be helped Heth,' Luke said. 'He had his own path to follow.'

'Yeah. But he was going off into the unknown in late autumn and might have ended up on the streets of Glasgow or London for all we knew. I never had a good feeling about it. And if he's not been seen since he left here then I was right.'

She stopped. Luke put his hand on her shoulder. The toddler crawled over and pulled herself unsteadily to her feet, gripped his leg. He picked her up and Heather went over to flick off the coffee machine and return the milk to the fridge.

'What on earth's happened to him?' she said. 'He said he'd write. But that was a big disappointment here. I knew it.'

'Any hint about his next stop?'

Luke thought about it.

'His friend,' he said. 'Alfie.'

Heather came back over. Recollected.

'He's someone else who'd disappeared,' she said. 'Chas had lost track of him, thought he'd got himself into some kind of trouble. He talked about finding him.'

She shook her head. 'Chas should have realised that his family were already looking for *him*. One vanished guy searching for another.'

I finished my coffee. It was good. Surprisingly hot. Those solar panels.

I thought about Alfie.

Wondered if Chas had followed up on his idea and returned to continue the search for his friend when his half-baked plans died here in the mud and rain. Maybe he'd trekked back out with the notion of returning to Lincolnshire. But what was Alfie up to that had Chas worrying about him?

I asked if Chas had told them anything more about his friend and the two dug up a hazy memory.

'The dude was in some kind of trouble,' Luke said. 'Mixed up with bad people. Maybe had issues with drugs. But the important thing is what's happened to Chas?'

Heather agreed. I handed her my mug.

'I intend to find out,' I said. I thanked them and promised to let them know then took my muddy feet back out and began the slow climb back to the ridge.

I beat the weather by a whisker. The rain hit just as I unlocked the car door. I jumped in and donned dry footwear as the world outside disappeared behind sheets of rain.

I drove back up the loch towards the Mallaig road. The squall blew out and the road steamed as I turned towards Fort William. A few hundred yards down I braked on impulse and pulled onto the verge. Walked a track that climbed up beneath dripping trees to the railway halt. Found a short platform serving a single track that looked like it hadn't seen a train in a couple of decades. The boom times of the fish trains out of Mallaig were long gone and the line was mostly surviving on steam excursions. I checked the timetable. It showed a two-hourly local service. So not quite abandoned. I pictured Chas up here, wondering whether to hitch or wait. But if he'd hiked over from Smirisary in the rain his motivation would likely have been shot. Better to shiver in the tiny railway shelter, thinking about the might-have-beens.

He'd waited, was my guess, then taken the train back to civilisation. But then what? Was he drawn back to Lincolnshire to try to squeeze more info out of Petra? If he'd done that she'd kept it from me. Or did he push Alfie to the back of his mind for a while and continue his wanderings? Maybe he'd travelled down into England and Wales looking for somewhere to hole up for the winter.

I'd reached the end of the line again. I had Chas in Smirisary the first week of October and then nothing. I needed inspiration. A break and a re-think. Figure out how to get back into the steps of the kid who'd left nothing but vague memories in his wake.

My best bet was clear: I needed to look at the things that didn't fit, the circus that had sprung up around him down south.

I walked back down to the road and fired up the Skoda and drove back to Glasgow.

CHAPTER SEVENTEEN
The pants he was wearing

My flight got me back to London mid-evening. I drove across the city through the dusk and parked at Battersea. Climbed up to my apartment. The sound of scratching and snuffling came from behind my door. Someone home. When I opened up Herbie pounced and clamped his teeth onto my shoe. It was a new trick he'd developed for the times I disappeared without permission. I yelled at him and got the door shut and lurched my way through to the kitchen where something was cooking. You move slowly with twenty kilograms locked onto your foot. As I reached the door Margot came out and shook her head.

'He's been so good all day,' she apologised.

I believed her. I also believed that she was behind this new habit. Herbie's objections to my absences and broken promises had started at precisely the same time as Margot's ever-understanding forgiveness of the same. I lurched and leaned, planted a kiss. Dropped my carry-on when I felt the silky glide of her short dress over her hips. Dresses like that needed all the hands you could spare. Margot gave things a few moments then said *Stop that!* Herbie dropped my foot and grinned up at her.

'Supper needs to be fast,' Margot said. 'We're heading out for that night you've been promising all week.'

Which was technically untrue. What I'd been doing all week was stalling. And Margot's theatre tickets were booked for tomorrow, which made *that* our big night out. So I guess what she had in mind was what most people think of as two people hanging out on a Friday night.

But hanging sounded good. I grabbed a quick shower then sat down for a supper of fresh-baked lasagne on leaves and spring onions. It was late in the day for pasta but I'd not eaten since my hotel breakfast and Margot had been out on the park with Herbie when I'd sent through my flight times, burning off ten lasagnes' worth of calories. So we both had deficits. And I had to consider the prospect of significant calorific expenditure later.

We ate fast and headed out.

Margot drove to save her expensively fragile dress from the lap passenger's claws. The Frogeye took its usual hammering from her decisive wheel work as we skirted Chelsea and raced towards Paddington. She'd been talking since we met about buying vintage herself but then she'd need to drive more carefully. We got to Paddington faster than my nerves would have liked but later than ideal for Friday night. Once we'd found a parking spot the short walk round to the Podium dropped my pulse back down to double figures and I was good to go.

Barney waved us through for a tenner each – canines go free – and we found a table at the back with two seats spare that we worked together by a process akin to musical chairs. Juke came over and planted a beer for me and juice for Margot, a packet of pork scratchings for the floor-level clientele. I handed back a monster tip and he gave me the thumbs up with dancing eyebrows and a sly head tilt towards the lady. I wiggled my own eyebrows and grinned back. Lifted my beer.

Friday nights have two live sets at the Podium. We'd missed the first and had thirty minutes of buzz to hold any conversation we were planning to hold. Margot kicked things off with the reprimand she'd held off at Battersea.

'I'm starting to get used to your schedule, Eddie. The weeks where a Monday night out means 10 p.m. Friday.'

'You're hardly the nine-to-five woman yourself, Marg. What about all those horror stories about your friends' awful ordered lives?'

'I guess I'm not complaining, Eddie. Unpredictability is the spice of life. And unplanned self-time is opportunity if you look at it the right way.'

'No one's ever told me that before.'

She leaned and smiled. Touched glasses.

'My problem's always been the opposite. Guys who get too close and take it wrong when I ease them back. You're the first guy who doesn't need pushing. There but not there.'

'You've got me to a tee. Here when I'm not.' I chinked and sipped. 'I've been waiting to meet a girl who understands that concept.'

She grinned. Planted her glass.

'But let it be known,' she said, 'that if I ever tell you I *need* you, somewhere, sometime, then you'd better be there.'

'Depend on it. There's not an undercover operation or car chase that I wouldn't put on hold for you, Margot. Just say the word. I'll be there in spirit *and* body.'

'So cutting to the chase: tomorrow's theatre tickets are safe?'

'Safe as houses. Wild horses and all that...'

'It's the wild horses I'm worried about. Have you anything galloping loose at the moment?'

'Nothing I can see. I've hit what you'd call a lull in activities. The landscape's bare. I'm standing in a field of emptiness. I'm surrounded by metaphorical nothingness.'

'You've not sighted your missing boy?'

'I followed him up to the Highlands yesterday. Found barely a shadow.'

'Okay, but he'd been there? You must be closing the gap.'

'I'm seven hundred miles and three months down the trail. Problem is, all everyone recalls is him moving on. And something is up: I'm tripping over dodgy people everywhere who shouldn't be part of the thing and being watched by others who've no reason to do so.'

I brought her up to date. Left out names. The names didn't matter. She could see the tangle without needing specifics.

She stretched and pushed her hair back. Her dress flowed over her figure in an alarming way.

'So your kid's not what he seems,' she concluded. 'He *isn't* the average Joe you thought you were following.'

'Problem is, that's exactly what he is. Just a kid taking a year out.'

But Margot had it right. There was something about Chas Abbott I was missing. The theory that all the oddities that had sprang up around my search were unrelated, maybe linked only to his pal Alfie or to something else entirely, wasn't convincing me.

And if unravelling twelve weeks of the boy's two year mystery tour was progress it hardly seemed like that: all it came down to right now was another last sighting of him walking away from disappointment in the Highlands. It was hard to say whether I was any closer to him than I'd been ten days ago.

A quartet set up on the Podium's tiny stage. Got busy. Movement and amp. screech, bass riffs and horn trills. Margot took another sip of her juice and leaned closer. Came back to her previous topic.

'It's the funniest damn thing,' she said.

I looked at her.

'My whole disastrous love life has been a fight to avoid being smothered. I want a guy but I don't want my life to be defined by him. And now the shoe's on the other damn foot. You're a guy who's never here, and suddenly up pops this pain-in-the-backside longing to follow you round and stare over your shoulder.'

I gave her puzzled. This was out of the blue.

'A foot-slogging private eye following a kid who's hiked into obscurity. The damn thing's been bugging me all week, Eddie. Every time I'm trying to focus and magic up the next little episode of my mad fictional character, I'm distracted by serious cravings to be doing something even more ludicrous, following you down some dusty road as you chase ghosts. I almost called you a hundred times this week. And that's scary.'

Which I didn't dispute. If I'd had an inkling of this I'd have been putting the tailing vehicles down to her.

'You'd be disappointed staring over *this* shoulder,' I said. 'The P.I.'s reality is sore feet and frustration. Third-rate hotel rooms and endless dead ends. We just do the job as best we can and deliver the goods. And the ghosts we're chasing are never our own.'

'But the intrigue! Never knowing which fork in the road is the right one, never knowing what trap or red herring is waiting. Every day a new challenge.'

I bent and handed down pork scratchings to conceal my laugh. Jaws worked beneath the table. Teeth crunched. The room shook. When I had control again I came back up.

'Intrigue is usually thin on the ground,' I said. 'Mostly we just serve notices and check cooked books. And what's round the corner is likely to be bunched fists or a bat. The appeal of endlessly running for your life wouldn't last.'

'I'm not buying it. You've told me too many stories and there's the same element in all of them. The meandering trail, ghosts in the shadows. You told me you'd never do anything else. Addiction was what you called it: the allure of the unknown.'

I held my grin. She was right. The unknown. Always draws you in. And the allure hadn't exactly diminished this last week for lack of anything coming into focus. You might even describe a simple missing person case that was taking on the characteristic of a hydra *alluring*.

I swallowed beer. Planted the glass. We had another couple of minutes before the set.

'Tell me about Edgar,' I said. 'What's he been up to this week?'

She smiled.

'Since when were you so interested in my strip?'

'Since always. I buy the rag for Edgar. I told you. And I've gone a week without a humour fix.'

'Well I've still not figured out how a manic strip character fits the detective's world view. What are you always telling me? Fantasy is what you strip away to get at the next wage packet? Give me cold truth, etc etc.'

'Fantasy has its place. I model my behaviour on Edgar. I'm just not so loud.'

'Liar. Edgar is a lout, dressed up as middle class respectability. You're a gentleman, Eddie, even if you hate the word. He and you are the opposite.'

'Not many people call me a gentleman. You might be off target there.'

She laughed and sat back.

'I talk to Lucy, remember. She once told me you were the first real gentleman she'd ever met. I thought it was a negative at first. Pictured stiff-upper, retentive. But now I know what she was talking about.'

I smiled back. Damned if I did. I've always believed that right is right and wrong is wrong and good breeding is having the sense to see the difference. And if that defines a gentleman then I'm guilty. But Lucy was attracted to me because she thought I needed looking after, simple as that.

'Okay,' Margot said, 'Edgar: I'll tell you what happened. We picked up another lawsuit.'

I opened my eyes.

'The second in five years. It was Wednesday's strip. Flayed another peer of the realm. Seemed Edgar was too close to the bone in his speculation about the good Lord's extramarital interests.'

'I can't wait to catch up. Is the paper scared?'

'The paper's over the moon. Wally called me today. Says they'll cover legal costs out of circulation boost. And that's only if they fail to prove that the guy's a serial predator, which they won't. My guess is that the guy will take the weekend to cool down then settle, save having his face on the front of the tabloids for the next twelve months. But it's the potential settlement that's Wally's concern: he wants court time.'

'Tell Wally if he needs dirt to back up his defence he can give me a call.'

'You're top of the list, Eddie. I assume you'd put Lucy on it.'

'None other. The guy better not have taken a leak without washing his hands. But if you ever start up that new strip you mentioned – the deranged P.I. – give me some warning. I'll get my own retirement plan together.'

'Well here's the warning: I'm going ahead. It's my next project. The guy's called Axegrinder and he's old school hard-boiled. And he's going to make a few people's hair stand on end. Because he'll be investigating the people who don't want investigating. I've already worked up a couple of proofs to test the market. Maybe I'll give you a peek.'

I grinned. Clamped my lips. Tried to quell the fear that Axegrinder might turn out to be a little too close to home. He'd be a gentleman for sure.

~~~~~

The second set extended to two a.m. so it was late when we rolled out of the Podium. Margot slalomed the Sprite through the early hours traffic and got us back to my place in the blink of an eye. Either a record run or I'd nodded off. Herbie huffed up the stairs ahead of us and slurped his milk then hit his bed. I hit my own bed but then Margot slipped off her dress in a way that knocked sleep out of my head and by the time we were both too tired to make any further moves the hint of dawn was in my skylight and a late start to the day was on the cards.

My phone pulled me from the depths at a few minutes after eight.

I groaned. Picked up.

'Luce! We were talking about you last night.'

'That's spooky. I almost called. Decided to wait until this morning though in case I was interrupting any funny business.'

'I'm guessing there's a reason for this call?'

'So I was right! A heavy night. Give it half an hour before you wake Margot. She'll appreciate the change of mood.'

'Still waiting for that reason...'

'I've been busy. That's the reason.'

I perked up. When Lucy got busy something was apt to pop out of the bottle. I climbed out of bed. Padded through to the kitchen.

'What have you got?'

'I've got Tickner's client. The guy who's watching you.'

I grabbed a filter. Topped up the water.

'Tell me.'

'I used Sean's snap and the Kingston address. Dug around and had a chat with Philippa. Found him. Looks like you've got a big fish on your tail, Eddie.'

'How big?'

'You remember that Sean followed the guy into the merchant bank building? Holland International? Well the guy's more than a worker ant. He's Clark Holland. The grandson of the old man himself.'

I heaped a mountain of Buckaroo into the filter and flicked the switch. Waited for the aroma. But I'd already felt a kick as good as any extra-strength coffee could deliver.

The old man Lucy was referring to was Max Holland the company's multi-billionaire founder. Sir Max was one of Margot's upper echelon, the entrepreneurial autocrat who'd built Holland International into the fourth biggest company in the UK.

More accurately: former upper echelon; former entrepreneur.

Because two months ago Max and his son Marcus had forfeited all their privileges and power when their company Gulfstream took a dive into the Gulf of Mexico on a flight into Miami leaving the company headless and the world of the uber-privileged in shock at how the tiniest glitch in a piece of machinery can count for more than all the majority shareholdings and power networks in the world.

If I recalled the news, the two of them had been picked up within minutes of the ditching, but all to no avail. Marcus was DOA and Max lived for only a couple of days before they switched off his life-support. The two days was a testament to the combined power of money and medical science but in the end Max ended up in the same place we all do. Two days after the accident the Holland fortune was up for grabs.

The story had caught my peripheral attention but hadn't stuck. I was busy with a case over in the West Country at the time.

'So how about that,' Lucy summarised: 'You're being stalked by big money.'

I walked through and watched the street. Tickner's people were probably down there right now but the anarchy of parked cars gave them unassailable cover. I couldn't even spot the Frogeye. With any luck Margot would recall the spot.

'Just how big?' I said.

'We're talking ten billion-ish. All due to the old guy's two surviving grandkids. One of whom is Clark. He and his sister get everything.'

'Excluding the Gulfstream.'

'Minus the Gulfstream and the pants the old man was wearing. But that will leave Clark and his sister in the UK's top ten. We're talking five billion each.'

'So why are these people onto me? I'd be inclined to think I'm misreading this. Tickner must work for a lot of people. But this twenty-four seven assignment is costing someone *big* money. And when Terry takes time out for a forty minute chinwag right in the middle of the job I can't help thinking that the guy he's talking to is the one who's financing the operation. Especially when that guy turns out to have the means. So I'm buying Clark as the client. Just a bigger client than we were imagining.'

'So why would a zillionaire be interested in you – or Chas?'

'That's the question. They've stayed on my tail all week and they can see I'm searching for someone. Which means they must be interested in that same person.'

'That's crazy. Chas is just an ordinary kid. And who knew you were looking for him except his mother and sister?'

'No one. That's the puzzle. Tickner's people were with me the second I started looking.'

'So is it Chas they're interested in? Or you?'

I unlatched the window and swung it open. Let in fresh air and street noise. Distant traffic.

'Neither makes sense. But there's no reason anyone should be interested in me.'

'It's Chas,' Lucy said.

I grinned. Took a few deep breaths. Lucy had already decided this before she called. Her question had been rhetorical. Lucy got off on things getting complicated, not being what they should.

'If we can find an obvious connection between a billionaire family and a disoriented university graduate then you might be right, Luce.'

Though it was hard to imagine the connection. Chas Abbott was the archetypal nobody in the grand scheme of things. Valued and missed only by his family. He hadn't left a single mark on the wider world. And for two years he'd *literally* been a nobody. Dropped out of existence. The ghost on the dusty road.

I took a few more breaths and came fully awake. Confusion and oxygen mixed. I was ready to go.

But not today. The weekend was accounted for.

Margot and I had the two days set in stone, unchangeable if I wanted to keep her, which I did. The commitment was a good thing. Something solid to ground me for a couple of days.

Sometimes I actually keep promises. I had the sense and willpower to protect the things that mattered.

All I was lacking was an off switch.

CHAPTER EIGHTEEN
Room to swing cat

The weekend went the way of all weekends, and if I didn't entirely free myself from the urge to gnaw at knots neither did I spend too much time trying to explain things that weren't explainable. Boot leather, spadework and time were going to be needed before enlightenment came calling. What was harder to push aside was a picture in my head of Chas Abbott moving relentlessly away. I'd zero rationale to justify that picture but psychology's a funny thing. Every time I caught myself relaxing, drinking a beer or reading a theatre programme I saw the image of striding boots. In my misfiring psychology Chas Abbott never slept.

I drove to the office extra early on Monday morning to allow for my monthly detour up to Willesden to drop Herbie off with William Mullan, the old down-and-out from whom I'd inherited him. The two had been a team back then, touring the capital's streets for four years until William's health gave out right after I'd intervened to rescue him from a couple of muggers. The old guy survived his subsequent medical crisis but his days on the streets were numbered and the council's prohibition on pets in their sheltered accommodations resulted in the Staffie's forcible retraining as assistant to London's coolest detective.

The ban didn't apply to visiting pets so once a month, when William's sister came in from Amersham to escort him on a day out, Herbie showed up to spend the day in shameless pan-handling for handouts. If William had been threatened with losing his canine he'd have given up his warm home and hit the streets again. But the compromise worked. Herbie was back with the old guy once a month and that was enough. All Herbie had to do was remember the pining routine, an act that crescendoed at pick-up time as we made an exit that convinced William his dog would be counting the days to their next reunion. The tail-down parting continued unstoppably until Herbie had jumped into the car and had his paws on the dash.

Edgware Road traffic was the usual morass. I fought it both ways and got back to Paddington a little after eight. The lawyers' offices were still closed up as I jogged up two flights to our landing and turned the lock. I rotated the sign and fired up the coffee machine and went through to open the sash. Then I sat back in my Herman Miller executive chair and swivelled it to get my feet onto the sill whilst I waited for inspiration.

The Holland family connection was intriguing but a missing person case works fine without intrigue. Best case: the connection might give me somewhere to dig if I lost the trail. Which was decidedly on the cards unless I could pick up Chas' direction after Smirisary. Leaving me contemplating a long drive back out to Low Rasen to push the girl Petra a little harder to find out what she'd almost told me before our pub chat was interrupted.

I was sensing a connection between the guys who'd done the interrupting and the people who'd come looking for Chas' friend Alfie in London, who might also connect to the Eastern Europeans at the Streatham shop.

My crystal ball warned of diversions ahead, way off-centre from the dusty track I'd been following.

I listened to the coffee machine coughing over the background of Westway traffic and trains as I waited for the inspiration. But for the moment nothing came.

Then the outer door opened and I heard unfamiliar steps. I pulled my feet off the sill and swivelled to face my desk just as two guys walked into my office and suddenly the circus was on again.

The first guy instinctively ducked below the lintel as he came through, saving his head from damage. He was just as tall as I remembered.

Longhair.

The guy from the *Fizikun* shop.

His messy locks were still dropping to his shoulders, which were covered today in a black leather jacket over a black tee-shirt and black jeans. I didn't spot what colour his socks were. What I saw was that he had a baseball bat.

The guy behind him was of the same ilk but wearing a buzz cut which would have made him the dapper one if he wasn't wearing a track suit. He didn't look any happier than Longhair.

The two halted side-by-side just inside the door.

I smiled. Tried to keep my eyes off the bat.

'Gentlemen,' I said. 'Welcome to Eagle Eye. How may we be of assistance?'

Longhair looked at me and thought about it.

'Question is,' he said, 'what *we* can do for you? Make you understand.'

I lifted my feet onto my desk. Gave him a smile with teeth.

'Understand what?'

'Understand that you stop messing our business.'

I held the smile.

'And what business would that be?'

Longhair held his stare. He wasn't smiling.

'Okay,' he said. 'Let's stop being funny-man. I don' like.'

He shook his head and waggled the bat.

I opened my hands.

'Call me obtuse,' I said, 'but I don't know you and I don't know why you're here. Did I miss your name in the appointments book?'

'You don't need appointment book. *We* make appointment.'

'Got it. Though I'm still no nearer to figuring out what you want.'

Longhair motioned to Buzzcut who walked across to the other side of my desk and stood under my Geoff Boycott poster. Then Longhair stepped forward to stand right behind the roll top shelving just beyond my feet. Now I had them left and right like two ugly paperweights over my top sill.

I could no longer see the bat but the pat-pat-pat sound from behind my desk told me it was still there, smacking against the guy's leg.

'Why you come the shop?' Longhair asked.

'I told you. I was looking for someone who worked there.'

'He no work there,' he said. 'And we no stupid.' He leaned forwards a little and hefted the bat to wave it between himself and his pal.

'You know who we are?'

'I'm assuming you're Sales. But I've got all the fitness gear I need.'

The two looked at each other.

'He think is funny,' Longhair said.

Buzzcut concurred.

'Funny guy,' he said.

'What I think...' – Longhair was talking to me again – '...is you been

145

watching us. Poking nose.'

I disagreed.

'I've been watching nobody. Seems you people are the ones chasing me.'

'Poking nose,' Longhair repeated. 'Messing our affairs. This *Alfie:* why you ask about him?'

Alfie!

If I'd any doubts that these people had come into the picture because of Alfie they'd just evaporated. They knew the boy – and they assumed that if he was in trouble then someone might come to *them* for answers.

'You're right,' I said. 'I am interested in Alfie. And if that means I should be interested in *you* then point taken.'

Pat-pat-pat.

Crash!

The bat hit the roll top's side board and the desk jumped half an inch across the floor despite the weight of my feet. Things toppled from the shelves. The desktop mess got messier. I pushed back and got my feet onto the floor.

'I ask you,' Longhair said: 'You know who we are?'

I grinned to cover tension. Wondered how far down the countdown we were before these two cut up rough. Wondered what time Shaughnessy would be in. Sean was good with bats. I could just about handle these two at a push but I saw collateral damage looming. My desk was over a hundred years old, a genuine work of art in varnished walnut and brass. And fragile. Now it had a nasty crack in the left side that might not take another impact. If Sean was here he'd appreciate the delicacy of the situation. Help ease these two out with minimal repair costs. Maybe my best tactic was to stall for time. I answered Longhair's question.

'I truly don't know who you are,' I said. 'But if I was into wild guesses I'd say you're a bunch of thugs involved in business that's not legit. Thugs who rope in kids like Alfie. Which has me thinking of drugs. And I'm sensing that you're behind anything that might have happened to him, though I don't know that detail either. So I guess I'll have to find *out* who you are. If you happened to have a card handy that could save me some time.'

Longhair locked me in his stare for a few more seconds then spoke quietly.

'Funny man,' he said. 'But we no have card. And I think you do know 'bout us. I think you been spying.'

Pat-pat-pat. Smackity-smack.

'Snooping everywhere. In shop. In Linc'shire. Everywhere. So I want know: who 'as sent you?'

'Sorry, fellas,' I said. 'We don't share client business.'

'No. You talk.'

He started to come round his side of the desk and Buzzcut moved round the other. One each side of me as I sat in the middle feeling a little tense. I'd already decided that Buzzcut would be the first to go down if things got out of hand. Good practice is to go for the one with the weapon but when *that* guy is bigger than the door he came in through then the pragmatic option is to take out the lesser threat, get a body between you and the weapon. I didn't know when this chinwag would peter out but I didn't sense anything good coming after. I was still listening for the Shaughnessy's Yamaha.

'Who else know 'bout Linc'shire?' Longhair said.

'Are you telling me there's something to know?'

'And Streatham. Who know?'

'As I said, I can't go into detail. But I can't deny that you've caught my interest. What *is* happening in Lincolnshire?'

In reply Longhair stepped forward, clear of the desk and changed my plan. No way to get at Buzzcut before Longhair swung the bat. So if things took a turn the big guy was number one.

He'd stopped a yard and a half to my left, bat angled out from his leg.

'Who you work for?' he repeated.

'Sorry, fellas. No can tell.'

'My guess is Alfie people. But the job is over. You tell Alfie client: *finito*. Job finish. And we no see you again. That what I come to say. Finish! Or you regret. You understand?'

'More than you realise.'

'An' let me show how serious.'

In a flash he raised the bat and swung it two handed at the desk's rear shelving. The wood disintegrated like balsa. The tiny rear drawers exploded, ejected stationery and junk into the air. I was up before the bat could swing again but now Buzzcut moved on my right and suddenly I was looking into the muzzle of an automatic pistol. A squat Smith & Wesson.

'Sit,' Buzzcut said.

He came closer, gun steady, and his eyes had an intensity that said he was happy whichever way I chose to play things. I sat back down.

Longhair hefted the bat and threw a bright smile.

'Thank you,' he said. 'Is better. Room to swing cat.'

Then he swung.

The bat sliced across the remains of the roll top shelving, launching the toppled contents into low orbit. Another swing, hard and vicious, and the Anglepoise lamp exploded into a million pieces. A foot from my face the muzzle of the Smith & Wesson held steady. Then the bat rose high and another max effort splintered the last of the shelving.

Then Longhair stepped back round the desk and put the bat through the glass on my Time Recorder clocking machine. The clock's hands were smashed loose and rotated down. Time stopped and reversed to six-thirty as Longhair moved on, swinging fast and viciously. The bat tore down my Fred Trueman poster and scarred the tatty floral wallpaper behind it then came through in a wide swing that exploded the barometer in a hail of glass. Pressure jumped to thirty-one inches but give the thing its due – it stayed on the wall, though the way Longhair was going I might not have a wall in ten seconds.

I was watching Buzzcut in my periphery. He was ignoring the demolition, holding the gun on me with a tight-lipped smile. The muzzle was six inches from my face, far closer than it should have been. Training. The thing these criminals lack.

Longhair was working up a sweat. He raised the bat and demolished the inkjet, which I'd been thinking of junking due to the exorbitant cartridge prices. Then he hefted the bat wide and aimed at my signed and framed Geoff Boycott poster and I finally jumped up with a yell.

Buzzcut's eyes flicked round to see what had rattled me and by the time he sensed a ruse I'd got his gun hand in mine and wrapped his wrist back. Then I locked his elbow and heaved and he hit the wall by the window. As he rebounded I pulled the gun arm through then released the elbow and pushed it through the window glass and the gun went off in a blast of flame and cordite. But it was still pointing up and not at me. Plaster showered down as Buzzcut's free fist swung in and almost knocked my head off. The fist had two demon-face rings with illegally sharpened ears that ripped my cheek but I hardly noticed. I stayed focused on the gun. Launched myself backwards pulling the arm with me and used the guy's momentum to trip him and throw him down. He hit the deck and I dropped onto his stomach, knees-first with my ears ringing and blood seeping from the lacerations in my face. The gun fired again then dropped free. More plaster came down to mix with the blood seeping from both of us onto the carpet. Seemed the glass had sliced Buzzcut's upper arm, right through the track suit. I pushed away and grabbed the gun, but then my roll top levitated and crashed down onto both of us as Longhair came back into the action. The desk toppled my chair, which protected me, but Buzzcut caught the thing smack in his face and his head snapped back onto the floor. He was out. But he wasn't my problem. The threat now was Longhair who'd leapt the mess and was swinging the bat up to crack my skull.

We were in the corner, with a mess of chair and desk parts piled around me, and the limited space slowed Longhair for the moment I needed to raise the gun and point it his way. But incredibly the thing didn't deter him. He swung the bat down and dug a hole in the plaster as I rolled away, then swung again as I came to my feet and caught me a whack on the upper arm that almost broke it. But it was the wrong arm. I kept my balance and raised the gun right into his face and the sight of its muzzle half an inch from his nose finally registered. The lunatic froze and eased the bat down. Then a knowing sneer came onto his face and for a sec. I thought he was going to come at me, nose be damned but the sneer was just his acknowledgement that if I wasn't squeamish about putting a round into him neither was I badass enough simply to shoot him for the hell of it. His smile was the one of a guy who still held the advantage. And whose message still stood.

The message was: we can mess you up.

Behind me Buzzcut was resurfacing. He heaved and grunted and pulled himself from under the roll top, still on his back, still seeping blood into my carpet. He cursed and took a kick at the desk which detached the remaining side panel. Longhair had stepped back and I was no longer within bat range which gave me space to re-orient the gun. I pointed it at the floored guy's torso.

'Break anything else,' I said, 'and you leave in a bag.'

Buzzcut wasn't into the subtleties of the situation. He wasn't sizing me up and weighing consequences. He just looked at my face and saw that he was within an inch of serious hurt, of far more pain than his gushing arm was delivering. The numbness in my own left arm had begun to fade and that pain was coming through nicely despite the adrenaline rush. I was going to know about this later.

I snapped back to the here and now as Longhair stepped further away and swung the bat casually to clear the mantelpiece of more junk. He was still grinning, throwing me a dare. If he'd had a gun of his own we'd have had an interesting situation.

'Okay,' he said. 'We through. *Vali!*' He snapped his fingers. Gestured towards me. 'The gun.'

The gun stayed pointed at Vali's chest.

'Feel free to try,' I said.

Vali didn't try. He got himself to his feet and held his dripping arm and gave me a look that said he'd be happy to take on the odds if he'd only had the means. But his bleeding arm and shaky limbs weren't up to fast work.

Across the room Longhair laughed. Pointed the bat at me.

'Tough guy,' he said, 'now you got gun.'

Which was a little illogical since I'd taken the gun from them, but Longhair knew it. He was just baiting me.

We held our stand-off a moment longer then Longhair yelled something to his guy and Vali struggled clear of the mess and made his way to the door.

Longhair let him go through then turned to tap the bat on one of my club chairs.

'Keep the shooter,' he said. 'Memento. But if you come near our business again I kill you. You and your client. Say to him that. Show him gun.'

Then he smacked the bat a final time on my chair and left.

I stood by the broken window. Cool air flowed in, stinging my cheek as the blood trickled down. I found a tissue to dab the flow but my hand wouldn't rise all the way. My arm had the shakes. I guess the bat had hit some kind of nerve. I walked over and planted the gun onto the empty mantelpiece and went out to the bathroom. Pulled out the first aid kit and checked the mirror. A two-inch tear. Dramatic enough for stitches. I pulled the cut closed and secured it with plasters then covered the mess with gauze and more plaster. The blood more or less stopped and I rinsed my face with my good hand. It cleaned up fine, though I couldn't do anything about my shirt. Seemed a trip back home was now squeezed into my day's schedule, right after the detour to A&E.

The outer door opened and Lucy came in, nearly jumped out of her skin as I appeared. For a second she had lockjaw, which is something you rarely see. I grinned. My cheek stretched and turned to fire.

'Jeez, Eddie, what have you done?'

My grin held despite the pain. I'm all busted up and it's what have *I* done? Slipped on a banana skin, maybe. I pulled a brush and pan from the cupboard and walked through to my room and Lucy followed to deliver another shriek, this one louder.

'Holy cow, what the hell happened, Eddie?'

A serious banana skin.

The place looked like it had been bombed.

I walked over and lifted the desk onto its three remaining legs and cleared wood and the larger detritus from the carpet, watching for glass. Luckily Vali had smashed the window outwards so apart from the bloodstains the carpet was clear. I got my chair up and back in its place. Nothing broken there. Its left arm, which had been missing when the goons walked in, was still missing.

I heard a rumble outside and lifted the broken sash. Leaned out. Shaughnessy had spotted the glass on the tarmac and wheeled the Yamaha away. Kicked down the stand well clear. Then he looked up. I gave him the thumbs-up. All good. He stood a moment then disappeared round the building.

By the time he arrived upstairs I was brushing bits of inkjet into the dustpan and Lucy was stacking the contents of my roll top shelf drawers on the mantelpiece. My desk was looking shakier than it had when I first stood it up. It could stand fine on three legs but one of them had splintered and was giving, making a tricky angle for work.

Sean checked out the room.

'Who won?' he said.

I hefted the dustpan. Tapped debris into the back.

'I'd say it was a draw. But you know what they say about parties: you never win at home.'

'Yeah. This will take a tidy-over. Maybe you're attracting the wrong kind of client, Eddie.'

'This kind had bats,' I said. 'I guess that's what you'd call the wrong kind.'

'And hardware.'

He nodded across to the gun on the mantelpiece.

'That was their backup.'

Shaughnessy smiled.

'I take it things didn't go entirely the visitors' way.'

Then the outer door banged open and another body rolled through and into my room. This one was less friendly, topped by a face that was red with some kind of issue.

Bob Rook. Our legal neighbour.

He stopped a moment and looked round the room. His eyes were boggling.

'Really?' he said.

He was staring at the devastation.

'*This* is where we're at?'

Bob ran the solicitors business downstairs with his partner Gerry Lye. It was Gerry who usually did the negotiating when our paths crossed. I guess today was his day off. There was no other explanation for Bob heaving his three hundred pounds up to the top floor. Anger alone didn't account for the trip. He'd been angry many times but his rage had never propelled him this high. When he'd finished looking round the room he looked at me.

'The fuck's going on up here?' he said. 'The absolute *fuck?*'

Shaughnessy smiled at him.

'What's up, Bob?'

Rook switched from me to Sean. Then back to the room. Then back to me.

'What's up? What do you mean what's up? You telling me this is *normal?* Just another Monday morning in the demolition business?'

I took the prompt. Looked round the room myself. Had to agree it didn't look good, but since Bob had never been up here there was no way he could know what was normal. It had to be something else stoking his blood pressure.

'It was like a fucking bomb went off down there,' he said. *'Ten fucking bombs. I thought the roof was coming down.'*

'Maybe one of those jumbos,' I said. *'Though it would be a little off flight path.'*

'Jumbos hell! It's not jumbos that just put our lights out. And you scared the absolute *shit* out of our new paralegal. She's gone home crying. And do you know what? I heard a gunshot. I *heard* a frigging *gunshot.* So let me tell you: the cops are on their way right now.'

Shaughnessy and I looked at each other. If Rook hadn't been in such a state he'd have spotted the Smith & Wesson on the mantelpiece and his outrageous suspicions would have been confirmed.

'Bob,' I said, 'it probably sounded worse than it was. We just had a coupla things fall over. Like you say: Monday morning. You know the score.'

'Know *hell* the score! This building has been a disaster zone since you moved in, Flynn. You think this is the wild west? This is Paddington for Chrissakes.' He jabbed with his thumb. 'Go open an office in Millwall, *mate.'*

Bob was here to vent steam but it didn't seem to be working. The anger was still building. High blood does that. High blood and plaster flakes on your suit shoulders. Bob must have been on the middle floor when the jumbo flew past. I assumed that the medical needs of his paralegal explained his five minute delay in getting up our stairs but now he was here he was rapidly moving towards his own medical episode. Which could be a problem when the police arrived. They'd need a hefty stick of chalk to get the line round Bob Rook's carcass.

'Gee, Bob, I'm so sorry,' said Lucy. She hustled across and took him by the upper arm, eased him back through the door. Her other hand patted at his shoulder, getting the plaster off.

'Eddie was changing a light bulb and the stupid desk collapsed under him. Would you believe it? And I meant to ask: how's Natalie? That was a horrible fall of her own I heard. And it takes forever for tendons to heal.'

Bob was still open-mouth-boiling but he allowed himself to be propelled backwards into the near-normalcy of reception.

Shaughnessy and I followed them out, mouthing our own concerns over Natalie, who was probably someone we should have known.

'Bob, what can we say?' I said. 'You've got your troubles and we're just adding to them. What the hell are we doing bringing you up here? Let's clear things up and you won't hear a pin drop for the rest of the week. It'll be like we're not here. We truly hate to disturb you.'

'Not half as much as I do,' Rook said. 'And don't fob me off with platitudes, Flynn. We're going to take another look at that lease of yours. And we're going to take a look at *our* lease. We pay through the nose for this building and either this top floor riot-in-progress is going to end or the landlord's gonna be in court. And Natalie is fine, thank you Lucy, she's out of bed already.'

'*Already?* I heard it would be months.' Lucy shook her head in wonder. 'Your wife's one tough woman, Bob.'

'Oh, she's really a softie,' Bob contradicted. 'But yeah, she's tough. She breaks a leg and she's learning a new dance next day. I always tell her: if everyone was like you, my dear, laughing off their injuries, I'd be out of business.'

'Oh, *perish* the thought! And don't worry, Bob: women like Natalie are one in a million. It's the rest of us you're here for. We need all the medical and legal help you can give us. Did I tell you my uncle got knocked off his bike?'

'You didn't, Lucy, but if he's making a claim we're the right people. Tell him that. And tell your hoodlum bosses that I've not forgotten the hallway damage from twelve months ago nor the destruction of my parking spot, and if they think they can hold World War Three up here ever again they'd better think twice. Because next time I come up those stairs I'll be serving.'

'Message received,' I said, 'and once again noted. This won't happen again, Bob. Number one in our professional standards charter is "run a quiet business". So why not let Lucy help you back down? This last flight is steep. And we'll just get tidied up quiet as a mouse.'

Rook stood a moment, resisting Lucy's tug. Then jabbed a finger my way.

'You do it,' he said. 'Tidy up your whole damn act.'

Then he turned and let Lucy steer him stairwards. Diplomatic incident defused, though he launched one last fusillade as he went down.

'They're on their way,' he yelled back. 'I really did call them. And I'm gonna tell them exactly what I heard.'

Which gave us five minutes to get ship-shape. And maybe resuscitate the coffee machine. The thing had died during the excitement. I got the hotplate light back on and refilled the filter and waited for Lucy.

When she came back up she rushed into my office then came straight out.

'Who's got the gun?' she said.

'It's safe,' I said. 'Unless they check the chimney flue. Has Umberto really been knocked off his bike?' I wondered why she hadn't told me. Her uncle was a good old stick, old school Londoner, but he was a little frail nowadays.

'It was in nineteen fifty-seven,' Lucy said. 'But there's no statute of limitations in civil prosecutions. I bet Bob could get him compensation.'

I grinned.

'Is the offending party still alive even?'

'I doubt it. It was a horse.'

My grin stretched. Knowing Bob he'd still go after the beast if Lucy sweet-talked him. She was good that way. Probably Bob had ended up apologising to *her* downstairs. It's what we use her for. Defusing situations. Keeping undesirables out, though I was glad she wasn't here earlier.

She sorted out the drinks just as Harry appeared. He took his turn to tour my office with his mug of tea and came out shaking his head.

'This is the bunch mixed up in your missing kid search?'

'The very ones. Looks like I've stepped on someone's toes.'

We went through into the front office. Shaughnessy planted himself behind his desk.

'For a simple missing person gig we've a lot of funnies going on,' he said.

'My questions have threatened someone. And even if these guys are not tied to Chas they're linked for sure to friend Alfie.'

'Or were,' Shaughnessy said.

'Yeah. We're talking two years ago. But maybe Alfie is missing too. Which would put an ugly slant on our search for Chas.'

155

'You think these people are why Chas disappeared?' Shaughnessy said.

'Can't even guess. But if they were I'd be worried about getting him back. But we're going to have to find out about these people.'

'The Lincolnshire thing,' Harry said. 'That's gotta be drugs or something. It would explain why they're sensitive about you poking around near the farm.'

'Whatever it is, the kid Alfie is or was mixed up with it. And that means maybe Chas.'

'What about the other party?' Shaughnessy said. 'The Holland people: what's their link to all this?'

'Beats me. But they provide a little balance. Criminal types on one side, a billionaire-financed operation on the other. All for a missing boy.'

'Maybe none of them are connected,' Lucy said. 'The bad guys are linked to Alfie and just want you out of their hair and the billionaire people are after something else.'

I finished my coffee. Grinned at her. The First Rule of Investigation says that there's no such thing as coincidence. Things had heated up too quickly right after I started looking for Chas Abbott. None of it made any sense but I wasn't buying coincidence.

'We need to get to the bottom of what both parties are up to,' I said. 'That might be the best pointer to what's happened to Chas.'

Shaughnessy stood and turned to watch the street.

'If we dig at this Eastern European crew we're gonna attract comeback.'

'Hazard of the job. But I want clear ground. And maybe Chas is connected. First thing: I'm going to look at that farm.'

'And if you spot something dirty?' Shaughnessy was still watching the street.

I grinned. It hurt like hell.

'Then we'll mess up their operation. See how *they* feel.'

When Shaughnessy turned back he had that funny smile I'd never quite decoded.

'If it's a drugs operation they'll have soldiers up there,' he said.

'Undoubtedly.'

'Maybe we'll need reinforcements.'

Lucy sighed and raised her eyes skywards.

'Here we go,' she said. 'Another outing for Bernie.'

'That's an idea,' I said. 'Let's get him on standby.'

Bernie Locke was my old pal from Yorkshire, the man-mountain ex-marine who helped us out from time to time when we needed to balance the odds in a problematic case. Hiring Bernie didn't come cheap but even if Lucy held the firm's purse strings with the grip of a miser her fingers never moved faster than when she hit the speed dial to bring Bernie in. My office repairs already threatened to stretch our finances this month but Lucy couldn't resist the shivery frisson of opening the flood gates to invite one of Bernie's eye-watering invoices. It was like a child playing with fire.

There's an unwritten rule in our contracts that says that all escalations and expenses remotely linked to a case are billable to the client. So provided this client didn't renege we could cover Bernie's cheque.

'Fill him in,' I decided. 'The bastard won't refuse.'

'Wilco.'

'And take a dig at these Holland people. Rumours, history, anything that could connect to Chas or his family, though what that might be beats me.'

'I'm on it.'

The simple missing boy case was ramping up. Resources suddenly growing. But that's the business. You're as flexible as the client's chequebook.

Sean was tied up today with work for a young couple who were under attack from an unknown adversary intent on demolishing their lives with a campaign of theft and vandalism. He was a week in and had a theory that would be tested today. If the theory was good the case might be closed before he clocked off. He'd be free from tomorrow.

Harry had two notice-servings. He'd be clear by lunch.

'I'll take a look at these Streatham people,' he said. 'Someone will know them. Maybe your friend Percy has heard something.'

Percy Valan was one of my old Metropolitan Police C.I.s and no friend to anyone except the Governor of the Bank of England. If you wanted Percy to talk you came with a pocket full of readies. I'd held on to Percy even after I left the Met but his services came with an ill-judged attitude built on years of self importance to officialdom.

He'd agreed to feed me snippets but at double the Met's fee. And the deal was that he'd talk only to me, no company lackeys or go-betweens. I agreed the terms, and the first time I needed to talk to him I sent Harry along. Percy took offence when I didn't show personally and told Harry about the lackey thing and Harry hung him up by his trouser belt on some railings to think about life. Percy cursed and yelled but you can't unfasten a belt with the buckle under tension and Harry sat on a bench over the road until Percy made some decisions. When Percy invited him back over they agreed a new deal. Percy would talk to whoever the hell I sent and he'd take the government fee.

Percy had stopped wearing trouser belts for our meets, never knowing who'd turn up, but ditching the belt wasn't the solution. The issue was whether Harry took a disliking to you and there was nothing Percy could do to mitigate that. If he knew anything about the Eastern Europeans or the *Fizikun* shop he might be tempted to forgo the fee just to spite us, but Harry knew when the bastard was lying and Percy knew he knew. Bottom line: sprinting to your bank with a fistful of notes had more appeal than hanging from railings. If Percy knew anything at all Harry would get it.

My own plans were clear. My face was hurting like the devil and would hurt even more after thirty minutes in A&E and that would put me in a nice mood for the job I needed to do here in Town before I headed out to Lincolnshire.

We wrapped up and I closed the door on the mess in my office and headed out.

CHAPTER NINETEEN
Cosmetic surgeon

Medical matters swallowed most of the morning. I exited A&E a little before noon with my face patched back to something resembling normal and pain dulled by anaesthetic. The doc warned me against driving, with the repairs being so close to my eye, but my vision was fine. He couldn't prescribe anything for my poor temper so I left him to it.

I crossed the river and drove south. My left arm was giving me more than a little grief now, mostly when I shifted gears. Maybe I should have mentioned it whilst I had the doctors round me but then I'd have been tied up the rest of the day with X-rays and slings and stuff that might restrict my ability to drive. My guess was that the arm was just bad bruising, though that didn't put me in a better temper as I jigged through traffic.

I queued up a Parker MP3 and turned the Bird's squeals up to a pain-distracting volume and watched my rear-view.

Terry Tickner's black Range Rover was back there, working hard to stay with me. I grinned and got pain and flashes. Grinned harder. Terry would grin too if he knew.

I turned through Lambeth and worked the wheel to give Tickner a ride. Those Range Rovers will eat up any terrain but they're a little top heavy for nifty wheel-work. I increased the tempo until I knew Tickner's head was bouncing off his door post as he stuck with me. My previous Sprite, which was an original, would have been up a lamp post with the manoeuvres I was pulling but my newer wheels were a modern rebuild with suspension hard enough to shake your granny's dentures loose. Zero comfort, maximum road holding. With or without the Bird.

The Range Rover rocked and rolled but stayed with me like a bad migraine. In a fit of pique I swung the wheel at Clapham Common and drove a vicious and meaningless detour round Wandsworth and Garratt Green to make sure Tickner knew he was clocked. But he had to stay with me. He couldn't switch in any of his people whilst I was driving fast and at random. And a switch would be pointless.

When I hit Merton I slackened off. Recalled Harry's briefing and turned at the health centre to roll to a stop on double yellows outside the beauticians shop above which Tickner had his office. Tickner drove in right behind me. Coasted straight past and turned into the alley at the end of the block. Sixty seconds later he came out and walked back down. Stooped to open the Sprite's door. I had the hood up which made things tricky. He fought this way and that, worked his limbs and finally got himself in. Slammed the door. I'd switched to speakers and we sat a moment listening to Parker's frenetic Move fade-out. Then I killed the music and turned to watch Tickner's ugly face watching me.

'Nice little dance, Eddie,' he said after a moment. 'Hook, line and damn sinker.'

I grinned. He wasn't talking about our dash from Vauxhall.

'Technology,' I said. 'You can't live without it. Until it goes wrong.'

He thought about it. Gave me a kind of snarl.

'The truth is,' I said, 'that you can't beat the human eyeball for reliability. Take our little jaunt just now. You knew exactly who you were following even if it didn't get you anywhere.'

The quip didn't improve Tickner's mood. His GPS tracker had given him invaluable assistance in staying with me the last few days but when you follow the beam without line of sight it's always liable to catch you out. As it did yesterday. Energised by an athletic night with Margot I'd popped out first thing and jumped on a Number 344 down on the main road. Hopped off at the next stop but left Tickner's tracker under the back seat. I guess when the motion alert came through his people assumed that they'd missed me driving out and raced off towards Lambeth, smug in their confidence in gadgets. Problem was, they never got a sight of me. Just spent a puzzling morning wondering why I was wandering to and fro across the city to a fixed schedule. I guess the second or third time crossing the river behind the same bus they'd cottoned on.

Tickner was watching my face now with more than just polite interest. His professional eye: comparing the damage to that on his own cheek which was slashed by an old scar fit for a pirate captain.

'You've been mixing with the wrong people,' he concluded, still inspecting the damage.

Still no smile. Maybe he'd tailed the 344 himself.

'Story of my life. But what I'm wondering is whether you know something about it.'

'Not guilty,' he said.

'You're saying it's just a coincidence that I've got these people onto me and I've got *you* onto me?'

'Who*ever* is onto you, it's just that. So you don't know the artists?'

'Not yet. Neither do I know why you're following me around. But I'm going to find out. Unless you save me the trouble.'

Tickner shook his head.

'No can do, Eddie.'

'Come on, Terry. Your operation's busted. I know you've been right behind me the last ten days. Just enlighten me before you sign off.'

'Who says we're signing off?'

'Your client, most likely, when you tell him that we've clocked you. Maybe he'll want you to stand down.'

'And maybe he won't.'

'You mean you're staying with me whatever?'

'That's a decision for the client.'

'Well it's gonna be a tough assignment since I'll be giving you the slip every chance I get. And we know that tracking devices are out now unless you get them wholesale.'

'We'll be sure to point that out. The client will cost everything in.'

'Okay. So I'm going to have to ask your client myself. I'm just thinking that it won't reflect well on your firm if he finds himself in the spotlight...'

'It's a risk we'll take.'

'Come on Terry, give me a hint. Then maybe I'll decide that pushing back is not a priority right now. You can stay on my tail and save us both the trouble and embarrassment.'

Finally Tickner smiled.

'Good try, Eddie,' he said. 'And I assume that you really do know who our client is. But this is between you and him. We warned him that things might not stay discreet. Twenty-four seven on a professional isn't sustainable.'

'So what did you tell him? A week? A fortnight? We were onto you inside eight hours, Terry, if you're looking for feedback.'

Tickner dropped his smile. Watched the street.

'Well fuck you, Eddie. I knew you'd be sharp.'

'But discretion wasn't the make or break. You were told just to stay with us. As exemplified by our present chat.'

'My instructions are not up for discussion. And since you know the guy you'd better talk to him directly.'

'Is this about Chas Abbott?'

'Who?'

'Or is it about the people we've annoyed: the Eastern Europeans?'

'I've nothing to say, Eddie, except that I'm not working for any Eastern Europeans.'

'That wasn't my question.'

'Yeah. Well that wasn't an answer. I'm here as a courtesy, since you were clearly itching to talk. Clearing the air.'

'Got it,' I said. 'Then consider it cleared. Now get out. I've places to go. If you follow me it will be hard work.'

'Doubtless. But we'll see.'

He turned to fiddle with the door. Took a moment to figure it out then extracted himself and smacked the top. Went into his building.

I flicked the music back on but kept it low. Watched the building for five minutes. When I'd finished thinking I made a three-point turn that extended to five as I worked the wheel and gear lever with misbehaving muscles. My biceps felt like they were being torn apart. Once the car was facing the right way and my arm had settled to a vicious ache I drove out into the traffic.

My trip over here had delivered what I expected, which was the marginal satisfaction of seeing Terry Tickner on the back foot. I was still ninety percent sure that his client was interested in Chas Abbott but I'd been ninety percent sure when I drove over the river, so nothing gained there.

I checked my mirror and saw the BMW way back in the traffic. I pictured Tickner up behind his desk, coordinating things. By the time I was through Tooting the BMW had closed to twenty yards, sometimes a car back, sometimes right on my bumper. I pictured Tickner grinning as he pressed the blower to his ear, dispensing new tactics. Units two and three stand down. Take the afternoon off. Unit one, stay with the bastard. In or out of sight, it doesn't bloody matter.

Seemed I'd just saved Tickner's client five hundred quid a day as his operation ditched any pretence at discretion.

I flicked the volume up higher. Sighed.

A burning left arm, cheek feeling like the stitches were tearing themselves out and an unfathomable party sticking obstinately on my tail. Maybe Tickner's people would be right there next time the guys with bats showed up. Take a little collateral damage themselves.

All for a simple missing kid.

I snapped back, reminded myself that what mattered was finding the boy safe. Not for his family or for my wage-cheque or some kind of job satisfaction. Or even out of satisfaction at the prospect of messing up our Eastern Europeans' operation, which we were going to do. But because whatever Chas Abbott's connection to all of these people, and wherever he'd gone after Smirisary, the two-year silence said he probably needed help. When I'd signed the contract I'd had an open mind. People usually disappear because they want to. But that scenario was fast dissipating. I'd nothing bar my sixth sense but everything pointed to the same thing.

Chas Abbott was in deep trouble.

CHAPTER TWENTY
This conversation is closed

I called at Battersea for a shower and change of clothes then drove out to retrieve Herbie. Herbie raised his eyebrows at the mess on my face but decided that it was me in there and scooted over. William looked at my face too and told me to be *varry careful, my fren'*, like I was newly discovering a bad side of the world. I promised him I'd take extra special care and confirmed we'd be back next month.

It was too late in the day to head out to Lincolnshire but too early to make the house call I was planning so we drove back to Battersea and took a turn on the park then stopped off at Kiki's for a late, late lunch. Kiki's menu is a little avant-garde but they do great piadinas and the chef is not above sending out a couple of sausages at two quid apiece to satisfy his less discerning customers. When we were through we drove out through the last of the rush hour.

I checked my mirror. Tickner's BMW guy was on the evening shift. He slotted in and followed me on what was going to seem like an ironic trip once word got back.

It took an hour to get to Kingston and locate the property Shaughnessy had described close to the university. When I found it I pulled in and stopped in front of black electric gates that blocked a driveway curving away behind thick foliage.

I hopped out and watched Tickner's man roll to a stop fifty yards past the property. I grinned to let him know that he was clocked then pressed the bell. Waited ten seconds.

'Yeah?'

Curt. Faint annoyance above a hint of alarm. The alarm was understandable. I was the last person Clark Holland expected at his door.

I made a gate-opening gesture to the camera.

'Open up,' I told it. 'We need a chat.'

'Who the hell are you?'

'You know damn well. Open the gate.'

I repeated my hand gesture and hopped back into the car. Fired up the engine and nudged up to the metalwork. There was a few seconds' pause but then the gates swung back and I was in. I drove up the leafy driveway and steered round the curve leading to a modernist concrete and glass mansion, two floors of panoramic windows under a grey tiled roof.

Modest by billionaire standards but maybe Clark Holland hadn't yet been elevated to the top tier lifestyle. An heir-in-waiting, roughing it in a fifty million crash pad, though the Lamborghini parked in front of the house was the real deal. I pulled alongside it and killed the engine.

I was assuming that the finger that pressed the gate button was Clark's. The greeting had been too brusque for an assistant, and the innocent act had been dropped too quickly. And I knew Clark was home because Shaughnessy had tailed him here forty minutes ago.

I told Herbie to hold tight and hopped out. Walked up the steps to where the door had been opened by a short guy dressed in impeccable casual: bright clean jeans and branded golf shirt, soft leather brogues. The guy had the same tight face of overfed progeny I'd seen in Lucy's society pic., though the diet that shaped him was one of excess privilege. Clark was fit and tanned and his black curly hair was freshly styled. Maybe they had a barbers at the company complex. Maybe he put in gym time there, played his twice-weekly squash matches in the lunch hour. Maybe he was feeling a little jumpy since finding out that his investigation team had screwed up and brought me to his door.

'What do you want?' he said. He held the door. Stood his ground.

I wasn't in the mood. I pushed past him.

'Hey!' he said.

I walked across a galleried entrance hall clad in marble and antique wood and lit by a glass dome two stories up. An open doorway at the far side was blasting heavy metal. I went that way and arrived in a lounge the size of a small ballroom decorated in minimalist modern. Snow white furniture on slip-shiny Calacatta marble whose black streaking matched the four black obelisks guarding the corners of the room – Kharma speaker towers that would have cost more than my apartment. Soft leather sofas were scattered about to give you a choice of facing the crackling fire on a winter's night or the pool and gardens on today's summer evening. The full-width windows were rolled back to extend the space out across a pool deck where three people were killing time: a couple lounging in fully upholstered patio chairs and a girl swimming lengths. The couple were a man and woman in their early thirties, fit and tanned like Clark. Both exuded the same air of privilege that only inherited wealth brings. When I walked out the woman turned and started to smile before she realised she didn't know me. It was a nice smile. A stunning face, and stunning figure when she stood to show off shapely limbs set off by her trendy tennis outfit. The guy turned to see what had caught her attention. He was big, handsome, tanned to leather, bare chest showing off gym-honed muscle. He was wearing mirror shades but enough light got through for him to see my face and then Clark's as he scurried out behind me. Enough to bring him to his feet.

I admired the view for a moment – a couple of acres of landscaped grounds stretched away beyond the deck – then turned to Clark. His face had the same disapproval as at the door, though I guess it was a mixed emotion since I was here because of him. I nodded to the couple and said hi but they didn't reply. The girl in the pool kept swimming.

'What do you want?' Clark repeated.

I'd come for a quiet discussion, a private one, but the music and the audience made things tricky. But what the hell? If Clark wanted to keep our conversation private he'd tell his guests to shove off. I walked further across the deck and rocked on my toes by the pool's edge. Clark came to stand right behind me.

'I happened to be passing,' I said, 'with one of your guys on my tail. Thought I'd pop in.'

I sensed gritted teeth.

'I asked what you wanted.'

I turned.

'Think we should invite the guy in? It's been a thirsty drive.'

'Quit playing the fool,' Clark said. 'What do you want?'

The deck suite looked inviting. I walked round him and flopped down. Watched the pool girl.

'I was hoping to put that question to you,' I said. I craned my neck.

Clark towered over me.

'What do *you* want with *me*, Clark?'

Off to the side the woman was putting two and two together. She moved towards Clark. Put her hand on his arm. Shoulder to shoulder. Defensive.

'Darling,' she said.

Clark ignored her. For a second he was lost for words. I smiled at them both.

Finally Clark spoke.

'Yes, Flynn,' he said. 'We're keeping an eye on you. But I'm not going to discuss it.'

I dropped the smile. Went back to watching the pool. The girl was lapping it with an elegant, powerful crawl, oblivious to everything.

'Let's think about that,' I said. 'Look at the logic. I know you're watching me, which means I'll be working on that basis. So whatever you're hoping to find out – or that I'll find out for you – isn't going to happen. What will happen is I give your people the run-around and treble the cost of you staying near me. And those people learn nothing I don't want them to. What's the point of that?' I craned my neck again to look at Clark.

Saw that my logic hadn't impressed.

'We'll decide what's the point,' Clark said. 'And if we need more manpower we'll put it on. Whatever it takes.'

The muscled guy was watching us. He came into the conversation.

'This guy a problem?' he said.

I reoriented. Checked him out.

'If I am,' I said, 'your best option's the pool.'

'Leave it Howard,' the woman told him.

But Howard didn't leave it.

'Who is this shithead?' he said. He stepped closer but the woman held up a palm and this time her voice was curt.

'Leave it, Howard. There's no problem.'

I grinned at her.

'I hate to be contradictory,' I said, 'but I think there is. The problem that comes from your lover-boy here putting people on my tail then refusing to talk about it.'

The woman's face coloured. Now it was Clark's turn to smooth things over. He spoke to the other guy.

'Howard,' he said, 'how about grabbing a couple of beers? And kill the music.'

Both he and the woman looked at the guy to make it clear this was not an optional suggestion. Howard held his ground a moment and pulled off his shades to stare me out, like he was making hard decisions. But then he turned and walked into the house.

'Coming back to my point,' I said, 'I don't like being followed around. And skipping endless hoops to shrug your people off my tail is going to be hard work. So I'm not inclined to walk out of here until I know what the hell is going on.'

'And you're not going to know,' Clark said. 'So we're stuck.'

'If you want to make things difficult,' the woman said, 'feel free. As my brother said, we'll put ten times the manpower on you. So live with it.'

Things came together. The touch on Clark's arm. The power-play dismissal of Howard like a lackey. The matching attitude. The woman was Hillary Holland, Clark's sister. Maybe Howard was her husband. Lucy would check. But I could see the family resemblance now as the two watched me.

'You're not thinking this through,' I persisted. 'Whatever manpower you bring in I'll negate it. And what I don't want you to know about you won't know. But if I knew what you were after I could make a judgement. Maybe shared information would benefit us both. There may be common goals here. The problem is that you know and I don't.'

'Okay. So just assume that there aren't,' Hillary said.

'Assume this,' Clark added: 'our interest doesn't threaten you or your client. For us it's just a necessary chore.'

'That's quite an assertion,' I said. 'Which I'm not inclined to take at face value. To me you're a threat unless I know otherwise.'

'As you wish.'

'And I'm assuming that the interest we're talking about is to do with kid called Chas Abbott because that's the only job I'm on right now. If it's something else then you've been misinformed.'

The pool girl climbed out just then with a splash. Diverted my attention. She was tall and tanned, what you'd call drop-dead gorgeous as she padded towards us along the deck. Mid twenties, eye-catchingly lithe in her minimalist swim gear. She spotted me and flashed a smile, though as she dripped her way over and the damage on my face became clearer the smile faded. By the time she reached us her face was neutral at best. She pulled a towel off a table and leaned to plant a kiss on Clark's cheek. Clark was one for the girls, it seemed.

Clark and Hillary exchanged a glance. I sensed that they didn't want a wider audience right now. I wondered whether to push the girl back into the pool.

It would work but I'd be time-limited afterwards so I ignored her and came back to the point, which hadn't yet been disputed.

'Chas Abbott,' I said. 'You don't know where he is but for some reason you need to. So you're watching me. Hoping I'll get you there on the cheap.'

The siblings shook their heads simultaneously. The pool girl dripped sweetly.

'For the final time,' Hillary said, 'we're not discussing it. This conversation is closed.'

But it wasn't. Not unless they ganged up to lift my chair out through the house.

'The two things that really puzzle me,' I said, 'are firstly what possible interest you could have in a missing graduate, and secondly how the hell did you know to watch me right from the start. Actually, three things: why don't you just look for the boy yourself, if you're so keen to find him?'

'Please leave,' Clark said. 'Now.'

Howard reappeared and planted beer bottles. Stood to attention, ready to come back into equation.

I stayed where I was. I wasn't buying Clark and Hillary's brush-off, even though I still had no sensible theory to explain why they were interested in the kid. I needed something from them. Whatever the Hollands were up to might shed light on my search. And I needed every spark of light. Up to now I'd been chasing shadows.

And what I was sensing as I sat there was the power of these people, the assured righteousness of big money. The sense of being an outsider battering away at some castle walls without the least chance of getting in or knowing what was in there. The Hollands were a closed circle and their money was capable of keeping it closed as tightly as they wanted. Of letting them keep tabs on whomever they wanted.

But in the silence that enfolded our stand-off I saw how things were.

Castle walls. I wasn't going to breach them today.

I sighed and stood. Clark tensed, waited for a wrong move.

For a moment I wanted to push *him* into the pool but then Howard would come for me and probably he'd end up in the pool too. Then maybe Hillary would come clawing and she'd end up taking a splash right along with them. Leaving me alone with Miss Drop Dead, and maybe I'd have to throw her into the water after them for good measure. Hell, maybe I could jump in myself to cool off my frustration.

But maybe another time. I thanked Clark and Hillary for nothing and said I'd be in touch. Walked back through the house. Clark followed to help with the door. Herbie was watching as I came out down the steps. He'd have had them all in the pool if he'd been back there. If I ever returned to this house I'd remember that.

I fired up the car and rolled back down the driveway. As I reached the gates they opened magically, inviting me out.

Clark and Hillary Holland.

Watching me twenty-four seven.

None of it a threat to me or to my clients.

Empty reassurance.

More likely just arrogance: I didn't need to know their business so they weren't telling me.

But I did need to know.

Because my arm ached and my stitches felt like they were tearing themselves out and right now I felt threatened as hell.

And my surprise chat hadn't got me an inch nearer to Chas Abbott.

CHAPTER TWENTY-ONE
Meditation

'This is interesting,' Shaughnessy said.

He walked across concrete into the centre of the building. The clack of his boots echoed back with that barely discernible whispery delay that gives big enclosed spaces an air of listening.

He turned three-sixty and checked the place out. Breeze block base, slatted walls, corrugated iron high overhead. Plastic skylights beaming light and warmth in from the mid-day sun. Shaughnessy watched them for a moment, listening for sounds. There were none. The interesting thing about the place was that there was nothing interesting.

Just all that empty concrete, a few runs of suspended pipework up top, the odd crate lying about. Otherwise an empty shell.

Which made it three in a row.

He walked back over.

'My hunch,' he said, 'is that your hunch is on the mark.'

'It's on the mark,' I said. 'This place isn't kosher.'

This was the third building we'd poked our noses into. The third empty shell. Sterile. Unused. The structures had once housed poultry or pigs, maybe cattle in the winter, but there was no remnant of mess or muck, no whiff of once-resident livestock.

The sterile interiors had me assuming that the buildings hadn't been in use in the three years since the farm had been auctioned. Someone had bought Low Farm then left it to rot.

But the place wasn't abandoned. The farmhouse was in use. The black 4x4 driven by the two Eastern European guys who'd popped into the Thistle to see who was asking questions – Hat and Cough – was parked there and we'd watched people kicking around the house, standing and sitting, smoking. Bored. None of them farmers. And all linked to the people who'd wrecked my office yesterday. The *Fizikun* people.

So those people had this nice little farm out in the wilds of Lincolnshire that looked like any other farm until you looked closer.

Shaughnessy and I had trekked in over the fields under cover of hedgerows, watching out for any legit. farm workers who might want to know what we were doing on their land. But the fields and tracks were deserted. Likewise the farm, except for the house.

We'd watched the house for a while then come to look round the buildings. A task facilitated by the fact that security didn't seem to be a big thing here. No cameras or guys strolling round to make sure everything was quiet. Which *didn't* match our hunches about the place.

If these people were up to something dodgy, something that warranted a drive down to the pub when you heard that a guy was asking questions, something that sent instructions back to London to pop in on a nosey P.I., then you'd expect them to be a little tighter on security around their operation. But all we had was a deserted farm.

We'd found nothing, which was the wrong kind of oddity. Thousands of square feet of empty concrete didn't fit.

We went back out and checked the last two buildings. Had to be something somewhere.

But the last buildings were no different from the others. No one and nothing. Just concrete and dust. Odd bits of detritus from the seller's clear out three years ago. The farm had been sold as buildings-only. Equipment and stalls and cages gone. The most attractive option for auction, leaving the prospective buyer to kit out the place in line with his business plan.

Except this buyer didn't seem to have any plan.

We stood in the last building, listening to birds scratching on the roof, sunlight and silence inside. Shaughnessy nodded.

'They're up to something,' he said. 'Something that covers the purchase price of a place you're not going to use.'

'Camouflage. But where's the hidden stuff? I'd have put money on one of these sheds.'

Shaughnessy kicked at the concrete. Checked the skylights again. Listened.

'Obvious solution,' he said. 'There's somewhere else. But why are we not seeing it?'

I turned and started to pull open the access door then stepped back as the sound of a vehicle came round the buildings. We watched through the gap as the 4x4 rounded the corner and drove past between the barns. Disappeared behind them.

'That's where it is,' I said. All we'd noticed as we'd scouted the farm was a stand of trees fifty yards away behind the buildings. But the 4x4 wasn't heading towards nothing. We walked out and followed. The concrete continued past the last barn then switched to mud, but a gravel track angled off through high grass towards the trees.

The vehicle had reached the end of the track and was stopped at a gate in a nine-foot mesh fence that was barely visible in the shadows of the trees. We jogged across open ground to get to the fence fifty yards along from the gate. The fence ran tight beneath the trees and was topped with razor wire. At the gate a camera clocked everyone coming in. As we gained the shadows the 4x4 was just disappearing and a guy was pushing the gate closed behind it. The foliage was thin behind the fence at that point revealing a hint of open ground beyond.

We walked in towards the gate, watching for more cameras. There were none, but thirty yards from the gate was as close as we were going to get without coming into the field of view of the gate cam. Not close enough. The trees still obscured detail. Just those hints of open ground and maybe sheds and smaller structures in there.

We backtracked away from the gate and followed the fence for seventy yards until it cut into the trees and ran through towards the back of the area. We pushed through and came out on the far side. Followed the fence again to a better viewpoint of an open space inside it.

The 4x4 was parked in front of what looked like two more livestock sheds. Maybe a little smaller than the ones up at the main farm. Each a hundred feet in length. Eighty or so across.

And probably not empty.

I looked at Shaughnessy.

'That's it,' I said.

'No doubt. Whatever's going on it's going on in those sheds.'

An access door beside the main doors of the nearer shed opened and three figures came out and walked over to the 4x4. One of them was Hat, the guy who'd interrogated me in the Thistle the other night. He was wearing the same trilby at the same angle and looked like the one in charge. He stopped beside the vehicle, planted an elbow on its roof and gestured to the other two with a fag between his knuckles. Darting and circling motions. The other guys nodded and kicked their feet and watched the gate.

The other structures inside the fence turned out to be six static caravans lined up in a row opposite the sheds. Blinds covered their windows and there was no sign of life inside or out. We waited and watched.

Two minutes later one of the guys walked across to the gate and let a white van through that had come across from the farm. Deliveries.

The van stopped by the 4x4 and the driver jumped out and opened its rear doors. We were on the wrong side to see the interior but the guy didn't bring anything out. Just walked over for a chinwag with his pals. Waiting for something to come out of the sheds.

We waited again.

Five minutes later the access door to the nearer shed opened and a line of five figures came out and snaked over to the van. We were looking at a shuttle service. You'd imagine they'd put windows in for ferrying personnel but I guess the van was multi-use. Probably no seats. Which was not a problem because the journey would be short.

The van was taking the five kids I'd talked to last week back out to their cottage by the Thistle. Cookie, Gangly, Petra and two others. Now we knew where they worked.

What I was really looking for was Chas' face. Or Alfie's. Because if the Eastern Europeans' dodgy operation involved young workers then both Chas and his friend would fit the bill. Friend Alfie in particular: his connection to these people went right back to their busting into Ralph's place asking about him, and ratcheted up to dead cert when the two goons walked into my office after my *Fizikun* visit. And my speculation about these people hiring kids like Alfie was more than credible with what we were seeing at this remote and secure workplace in the middle of Little Nowhere, Lincolnshire.

Friend Alfie for sure had to be connected to this place.

But his face didn't appear.

The five went round the back of the van and climbed in and the driver continued his natter with Hat and his pals as if he hadn't noticed. I thought maybe he was waiting for a few more, that maybe Alfie would be next out of the shed, but that little line of people was it. The chinwag by the van eventually broke up and the driver closed the doors and jumped in. If the kids had got a little hot while they waited it didn't seem to worry him.

The van fired up and headed out.

'The workforce,' Shaughnessy said.

'Yeah. Whatever's going on in that shed they're paying these kids to do it.'

'The odd thing,' Shaughnessy said, 'is that they're keeping them out at that cottage.'

'We're missing something,' I agreed. 'They've got this operation secure behind the razor-wire and they've six static caravans in here. Perfect accommodation if you want to keep tabs on your workforce.'

'My thoughts,' Shaughnessy said. 'Whatever dirty operation they've got going the outside help is their weakest link. The biggest risk.'

'As exemplified by Petra talking to me. Letting your workforce run round to the pub to gas with P.I.s isn't great practice. The hired help should be inside the compound. We're missing a piece of the jigsaw.'

'Maybe they're accommodated outside *because* of the caravans,' Shaughnessy said.

'That's my guess. There's something here they don't want the kids to know about.'

The remaining party finally broke up. Hat and his sidekick jumped back into the 4x4 and the gate guy let them out and then walked back to the caravan nearest the gate and went in and the compound was deserted again. The sheds were silent bar the sound of ventilation fans.

'I think I see it,' I said.

We quit our surveillance and made a wide detour to get back out the way we'd come in, a two mile trek across the fields. We'd left the Frogeye and Shaughnessy's Yamaha behind a little pumping station on a deserted lane well away from the farm. Our equipment for a long night was waiting there. We could have taken it in on the first hike but then we'd have been lumbered with stuff we might not need and priority was to scout the farm, find the best way in and out, best hidey-holes.

I pulled warm clothing, a camouflage jacket and night vision scope from the boot. A two-way radio so we weren't dependent on signal. I'd have blacked my face if I'd had any boot polish but out of direct light people are much less visible than the movies make out. We'd go without. I pushed everything into my lightweight hiking rucksack along with my twelve-hour Thermos of black coffee and three convenience store sandwiches and was good to go. Shaughnessy had pretty much the same stuff minus the coffee. Then we hiked two miles back in and split up. It was just turning dark. Shaughnessy went off to watch the farmhouse and I headed back round our spot on the far side of the compound. Settled in amongst the shrubs. My view was aided by two security lights on the sheds. The lights weren't much but they saved my night scope. The two static caravans nearest to me were now lit behind their blinds. I pulled out my coffee. Chewed a sandwich.

Ten p.m. A cloudless night. Stars visible away from the compound's light. Temperature falling. I leaned back on an angled tree trunk and listened. An owl screeched. A nightjar connected, with a burst of modem chatter. A fox yelped out in the fields. The compound stayed still and empty. Just the hum of the shed's extractor fans. My guess was that they had a night shift working inside. Brought in whilst we were away.

Shaughnessy reported all quiet. People in the house doing pretty much nothing. TV and fag breaks. Occasional voices. The house was lit with its own security light but the rest of the farmyard was dark.

Two minutes after the call my handset clicked twice. I picked up and Shaughnessy reported a van rolling in. Driver out and chatting with Hat. Then the van was moving again, coming my way. Thirty seconds later I saw the lights coming up from the farm buildings. The van came into view and a guy came out from the shed and let it into the compound. I hefted my Leica.

Two men jumped out and started unloading packages. They propped the access door open, spilling light onto the dimly lit ground. Twenty packs went in, each the size of a sandbag. Then they manhandled an unlabelled drum across and inside whilst the gate guy hefted ten-litre plastic containers. A five minutes hiatus then the van guys reappeared carrying two duffle bags each and pushed them into the van. Then the third guy unlocked the gate and the van turned and disappeared back towards the farm. I took a last snap and stashed my telephoto. Called up Shaughnessy. His voice came over, quiet and close.

'They're going straight out,' he said.

'Looks like the place prefers its deliveries at night. Supplies coming in and produce going out. Night shift running full tilt.'

'They going to take more than one delivery?'

'The night is young.'

I cut the transmission.

Eleven p.m.

I settled back and waited. The night stayed clear but dark. No moon. Just the dim lighting of the compound beyond the fence and the hum of the fans. Outside the fence the night was alive with night birds and foxes, the occasional barking of a dog across distant fields.

Midnight.

One a.m.

The shed hummed peacefully on.

I finished my coffee and sandwich. Was good till morning.

Waiting is an art you develop. Focussed relaxation becomes second nature. An alert meditation. Impervious to the thought that the waiting might get you nowhere. You wait and watch and know that one in twenty hours will give you something back. It's the same whether you're in a parked car on a dark street in the cold wet hours watching a door that might never open or standing under a tree beside a farm building in deep countryside where unseen activity was ticking quietly out of sight.

Waiting and watching. Something I'm easy with. The twentieth hour always comes.

Two a.m.

My radio clicked.

Shaughnessy. More traffic. A van just come in. Chinwag ongoing. Hat out again, checking credentials, sharing a fag. Then the van moving. Coming my way.

The shed door opened and a guy walked across to open the gate and let it through. This one angled towards the static caravans and stopped at the end of the line nearest to me where the last caravan's windows were still lit. The van was an old Mazda minibus with tinted windows and an asthmatic engine that coughed and ran on for three seconds after the driver switched off. I snapped pictures with my low-light lens as he jumped out and pulled open the side door and made hurry-up gestures. Security and discretion were hardly an issue so I guess the guy just wanted to be done. Get home.

In response four young women climbed out and followed him

177

round to the caravan. The girls were young. Twenties. Or maybe teens. Each was hefting a carry-on bag.

They looked uncertain about their accommodation but the driver gestured them up the steps. Chop-chop. Get inside. So the four went up and in and the door closed behind them and the van turned and drove back out. Gate re-locked. Compound secure and quiet again.

The other side of the farm's operations.

The shed was drugs processing, the caravans the people-smuggling department. My guess was that the women had just arrived in the country. Maybe legally, maybe not, but there was no question what kind of tour company they'd signed up with: it was the type that travelled at night to places no one knew. The type whose PR department carried baseball bats.

In a couple of days the women would be gone and they'd never know where they'd been. But their hesitation on the caravan steps showed that they were beginning to sense the trouble and pain ahead.

I stashed my camera and went back to watching.

But that was it.

At three a.m. Shaughnessy reported that the farmhouse lights were off. The caravan lights had extinguished too and the compound was dead. Just the hum of the extractor system.

Five a.m. The compound lights switched off with the dawn.

Then at six the shed's access door banged open and the gate guy and four youths came out. Three men and a woman. I pulled my Leica back out and zoomed in.

The youths walked slowly across to a static caravan at the far side. No talk. Groggy from a night's work. Just taking a few moments of early sunshine. In no hurry to reach the caravan. It gave me time to snap faces.

And one in particular.

After they'd disappeared inside the caravan I pulled up the snap and double-checked.

My impression had been correct.

I'd hit the twentieth hour.

Alfie.

Chas Abbott's pal. Recognisable from the photo I'd been given on the houseboat. The same emaciated build, same messed up hair and pock-marked face.

I'd known it.

I was looking for Chas Abbott but Alfie had become his surrogate. Get to him and I'd be nearer Chas. And here was Alfie.

And if Chas' disappearance had anything to do with this operation then Alfie would know.

I wondered how long it had been since Alfie had been outside the gate.

And whether I was near the end of my search.

CHAPTER TWENTY-TWO
Lunatic

We gave it another hour then hiked back to the vehicles and drove into Grimsby where we found a Premier Inn on an industrial park by the docks. Cheap rooms and traffic music, the rep's Mecca. We picked up two rooms and grabbed a few hours kip then found an out-of-town pub serving lunch. Ate sandwiches and fries in a dead corner whilst we thought it through.

First order of business: a return call to Harry. He'd left a message re the *Fizikun* operation.

'I talked to some people,' he said, 'and your pal Percy. Which latter emptied the kitty but I got a couple of things to back up the whispers I was hearing so I guess it's an expense worth paying.'

'It probably is, though since we don't know that this is anything to do with Chas Abbott we could be on shaky ground with the billing.'

'Maybe our insurance will cover it. On the matter in hand: your Eastern European tag is spot on. *Fizikun* is a front for an Albanian operation running drugs and girls from South London. They bring them in, send them out.'

'That ties in with what we're seeing here. My guess is we're looking at the supply end of the business. Anything point to Lincolnshire?'

'Nada. The rumours only go so far. But these people are active from the Midlands to the south coast. The drugs and girls are processed at a hub unknown. One that shifts location periodically. I guess that would fit Lincolnshire.'

'Any IDs?'

'I've not picked up the big name but your long-haired guy with the bat is Roel Prifti. The operation's enforcer. His is the moniker for your office insurance.'

'Got it. Though recovery might be tricky unless the insurance people are dedicated.'

'If we go by the numbers being bandied about,' Harry continued, 'this operation is worth clearing up. These people are expanding their business in the UK, bringing grief to a lot of people. Word is that they run methamphetamines and cocaine, maybe cut the coke at their out-of-Town hub. I'm wondering whether they've got facilities up there amongst the cowsheds.'

'There's a production operation of some kind. Which they've managed to keep under wraps. Maybe the secret's in their moving around. Work a location three or four years then sell up, move on.'

'That could work if they kept the operation tight.'

'I think they have. It was just bad luck that our search for Chas took us across their path.'

'Or maybe not...'

'Maybe not. If Chas got tangled with these people through friend Alfie then *they* may be the reason for his disappearance. In which case luck doesn't come into it. We were going to get to them sooner or later.'

'You think these people have him?'

'He had this place in his sights when he left Scotland two years back.'

'He on the farm?'

'Alfie is. Which means we need to know what *he* knows. I'm giving it fifty-fifty that Chas returned here looking for him.'

'So we go in.'

'As planned. We throw a spanner into their operation and get hold of Alfie. Then we'll know. And whether the boy came back or not the board will be wiped clean. Prifti and his people can start filling out their own insurance forms.'

'When do you want me?'

'Tomorrow. I need another peek at the farm tonight. Give you and Bernie time to get here. Grimsby's a terrific place, by the way. Bernie will love it.'

'We staying unofficial?'

'Just until we've got eyes on the operation and talked to Alfie. Then we blow the whistle. The local people will want to coordinate with the Met. Move on Streatham before these people know what's hit them.'

'Sounds good.'

'Pack your bags.'

Harry rang off and I punched another number.

It picked with an explosive chuckle.

'Hey, me old pal! In trouble again! Lucy tells me you're walking wounded.'

I grinned. Flinched as the stitches fought back. And now the topic had come up the pain in my left arm blazed back with a vengeance.

'Bernie,' I said, 'when I need a nursemaid I've got you on speed-dial.'

'I'm your guy. Done my medics course. And no one died. We Marines are the go-to people whatever your situation. *Per Mare, Per Terror* and all that.'

'I'm reassured.'

'So what's the word?'

'Pack your bags. The party's tomorrow.'

'I heard you're looking for a kid.'

I stopped. Recalled our core business, the reason we were here. And how this whole thing might be a wild goose chase.

'Yeah,' I said. 'We're after a kid. But there's some people in our way. And they're not going to shift without persuasion.'

Bernie laughed. Nearly blew the phone's speaker.

'Persuasion is my middle name,' he said. 'Give me the details.'

I gave them then killed the line. Left Bernie to pack his grenades and nuclear bombs.

I grinned at Shaughnessy. Swigged the black coffee I'd ordered for the caffeine boost. Good for another night.

When we were through we returned to the hotel and got ready.

~~~~~

The second night shift clarified things. We watched the farm for twelve hours straight from six in the evening. Shaughnessy stayed with the farmhouse. I hid out in the woods behind the compound.

Watched the same routine as the previous night. Crew coming off shift at six p.m., packed into the van for the ride to the cottage. Kids looking to earn more dosh than they could hope to see elsewhere, accommodated away from the compound to limit their knowledge. If they suspected that the shed operated through the night they'd never met their counterparts who took that shift. Never had to worry about what the deal was and the implications for themselves. Never had to see women being shipped in and out, because they'd have worried about *that* for sure. Accommodating the day shift in the cottage was the lesser risk for the Albanians. High wages and implicit threats in place of the razor wire.

An hour after the day crew left the four-person night shift ambled across from their caravan accompanied by two of the Albanians, and I got a second look at Alfie as he walked over alongside the one girl in the group. None of the group looked worried in the sense of held-against-their-will worried but they weren't exactly bounding to work. My guess was that the Albanians had sold them some kind of deal, promises of sweeteners, to keep them placid, though it wasn't good enough to let them out of the gate.

They reached the shed, went in, and things settled down.

I waited and watched.

Two deliveries: at ten-thirty and just after midnight. Same as before. Sacks, containers, metal drums coming in. Produce going out.

Then five a.m. A third delivery. Different kind.

The Mazda minibus again. Bringing in six women. Dropping them at the caravan inside the compound. Young. Pretty. Tired. Maybe scared.

At six a.m. the night shift came out and Alfie and his pals walked back to their caravan with even less spring in their step than last night. They milled about outside the unit for a while, smoking in the early sun. Then at seven they were herded up the steps and out of sight.

We called it quits and walked out across misty fields.

Our best estimate was eight Albanians in residence at the farmhouse. Hat in charge.

Static caravans inside the compound housing the night shift and women in transit. The women would be in and out within a day or so. They were here to generate revenue and that wasn't going to happen at Low Rasen.

Three or four Albanians on shift inside the compound at any one time. Possibly armed, though we hadn't spotted weapons.

'We need to watch out for that,' Shaughnessy said. 'A couple of firearms and we're likely to have our hands full.'

'There'll be guns,' I said. 'This will be all about surprise and speed.'

'And Bernie.'

I caught the flicker of a smile on Shaughnessy's face. Between him and Bernie I couldn't say who was the more lethal, but so far only Bernie had put me in hospital so I had to see Shaughnessy as the soft touch. He'd described Bernie as "interesting" when they first met, which I took to be special forces parlance for "dangerous". Something I'd known since I was a kid in that hospital bed. And Bernie had taken a shine to Shaughnessy – some kind of inter-forces recognition – and told me he was glad he never had to mess with *that* one. Which was Bernie's parlance for "lunatic".

I guess they were both pretty near the mark.

But when surprise was our main weapon we needed to hit with a momentum that ended the game in seconds. And Bernie Locke gave us a nice edge in that respect, courtesy of his rocket-propelled seventeen stone and his strategy of dodging bullets by getting to the shooter before their trigger finger got a half-decent pull.

Surprise and overkill.

If we could get hold of the compound and sheds and get the security cam out of action, we could sit tight until the police came in. Without comms the house crew would be guessing. They'd come looking but we could stall them until the blue lights arrived.

Who would be Armed Response.

They'd take it from there.

We'd take a ticking off for not bringing the authorities in earlier, but if we handed this over now we'd be talking days to sort out plans and warrants, with Prifti and his crew already on alert back in London. We were already on borrowed time. The people here weren't looking for us yet but the London people would be keeping tabs on me for sure. And by the second or third day they failed to pick me up around Town they'd smell a rat. Low Farm would be on high alert – and maybe packing up for their next relocation. Assets and people moving out.

A week's stalling would turn up an empty farm.

Alternatively, if our plan was good, we might close the whole operation down in one night. And get the kid Alfie out.

And maybe find out if Chas Abbott was anywhere nearby.

We finalised details as we walked across the fields then headed back to our Grimsby digs.

Sleep eluded me for an hour whilst my arm and face played hell, giving my mind plenty of time to toss around all the what-ifs and how-mights. And to keep falling back to the thought that after all the fireworks, however things went at the farm, tomorrow might be just aches and pains and a blank sheet of paper regarding my main business.

Because so far I'd picked up no sense that Chas Abbott was linked to the operation at Low Farm, that he was anywhere near here. Friend Alfie might know nothing.

Leaving us with just a ground clearing. Removing the clutter to get a sight of where I stood as the dust cleared.

And that might be nothing more than square one, a blank sheet and a lost boy more distant than ever.

CHAPTER TWENTY-THREE
He went for Plan B

'These people could use a few lessons in security,' Harry said.

We were lying full length in the grass, ten yards from the compound fence at Low Rasen, fifty yards from the gate.

Harry had binocs to his eyes. He was camouflaged in grey slacks and a black herringbone jacket that I'd not seen before. Those eighties' fashions were really something. Strictly speaking there was colour in the herringbone, some kind of brown, but it wouldn't show up once night fell.

'They've two thousand feet of fencing,' he said, 'and just one gate cam. Then they bring the shed feeds out and tie everything up at a box in easy reach. What's the point of that?' He rolled his head to look at me. I was flat with my weight on my right side to save the left arm. 'You only need to reach through the fence with a pair of nail-clips and the house is blind.'

'We'll be on a tight schedule,' I pointed out.

'No prob.,' Harry said. 'Five secs tops. Plus two or three to get to the box. Call it eight max until the screens go blank. If they blink they'll miss it.'

'If we get lucky they might not check their screens for five minutes. Then if they waste time thinking about glitches and what-ifs we might have ten minutes before they come over.'

'That would be nice.'

'The key is the phones inside the compound. We'll need to nail those fast.'

'How many people you seeing in there?'

'Two or three plus the driver.'

'Sounds straightforward. We'll hardly need Bernie.'

He grinned and went back to his binocs. He knew the rule. Excess firepower saves a thousand tears. We'd one aim here: stamp out the compound activities fast and get the clear ground I needed to talk to the kid Alfie and take a gander for Chas Abbott. And if Chas wasn't here then the faster and harder the better. I didn't fancy a drawn out campaign with the Albanians.

We crawled back to the fence and risked an upright gait once we gained the tree shadows. Jogged round to my observation spot on the far side of the compound. We'd left rucksacks there with equipment and provisions. I pulled out a flask of coffee and munched another supermarket sandwich. Harry pulled out a flask of tea and tin of digestives. I double-clicked transmit and Shaughnessy came on and reported all quiet at the house. He didn't say what he was drinking.

Then just before six p.m. he came through again.

'Shuttle,' he said.

We watched the white van turn out from between the farm buildings and roll towards the gate. A guy came out and unfastened a chain and the van came in. Once it was parked up the day shift came out. Same as before. Cookie, Gangly, Petra, two others. They walked swiftly to the van and hopped in. Keen to get home. Those shifts were long and I didn't see the Albanians sending in quality lunches. Once they were on board the driver slammed the doors and drove out.

Ten minutes later a 4x4 came over and we got the supervisor shift change. Two guys from the shed and two from the static caravans headed back to the house for dinner as the night crew took over. Four of them. One locked the gate and disappeared into the caravan housing the girls. The other three headed into the shed, setting up. Then just before seven one of them reappeared and brought the night workers over from the static by the gate. The same group as last night, Alfie amongst them, shoulder to shoulder with the girl. Taking their time on the stroll over. Breathing fresh air. Shift changes were probably the only chance they got.

Then things settled down. Just the hum of the fans across an empty compound. The heat was dropping fast. The tree shadows lengthened across the bare earth.

Then a rustling in the undergrowth behind us and Bernie's black mass was suddenly on top of us. The rustling was for effect. If he'd had the whim he could have breathed down our necks for an hour before shocking the hell out of us with a chummy slap on the back.

He skipped the back-slapping this time and chucked out a beefy hand. Harry first then me.

'How do, pals?'

I hesitated taking his paw. Was rewarded when I did with the pain of bones almost breaking. Luckily we shake hands with our right. If I'd suffered his little ritual with my left I'd have been riding a stretcher out of there.

'Bin too long,' he declared. He was still pumping my hand as we played the game we'd played for two decades, which was for him to pretend he wasn't breaking my bones and me to pretend I didn't notice.

'How you bin keeping Eddie, me old pal?'

He threw a massive toothy grin at the plasterwork on my face.

I grinned back.

'Never better,' I said. 'Just that damn bus...'

Bernie rocked back with mirth and increased crush pressure. My hand was near cardiac arrest but I grinned back to show that this was all good fun. When I finally pulled clear Bernie was watching the compound.

'Hear you're looking to give these people grief.'

I gestured to my face.

'Payment for this.'

'The bus drivers.' He shook his head. 'Lucy tells me they messed up your office too. There's a message in there somewhere.'

'The message was: keep away from this compound.'

Bernie turned to Harry.

'So here we are. I guess they don't know our Eddie.' He dug for a memory. 'I threatened him once, way, way back. Just a friendly warning about a girl but he put my lights out. Right there on the school stage. Middle of Hamlet with five hundred paying customers looking on.'

'It was An Inspector Calls. And the girl was my sister, whom you were bent on deflowering after you'd warned me to keep clear. And your timing never was hot, Bernie. It's better to concentrate on your lines once the curtain's up.'

'Words of wisdom, pal. That's what I love about you. And how is the delectable Amber right now?'

'She's fine. I'll tell her you asked.'

'Out like a bloody light,' Bernie said. 'That's what you get when you put Eddie's nose out of joint. These Albanians don't know what they've started.'

'They soon will,' Harry said. 'Their operation's going off the air tonight.'

'Of which I've no doubt.' Bernie was back watching the compound. 'So what's the plan?'

I'd filled Bernie in earlier on the generalities, the reason we needed to clear the decks here – retaliation for my office aside. Now I gave him the tactical. He watched the compound and sheds and filed the plan.

'Their weak link is the separation from the house,' Harry said. 'The crew are sitting pretty at the farm, guarding the way in and depending on mobile comms and the gate cam to stay in touch. And I'm thinking the thing's become routine after three years. But when the gate opens for their vehicles the compound is exposed and if we go in then and kill the feed we'll have a free hand.'

'That's our plan,' I said.

Bernie nodded. Didn't post objections or treble his fee. Seemed the plan was good. As good as any can be with its own weak links.

Which were the uncontrolled elements: would any more crew come up here tonight? How well were they watching their screens at the farm? How quick were the compound people with their phones? And how many were armed?

There was only way to handle uncontrolled and unknown. Go in fast and hard. Take control before any of the factors become an obstacle.

Bernie grinned and sat down to wait. Harry and I finished our drinks and packed everything ready to take back out after the thing was done.

As dusk came on we moved round the compound to the farm side. Dropped down by the fence where it came out of the trees, watching the gate. The cam would have us in its field of view but we'd be distant dots, shadowed by foliage against the setting sun. They'd not see us. We settled in to watch.

~~~~~

At nine forty-five Shaughnessy called. Visitors.

A black Transit had checked in at the farmhouse. Driver out talking to our man Hat. Then the rear van doors were opened and a girl was coaxed down. Hat was chit-chattering with her, bouncing and joking. Then he escorted her into the house and the Transit driver jumped back in and drove our way. Shaughnessy caught a glimpse of other passengers as the door closed. Women. Maybe the girl was tonight's entertainment at the house. Things could get lonely out in Lincolnshire.

A minute later the van crossed towards the compound and a guy came out to unlocked a padlock, release the chain and swing the gate open. The van rolled through.

We let it go. Not dark enough and we didn't want to move in with a group of women milling about. Better if third parties were out of the way, tucked up in the caravans.

The van unloaded and came straight back out and disappeared back to the farm. The gate guy locked up and returned to the sheds.

Best estimate was that they had three people supervising in there plus one processing arrivals at the static caravans. Four total. Manageable.

The light faded and went, leaving the distant farm visible only as a halo of light above the barns. The compound to our right was just a dimly lit space, sheds on one side, static caravans on the other, the hum of the ventilation fans unceasing in the night.

At midnight my radio clicked again.

'Another van,' Shaughnessy reported. 'One crew. Nattering at the house.'

'Any passengers?'

'Nothing visible.'

'Okay.'

Maybe deliveries for the shed. Or more women. We'd not know until we were in the compound. I looked at Bernie and Harry. No way of avoiding the risk this time.

I hit transmit.

'We'll go on this one,' I told Shaughnessy.

'Got it.'

Five minutes later Shaughnessy reported the van moving. We were already crawling, closing the distance to the gate. Forty yards. Thirty.

A guy appeared at the gate and released the chain as the van rolled past us. We flattened ourselves then stood and sprinted in behind it, covered by the glare of its headlights. Harry veered off towards the control box and Bernie and I followed the vehicle straight in through the gate. We were in the driver's blind spot and hidden from the gate guy until it was too late. As the van cleared the gate I rushed the guy and hit him hard before he could reach behind his back. His lights went out and he dropped. I rolled him over and pulled out the gun he'd been grabbing for. A Glock 28. Not heavy firepower but it was lucky he'd been slow on the draw. I stashed it inside my belt then cinched ties round the guy's wrists and ankles.

One down.

I finished the guy's job for him. Got the gate closed as Harry jogged in beneath the dead cam. I left the chain loose and followed Bernie who was twenty yards away, still behind the van. It pulled up outside the main shed and the guy climbed out backwards right into the path of his fist. I heard the smack then nothing.

Two down.

Two more inside the shed supervising the night shift. One over in the caravans.

We were up two out of five with the farmhouse crew blind.

Harry and I reached Bernie and helped with more ties.

Across the compound a light showed in a caravan door as a guy appeared. Maybe coming out to see if he'd just heard something. Bernie and Harry were concealed by the van but I walked round sharpish and jumped into the cab and fired up. Drove over. The van coming towards him should have alerted the guy that something was off but there was nothing specific, nothing overt to tell him that he only had seconds. By the time I hopped out and he grasped the situation it was too late.

He swore in a language I didn't understand and pulled a knife. Stepped back and took a stance, still trying to figure things out, waiting for the stand-off that never came. I charged straight in and got a grip on the knife arm. As I ploughed past I twisted the wrist and pulled the guy round and down. Got the arm under my knee and pressed while I grabbed the wrist with two hands. The guy thrashed ineffectively as I shifted my grip, got it behind the hand and heaved. The wrist gave way with a snap. The guy yelled and got his legs drawn back to launch a vicious two-footed kick that knocked me away. But the knife came with me. I was already on my feet and moving back in as the guy heaved himself up, injured arm hanging useless.

I lobbed the knife into the trees then feinted left, like I was making for the bad arm again. The guy twisted away and took a right-hander on his temple. He staggered and struggled for balance and didn't see the uppercut that caught him under his chin. His eyeballs rolled and he sank to his knees and I pulled more ties from my jacket and eased him down all the way. Secured wrists and ankles. Moans from deep in his semi-conscious attested to the pain. Lucky he was out when I manhandled him across and rolled him under the nearest caravan to leave the compound clear. But lights had gone on in a second caravan. The women, wondering what was happening outside.

Its door burst open.

Not a woman.

Another goon, dressed only in pants, hair messed. Another knife.

Seemed we'd underestimated the numbers.

I backed away round the van, gaining distance and breathing space. But this guy was a little less confused than the first, even if he'd come straight from his bed. He followed me round and I backed away. He took it slow, checking me again. Then he snarled and moved in holding his knife in a relaxed grip out to the side. He was big but agile. No easy touch.

I went for the unexpected. Stepped rapidly towards him which put him into a stance with the knife gleaming dangerously under the compound lights. I kept coming to maintain his focus and in a second he'd made his decision and came at me. Didn't see Bernie who stepped in from the side and clocked him with a brick. The guy slammed into me but his knife arm was no longer up. He bounced off and jumped and jittered and did a kind of tango before he went down onto the concrete.

Bernie tossed the brick away and grinned. I grinned right back as a memory flash put me on the ground in place of the guy, way back when. I was staring at blue sky from flat out on the school cricket pitch after a follow-through from one of Bernie's vicious stumpings caught me on the chin as I dived for the crease. That same grin had been swimming above me as Bernie yelled his appeal. And burned solidly in my memory was the fact that my bat was grounded when the bails flew, a fact that the umpire affirmed in the face of Bernie's aggrieved appeals. When the umpire got shirty, maybe thinking about the school's insurance, Bernie's grin held fast. He reached out a helping paw and pulled me up, told me I'd got lucky, and I pondered my luck for the next hour on a cot in the medical room whilst the school decided whether we could dispense with a hospital visit and guaranteed black mark against the institution. Luckily for Bernie his parents were well in at the school. He kept his place on the first eleven and expulsion was never even mentioned.

We secured our third body and walked round to check the other caravans for further surprises but nothing else moved. Just the lights behind the blinds in the end caravans.

The compound was peaceful again. Downed crew out of sight. If anyone came up prematurely from the farm they'd see nothing.

Which turned out to be a good thing because Shaughnessy called through right then.

'Two coming over,' he said. 'Guns.'

He was watching a pair of Albanians who'd exited the farmhouse and were walking smartish towards the barns. Seemed they'd spotted the dead feed.

I checked my watch. Two minutes since Harry cut the line. Way on the low side. Sometimes you don't get the break.

'Can you hold them?'

'Yes. But the house crew will be looking for a quick report-back. I'd say you've got five minutes.'

The radio clicked off.

Five minutes would do.

Harry was at the gate. He left the bad guys' chain hanging and wrapped his own twenty mill. chain round the post. His substitute had hex links, case-hardened steel. Uncuttable. He secured it with a padlock of his own. Equally indestructible.

No one was coming into the compound no matter when they arrived.

Next job: we went into the active shed. Me then Harry then Bernie.

The small access door was offset from the main doors. It let us in behind the cover of a parked forklift. The shed stretched a hundred feet back, divided part way down by a chest-high wall. Beyond the wall, shadows faded to dark. This side of the wall, industry. Light and sound, activity. Six work tables back-to-back in three pairs, cluttered with retort stands, flasks and trays. A row of sinks behind them, fed by exposed copper pipes. Drums and casks, stacked crates, hanging plastic suits. Chairs round the tables with the four nightshift crew working away with goggles and gloves. Three had their backs to us. The one facing us was Alfie, busy at a tray. Something alerted him and he looked up. Spotted us just before the two guys supervising the operation. They were sitting in armchairs over by the far wall, watching TV with beer cans in their fists. I guess night shifts were a little dull, which explained their inattention and slow reaction. I was half way round the tables, dodging containers and buckets and sacks, before they clocked me.

Instant understanding. Boredom switching to red alert.

They were up and moving in a flash and we switched to a sprint as the two pulled out knives. The left guy had a vicious looking karambit in his hand. The right one came out with the blade of a push knife projecting from his fist.

Alfie jumped up as I sprinted round, knocking me off course but the deviation let me pick up a retort stand from a cluster by the dividing wall. Not a recognised combat weapon but the stands are necessarily steel and have nasty heavy bases if they catch you. Harry was behind me and Bernie was sprinting round the far side of the tables.

I swung the retort stand at the nearer guy and he ducked and lunged. The bastard was fast, an old hand, and the knife sliced the air and contacted my good cheek. I turned and stepped sideways to get room for a second swing but Harry had barrelled through and his momentum took them both down into a mess of drums and bottles. He rolled with the guy, got a grip on the knife arm.

I came back in and stepped on the arm to hold it down. In my periphery a table levitated. Bernie, taking the simple option of heaving it at the second guy. The guy stabbed viciously with his push and its blade went deep into the wood which was bad news for him as Bernie steam-rollered forwards. The blade was stuck and the guy went backwards over his comfy chair and was crushed by the table with Bernie's weight atop it.

I fought the knife from the first guy's hand as blood welled from my cheek. The guy's grip was like steel until Harry sent in a second pile-driver which settled the argument. The guy fell back dazed and gasping amongst broken glass. Bernie's opponent was still trapped between the chair and the table as he applied his weight. The guy had finally extracted his push knife but since he couldn't see round the table his flailing arm achieved nothing. I stepped across and put the retort stand to use. The push went skittering.

Then we got the guys secure and the place was under control.

Unknowns and uncontrollables negated.

The action ended almost as suddenly as it had started as Alfie and the workers stood rigid with terror. Maybe thinking of gang rivals, collateral damage. The girl reacted first and scurried towards the door but Harry intercepted her and brought her back.

'Take it easy,' I told them. 'You're not in danger.'

The blood running down my cheek made that assertion a little questionable but they calmed, stood in a huddle behind the tables, pulling off their gear.

My assertion re danger had a hole or two in it with a crew of armed thugs holed up two hundred yards away at the farmhouse but we had to make do with where we were. Once we'd confirmed no more bad guys in the caravans, and if the gate held, and once the blue lights appeared on the farm track then the danger would be gone.

'We're here to help,' I told the group. 'This operation is being closed down.'

I ripped a tissue from a roll above one of the sinks and dabbed at my cheek. Hard to tell the cut's length without a mirror but it felt significant. Maybe it would balance the damage from the *Fizikun* visit.

One of the kids got brave and asked who the hell we were.

He was a teen, tall and gaunt, didn't look entirely there. I guess the 'here to help' was another assertion he might find questionable. Because if he'd heard right we were talking about termination of employment. About lifestyle change.

'We'll explain later,' I said. 'Right now we just need to be calm whilst things get sorted.'

Bernie grinned broadly at the group. If that didn't calm them nothing would. Harry was over by the tables, lifting stuff, pushing and swirling jars, sniffing.

'Cutting *and* crack production,' he reported. 'You people have multiple skills.'

'We do what we're told,' Gaunt said. 'And these people are going to be all over you, man.'

Bernie broadened his smile. Looked round.

'Only if we untie them,' he said.

I came back to the point.

'What happens now is we go over to the caravans and sit tight whilst we call in help. This will be a police operation from now on. When they tell you it's safe to come out you come out. They'll want to talk to you.'

The guy started to argue but Alfie tugged at his arm and got him moving after the others and Harry and Bernie shepherded them towards the door to continue the discussion in the caravan.

I held back and made the call. Connected to Nettleham. Fought bureaucracy for five minutes until a night shift sergeant grasped the situation. When he heard the word "guns" things got tense. He trawled for personal details and consulted his computer before he pulled the chain and told me to sit tight. Five minutes later he came back on and told me they'd have people here in forty.

Forty minutes was pushing the limits. The people at the house weren't going to wait that long. I sensed a confrontation in the offing. Called Shaughnessy.

He was back opposite the farmhouse. Didn't mention the two guys he'd neutralised. I guessed they were stashed out of sight, contemplating life.

The two plus the five in the compound made seven of the Albanians out of the game. My guess was that there were no more than three or four of them left in the house. Maybe forty minutes was doable. Shaughnessy concurred. Said he'd keep me posted.

I walked out and met Harry and Bernie coming back from the caravan and we walked to the far units which had lights behind their blinds. The girls' accommodation. Harry and Bernie took one caravan, I hopped up and knocked on the door to the other. We needed to make sure there were no more bad guys in the compound, and that the girls stayed out of sight.

My door opened and a girl in her late teens blinked out into the night. I went in and found eight of them, disturbed from their sleep. Only two spoke rudimentary English. It was enough to get the message across. The Albanians were no longer in charge but there could still be fireworks. I told them to stay put no matter what.

A hundred questions and a similar number of curses and finger-jabs came my way but I waved them off and went back out to meet Bernie and Harry.

I brought them up to speed on the police armed response. ETA now thirty minutes. The farmhouse people weren't going to give us that long so when they came over from the house the best option was to keep them confused – and more importantly outside the compound. Thirty should be doable.

Then Shaughnessy called again.

The Albanians were out of the house, heading our way.

CHAPTER TWENTY-FOUR

You've got guns, we've got guns

I guess the dead feeds and the fact that the two guys they'd sent over to investigate were now AWOL had rung alarm bells. Hat and four of his people were jogging out between the barns. Shaughnessy reported progress until we could see for ourselves. We watched as five figures spread out and crossed the open ground.

Harry and Bernie backed off between the caravans and I found cover in the shadows between the sheds.

Hat was still wearing his hat. He probably slept in it. He was on the blower as they marched towards the gate, still trying to contact his people. The call came up dud and he pocketed the phone as he reached the gate. He grabbed the metalwork and gave it a good shake, calling out as he gestured to a sidekick to get the thing open. The guy reached from outside with a key to release the padlock. It took him thirty seconds to figure out that the key didn't fit. Then Hat swore and pulled him away and stood watching the compound whilst the cogs meshed.

He was trying to figure out why the world had just turned alien. Cam feeds dead. People missing. New lock on the gate.

It didn't take him long.

When reality seeped in Hat cursed loudly and lifted a leg to kick the gate with the sole of his foot. The metalwork shimmered and clattered against the chain and he let loose a second kick then a third. Then pressed his face to the metal to scan the compound and yelled again – illogically – for his guys to show themselves. The compound stayed quiet.

Hat stood back finally and held his arms wide. Yelled into the night.

'Hey! You in there! What the hell you playing?'

I kept quiet. Right now, silence and an empty compound ensured confusion and confusion bought us time. Hat had guessed what was up but he was still processing the information, trying to figure who and how and what. I guess the possibility that the farm might be invaded had never occurred to him. He called out again.

198

'Who you are, silly fuckers? What your flaming game? You want mess with our operation? You fucking *crazy?*'

No response. Fifty yards out, behind Hat and his crew, I spotted a shape crossing from the farm buildings to gain the shadows further along the fence.

Shaughnessy.

'Whoev' in hell name you are, open fucking gate! Now!'

Another kick, this one savage enough to bounce Hat backwards. He struggled to keep his balance then pulled out a gun and loosed off a single shot then three more that cracked the night air. The guy was starting to lose it.

His profanity continued in two languages. We kept quiet. Twenty-three minutes, though the police sergeant's ETA had been nothing more than an estimate. Armed Response doesn't run to a timetable. But there was a certain comfort in counting down. If we could keep Hat and his crew on the back foot, keep them outside the fence for a while, then this could end as we'd intended. Things would go off the boil pretty fast once the Albanians spotted the blue lights coming in.

Two more minutes ticked away whilst Hat and his pals huddled in a noisy confab, still struggling with disbelief: the unthinkable situation of the compound and its crew in someone else's hands. Hat gestured and barked and one of his guys climbed onto the fence but the razor wire defeated him. He tried to show willing but once the blood was seeping from his fingers his determination evaporated. He thrashed and rattled the fence for effect then slid back down. Hat stepped up to yell in his face and the guy yelled something back in Albanian, probably something along the lines of "If you're so keen why don't you hop over the razor wire yourself, pal?"

Hat didn't hop over. Shredding himself on the fence wouldn't get the gate open. And anyone dropping into the compound might not come back. Because the enemy was waiting in there for sure, armed with confiscated guns for sure.

Hat took a moment to find a solution.

Opted for crude. He lifted his gun which was a hefty automatic. Rested its barrel on a fence link and loosed off a slow fusillade at the nearest caravan where he speculated that his night shift were skiving. Windows blew. Thin walls tore like paper.

And just like that the situation turned bad. I'd anticipated guns.

The Chase Street visit had told me that. What I didn't expect was the insane tactic of using firearms as a line of first resort. What I didn't expect was Hat and his temper. The tactic of prising us out by blasting willy-nilly at the people inside the caravans. The instant Hat put his weapon on target we were in a whole new situation.

Uncertainty and confusion was no longer going to work as a stalling tactic. Hat's response to the uncontrolled and unknown was to wreak havoc.

The shots ceased for a moment as Hat slotted in a new mag. I yelled over.

'Take it easy people. This won't get you in.'

Hat stopped. Scanned the compound to locate the source of the words. Vectored in on my direction. And by the time he'd placed us he'd also placed my voice.

'Hey! I knew it! Little car guy. City detective. What in the name of god you doin' here interfering my operation? What in the name of hell? You *crazy* man?'

Seemed somebody was.

I stayed under cover. Reverted to silence. But Hat was all for continuing the discourse.

'You listening, Mr Detective? I know you. We told you stay away. We *told* you *stay away!* So what you doing?'

His pistol came up again, pointing my way this time and six or seven rounds cracked across the compound and chipped wood and concrete. Shrapnel flew. A shard ricocheted and caught me on the forehead.

'That's not gonna work,' I yelled. 'We're dug in. And the caravans are empty. We're in here and you're out there and there's no way in.'

Hat barked a laugh.

'And we shoot you fucking head off if you try to leave. So what you goin' do about that, Mr Private Eye?'

'What we're doing is holding the fort. You've got half your guys missing and a lab that's out of operation and you've got cops on their way. ETA ten minutes.'

That fantasy time-schedule again. Twenty minutes had just become ten.

Hat thought about this then stepped forward and kicked the gate again, venting his anger. If he'd had a few hours the thing would have been down.

'You no police coming you shit-piece. You think I'm stupid? You here big tough guy fuckin' hero, saving the people. Only you stuck in there and our friends from London gonna be here just soon as I call.'

'That's a bad bluff to call,' I yelled. 'Of course we called the police. We've got signal, just like you. And how long before your reinforcements show up? Four hours? Six? Your operation's shot here. Nothing to salvage. If you shift now you might just get out.'

'Fuck we move. We're coming in there to put you in dirt, detective-man.'

Then Hat told his people to hang tight and headed off back to the farm. Shaughnessy was too far back along the fence. An opportunity missed. If he'd got to Hat the show would have been over.

A couple more minutes ticked by. Eighteen to go.

Then I heard the growl of machinery and a tractor rolled out from the farm complex. It ignored the curve of the track. Angled straight towards the gate.

It came full tilt towards the compound's light. It was a John Deere kitted out with front weights that added a couple of tons of momentum, and Hat just drove straight at the gate and demolished it. He was out of the cab, gun raised, before the thing had stopped moving.

I'd already made my move. The space between the sheds was a trap. I sprinted out and dove in through the lab access door before Hat got his bearings. Shifted fast as Hat spotted me and raised his weapon to loose off a few rounds. The access door metal popped and turned into a sieve but I was already behind the main doors looking out through a gap.

The Albanians were in. Three of them were with Hat, moving towards the shed. The fourth was heading towards the caravans, looking for their missing people.

As Hat and his pals came in through the access door I retreated across the lab area and crouched behind the low wall that divided the building.

A few seconds later Hat and his crew appeared in the lab. Trod glass and debris as they checked out their messed up production facility and their guys trussed up on the floor. Hat barked a heartfelt curse at them and turned to loose five shots in my general direction.

Bullets drilled corrugated iron. Breeze block and wood chipped and flew.

'Where you are, Mr Detective? Show your face my friend.'

I didn't comply. I liked my face the way it was.

'*Gjonny!* Go round.'

One of his sidekicks angled towards the end of the low wall. If he had a gun and got his sights on me I'd be in trouble. I scampered at a crouch for the deep shadows of the far end, pulled the confiscated Glock from my belt. Hat spotted movement and loosed off another volley as I crashed down in the dark amongst a mess of crates and drums. The cover was flimsy, no match for a heavy automatic or the MAC-11 the guy who'd rounded the wall was pointing my way. I loosed off a few rounds to divert their attention and scrambled along the shed's end wall under cover. When I peered out, Hat was crouched on the far side of the dividing wall and his MAC pal was kneeling behind a drum ten feet nearer. They'd lost me in the shadows and if they came my way my bullets would find them before they found me. Time for caution.

I lifted the radio and gave Shaughnessy the situation. Backup needed ASAP. Sean was already inside the compound with Bernie and Harry, securing Hat's guy who'd gone to check the caravans. Bernie's voice came on.

'You clear of the doors?' he said.

'Hiding in the back. The bad guys have the lab.'

'Don't move,' Bernie said.

I grinned. Repeated the info I'd given Shaughnessy on weaponry in play.

'Stay put,' Bernie repeated. The radio clicked off.

Then Hat called again.

'Come out, hands up,' he yelled. 'Throw gun. Or we kill you right here.'

I kept quiet. It would take more than verbal baiting to get my position.

'You screw with us,' Hat yelled, 'and think you get away? You *mother-bitch*. You mess our equipment? Our *production?* Bad mistake Mr Detective.'

Silence.

'You no talkin'? Wassup? You goin' hide there till you full of holes?' He called across to his pal behind the drum.

'Gjonny!'

Johnny replied by ducking out and loosing off twenty rounds from the MAC. All guesswork but twenty rounds go a long way in a confined space. Crates shattered around me. Drums rang and clattered and woodwork spat dust and splinters. I stayed flat behind a wooden crate that took two rounds and jumped six inches but stayed intact. Debris rained down.

Hat's plan was to draw fire and locate me but I had eighty feet of shadows and junk in my favour and it wasn't going to happen. Hat and his pals would have to take that walk.

'Last chance,' Hat called. 'I'm trying help you here. Get you out alive. Take care of things. What point of dying for stupid client? Come out! Let's talk. Forget damage. We sort things out. Send you home.'

I resisted the offer. Stayed flat on the floor, gun aiming out between my two crates. Limited line of fire but I had both Johnny and Hat covered.

'You listening?' Hat said. 'I help you out. Explain to boss all misunderstanding. You go home safe.'

Silence. The only explanation Hat was ever going to give his boss was how many bullets he'd put into me.

Then he kind of lost it.

'Why you no listening, you Mr *fuck* Detective? You... go... *home!'*

His final three words were punctuated by shots as he planted bullets all around my position. Seemed I'd be going home in pieces. And his instincts had sharpened. He'd sensed my position and was directing his fire on the shadows right around me. I estimated thirty seconds before I needed to come into this and give him the one-sided firefight he wanted.

Then all hell broke loose.

The barn doors behind the lab blew apart like they'd been bombed. One of them ripped free of its top rail and slammed down onto the lab tables, scattering attached plumbing and sinks in all directions and the John Deere reared and roared up onto the mess like a rhino on heat. The door shattered and metal sheeting crumpled and the tractor returned to earth with a crash that shook the building. That two tons of front loading.

Hat and Johnny spun round and ducked then loosed off rounds blindly as they processed what was coming at them. But whoever had been in the cab had dived out into the protection of the far side as the tractor rolled across the lab and tried to punch a hole in the shed wall. The guy we'd trussed up in the armchair got a lucky break. His chair flipped over and rolled him away from the thrashing behemoth.

I was up and running from the first impact, firing over the Albanians' heads as they were torn between targets. For a moment there was pandemonium. Hat's man *Gjonny* sensed the rounds coming in over his head and rolled instinctively for cover but by the time Hat and his other guys spun round we were on them. Shaughnessy leapt the door debris and put gunman Johnny down hard and I vaulted the low wall and caught my foot on it which angled me perfectly for a head in Hat's gut. His automatic spat bullets all ways as he staggered backwards but he kept his feet and his cool sufficiently to register Shaughnessy in his peripheral vision, and the MAC that was pointed his way point blank. He realised that this was a firefight he wasn't going to win. He yelled to his guys and sprinted sideways back to the access door and the group scarpered and were gone. All except *Gjonny* who was struggling to his feet until Bernie appeared and put him down hard on the glass and debris.

They were down to four, outside the shed. Had lost two of their three guns.

Though one of them wasn't going to help. Shaughnessy checked his magazine and threw the weapon away into the shadows then strode across and killed the lights. The missing barn doors gave a nice view of the compound, illuminated but empty. Hat and his people had ducked out of sight to re-think tactics.

I dusted myself off. Cursed.

'We screwed up,' I said.

Our plan had depended on us getting eyes on what was going on in the compound then sitting tight behind the locked gate until help arrived. Had depended on Hat and his pals taking a while to respond to their blank screens. And depended on them being outside the fence when help arrived.

'We got unlucky,' Shaughnessy concurred.

'We shouldn't have depended on luck.'

Something I'd said a million times. I'm planning to have the phrase engraved on my headstone.

'How long have we got?' Bernie was eyeing the compound, watching for movement.

'Fifteen, more or less.'

'Okay. We can keep them on the back foot for that long.'

'Maybe twenty. Worst case, thirty.'

Bernie looked at me. Went back to watching the compound.

A couple of minutes ticked by and Hat and his crew stayed clear. The real screw-up was theirs. They'd handed over most of their weaponry, and getting back into the shed wasn't an option. And their reinforcements were hours away. And despite his earlier words Hat had to assume that I wasn't bluffing about the cops.

Stalemate. The clock ticking.

If the Albanians were going to run it needed to be soon.

Another two minutes ticked by.

Then Hat stepped out from round the neighbouring shed and walked to the middle of the compound where we could see him. Over by the caravans two of his people showed themselves again, though they stayed back.

Parley time.

'Okay, Flynn, last chance. Come out now and we stand back. Let you go. You've got guns, we've got guns. Someone get hurt soon. Better call it a day. No spill milk.'

'How about *we* let *you* go?' I retorted. 'We've got the firepower and the reinforcements on their way.'

'I tell you again,' Hat said. 'Someone get hurt. I'm givin' you way out, here. Skedaddle. Go home. We catch up later.'

I grinned across at Shaughnessy and Bernie. Bernie grinned back. Shook his head.

'You listening?' Hat's voice was rising again. That anger management thing. 'Stop playing stupid, Flynn. Come out, all you. Come out an' go home!'

We stayed put.

So Hat raised his gun and four shots cracked out. The corrugated iron rang again. A string of slow profanity followed the rounds in through the empty shed doorway. Shaughnessy looked at me and raised an eyebrow. This wasn't good. We were concealed in the dark. Hat had no targets. But if he continued placing shots then sooner or later he'd get lucky. I didn't know how many rounds he had left in his magazine but if he clipped in another he'd go down.

Hat knew it. Knew he could only toy with us for so long. He was watching us and watching the compound, looking for inspiration. Then he saw it. Gestured to his people and they sprinted across to the second to last caravan where a girl was watching from the darkened doorway. Harry had the end unit and its occupants sealed up tight but we couldn't cover everything. What the hell the girl was thinking was beyond me. We'd told them to stay put, keep the doors locked. But curiosity is a funny thing. The explanation for most stupid things.

The girl stepped back and slammed the door but the goons were there before she could get it locked. Kicked it in and dragged her out and strong-armed her down the steps and out across the compound. She was young, seventeen or eighteen, slim with long black hair and a wasted expression on her face. Which switched to fear as they dragged her out.

Hat lunged and gripped her arm and pulled her in front of him. Looked back over at our shed and suddenly control was sliding again.

The girl struggled ineffectually but Hat held her tight.

'Okay, Mr Detective. I got my bullet-proof vest. So how 'bout I come in there an' shoot your balls off?'

His gun came up again and three more rounds spat across the compound and hit metalwork behind us in the dark.

'Show your faces *ndyra nëna*. This your last chance.'

'Give up, you idiot,' I yelled back. 'You're wasting time you don't have. And if you hurt the girl your time is up.'

'You think I'm going hurt the girl?' Hat's voice was rising. Losing it again. His agitation shook the girl, adding to her own struggles. Suddenly he pushed her forward, away from him, and took three steps back.

'Let me give demonstration,' he said. He raised his gun. Took aim as the girl turned to face him.

I saw what was about to happen.

The girl was still blocking any line of fire I might have drawn on Hat and I took the only action that might save her life, leapt out over the debris and sprinted towards her as Hat fired the first shot. The round flew deliberately high but it was clear where the next bullet would go. Hat lowered his aim and I took the girl down hard, heard her scream before her face met the ground. Hat yelled again and placed three more shots close enough to feel but just wide, toying, keeping me in play for a few more seconds whilst he reached for a fresh magazine. I covered the girl's body and reached to pull the Glock from my belt. The thing tugged and caught and wasn't going to save me as Hat took a stance and pointed the weapon.

'I told you!' he yelled. 'I *fucking* told you. You piece detective shit.'

Two figures streaked out from cover in my peripheral vision. Shaughnessy and Bernie, racing for the maniac in a contest they couldn't win. They'd take Hat but they still had ten yards to cover and that was bad news for me. Down at the far caravan Harry was leaping the steps but he was far too far.

Hat yelled at the thrill of it, put his gun on me and pulled the trigger.

The shots nearly deafened me but they dug up the earth a yard wide and then tracked away to arc off into the night as a steam-train hit the Albanian from the rear and smashed him off his feet. A figure had sprinted in through the broken gate. Hit him like a wrecking ball.

An instant later Shaughnessy and Bernie joined the ruck and Hat and his gun were buried.

I rolled off the girl and was up and pulling out the gun, scanning for any of Hat's remaining crew. But we were alone. Hat's soldiers were just shadows, jogging back to the farm to grab their vehicles.

I coaxed the girl to her feet and steadied her. She was wearing pyjamas that were torn and dusty and staining red where her damaged nose dripped blood. Just a bust vein, with any luck. She'd smacked the ground pretty hard. Tears streaked the dirt on her face and she was trembling under my touch. She spoke in a language I didn't understand. Terrified.

Same with me.

That gun had been right on me and Hat wasn't about to extend the game once he'd decided to take me out. Shaughnessy and Bernie would have got to him but by then I'd be gone, and maybe the girl.

Harry jogged up and took over with the girl whilst I continued watching for a counterattack. But none was coming. We had control again. So I walked over to see who the hell had taken Hat down a tenth of a second before he took me out.

The ruck had broken up. Hat had been pulled upright, leaving his trilby on the ground. Still raging, though the rage was muted by Bernie's hefty biceps locked in a choke hold. So maybe not rage. The crimson face was probably asphyxiation. Bernie's not the delicate type. I resisted the urge to plant a massive kick and looked instead for our guest intruder.

ID'd him.

Grinned.

I should have known.

Terry Tickner was brushing dust off his jacket and looking at me like he wanted to shoot me himself.

'Time to sharpen your act, Eddie,' he said. 'You're gonna get someone killed one of these days.'

I held the grin. Ate shit.

'Give me your number,' I said. 'If we get any more dicey situations I'll give you a call.'

'I won't be there.' Tickner wasn't smiling. 'This was a one-off.'

'Got it. But much appreciated, Terry. My life was just about to flash before my eyes.'

'If it hadn't already flashed it was too late,' he said. 'You had half a second maximum.'

'I was coming from behind for sure. So call this a misjudgement. I'm just glad you called by.'

'Good move, pal,' Bernie said. 'This little bugger had us cold.' He shook Hat like a hound shakes a rabbit. The Albanian's feet skittered and stamped and one of his feet flattened his discarded hat. 'And Edward here,' he noted, 'is the one signs my invoices.'

There you go: Bernie the goddamn comedian. He's holding a gangster in a choke hold and instead of putting him down and securing him, which any basic military training would tell you to do, he's focused on the humour. And Bernie knew as well as I did that Lucy handles the invoices. He'd have got his paycheque no matter how things ended tonight.

I looked at Shaughnessy for help. He shook his head.

I came back to Tickner.

'I guess it's gonna sound ungrateful,' I said, 'but what the hell were you doing sneaking around out here? Have you put another bug on my car?'

Tickner was focused on dusting himself off. I spotted a tear at his jacket shoulder that he hadn't yet noticed. With any luck he'd stay ignorant until he was back home.

'Yeah,' he said. 'It does sound ungrateful after I just saved your goddamned neck.' He didn't answer my question. 'These guys,' – he gestured towards Hat – 'I assume they're the Eastern Europeans you annoyed.'

'The very ones. And they're still annoyed.'

In demonstration of which Hat planted a vicious back-heel on Bernie's shin. Bernie grunted and lifted the guy. Upended him and dropped him hard onto the ground. The Albanian's head touched down in his ruined hat but it didn't protect him. Dust clouded skywards and the guy's eyes went up. He dropped and lay quiet. Bernie knelt and planted a knee to stabilise the situation whilst Shaughnessy fastened ties round his wrists. I was still watching Tickner.

'Ingratitude aside,' I said, 'I'm still wondering why, or how, you ended up here.'

'I'm just following my brief. Staying close. My people reported you coming back out this way and I followed. I've been driving round this area for twenty-four hours. Had just about given up when the big guy's Land Rover appeared.' He nodded to Bernie. 'The speed he was doing, taking out hedges left and right, caught my attention. Farmers don't drive vintage vehicles and they're not suicidal. So I smelled a rat. Followed him right to your car. And bingo. I've been watching all evening.'

'Hats off,' I said. 'We never saw you. But I guess we weren't looking.'

T plus five.

Armed response now officially late.

We checked that Hat and his people were secure and went over to the caravans and I went in to talk to Alfie. The static was a cramped mess of tiny kitchen and lounge, cubicles further in. The night shift's prison cells.

They were all there, sitting in the rudimentary lounge area. Alfie was sitting with his girl friend, arm round her shoulder in what he intended as a protective hold but looked kind of desperate. Fact is, they'd had no protection against anything in this compound. He reacted with a start when I called his name. Looked up, scared.

'Relax,' I told him and the room. 'It's all over.' But Alfie stayed nervous as he tried to figure out why I knew his name.

'I've been looking for you,' I explained.

Now he looked more scared than ever.

'Take it easy,' I repeated. 'The operation here is finished. The police are on their way. But I'm just wondering what got you people confined to this compound.'

The question was addressed to the four of them but I was looking at Alfie. He looked round for backup but the others stayed quiet. The guy looked even worse than his photo. He'd not combed his hair in a year and his bony frame would fail a scarecrow recruitment drive. His jumpy eyes, restless limbs, didn't point to good health. Then he shrugged and found his voice.

'We tried to leave,' he said. 'That's why they put us in here.'

As I'd guessed.

'The deal was that we could quit working here anytime. Just give them notice and keep quiet afterwards. But when Lynette tried to leave...' – he pulled the girl closer – 'she disappeared. So I got scared and ran. But they caught me. Put me in here with her and the others. Gave us a new deal. We'd be under lock and key until the end of our contracts then we'd get our back pay.'

'And you believed that?'

'Sure. Maybe. Who knows? We didn't have much choice. No one knows we're here. Not even the guys on the day shift. Two friggin' years we've been here.'

All just part of the Albanians' tight security. Any sign their paid workers were having second thoughts, thinking about retirement, they just picked them up and transferred them to the slave brigade. And Alfie was right to have doubts about the deal. There was only one way out of this compound.

I came to the point.

'Your friend Chas. Is he around?'

Alfie just looked at me.

'Is he working for these people?'

Still that look. Like he didn't know what the hell I was talking about. I took a breath. This was blood from stone.

'I came here looking for you, Alfie,' I said, 'because I was looking for Chas and apparently he was searching for you. Did you get him involved with these people?'

But Alfie still wasn't on wavelength. He just shook his head and looked at his pals. Looked round at the strangers crowding the caravan and maybe looking just as threatening as the Albanians.

'I don't know anything about Chas,' he said. 'Last time I saw him was in London before they picked me up. That was two years ago.'

'Okay: we already had Chas with you in London. Which is where you'd run after you got cold feet here. And where they picked you back up. But I'm thinking that his contact with you put him in the Albanians' sights.'

'He's never had any contact with the gang.'

'Did they never mention him? Ask about him? Because no one's seen Chas for nearly two years – almost as long as you. If there's anything you know then I need it.'

'There's nothing,' Alfie repeated. 'I swear it.'

'Well I disagree. There is something. I think he came into contact with these people because of his association with you. Maybe you should know that, in case it helps the feel-good factor for the mess you've made of your own life.'

'Hey! Fuck you, mister. What happens in my life is nothing to do with Chas. I've not dragged him into anything.'

'Did you know he came here?'

No answer. Alfie just looked lost. His eyes flicked between us all. His co-workers looked lost too.

'What puzzles me,' I said, 'is that Chas sounded like a regular kid. Finished his education. Was never in trouble. So what was he doing mixing with someone like you?'

Alfie switched back to me.

'Well fuck you again,' he said. 'People don't ask permission to make friends. Chas and me were cool. Got on. It's something you wouldn't understand, being some kind of thug.'

Thug. I'd been called worse. But this time I had the scars on my face to back up the boy's assertion. The way I looked right now a grizzly bear would turn the other way. But I was digressing, a trick to help keep the lid on anger and despair, the bad feeling that this was all for nothing.

'Think back to London,' I said. 'Did Chas say anything about his plans?'

'He was off on a trip. Taking a year. All kinda vague.'

'And he never mentioned coming to this area?'

'No.'

Because the idea of coming to Low Rasen started only after Alfie disappeared, failed to show up for another night out, didn't answer his phone. Low Rasen was on Chas' mind from then on. And his concern for his friend took him down a diversion from his year's wanderings that had probably brought something bad down on him. And friend Alfie had missed the whole thing. I wondered if anyone had tried looking for *him* when he went missing.

'Was Chas his normal self when you split?'

'He was okay. A little lost. I don't know. Man, I just wanna get out of here.'

Same with me. I was still listening for the vehicles.

Maybe Chas had come back here after Scotland, maybe he hadn't. If he had, no one knew. And if he hadn't then I was going to have to pick up his trail from scratch and this whole damn thing, this *war* we'd just fought, would be nothing but a dead end.

Leaving me standing again on a dusty road looking at a shimmering horizon and a mirage that never got closer.

CHAPTER TWENTY-FIVE
That brings me to the bad news

Armed Response showed up ten minutes later .

Blue lights lit up the farm buildings like Guy Fawkes night and the OIC talked to me over my phone courtesy of a patch through Lincoln. I explained that the known bad guys were neutralised. Suggested a precautionary check on the farmhouse. Distant yells and crashes attested to their compliance then the unit switched targets. Vehicles rolled up from the farm, dispersing people left and right into the darkness. We told the kids and girls to stay put in the caravans and went to stand in the centre of the compound trying to look non-threatening.

The lead vehicle stopped twenty yards from the gate and the guy in charge jumped out and told us to come through. We filed out into the glare of the police spots for the obligatory pat-down and ID check. After which bureaucracy moved into high gear. Self-proclaimed good guys or not, the only good guys the cops recognised in situations like this were the ones cuffed and face down on the ground. They dispensed with that formality but the Chief Super I'd guided in planted us in three of their vehicles under armed guard and stumped off to see what was what. Ended up less impressed than when he'd arrived as their sweep picked up the treasure trove of bodies, guns and knives scattered everywhere.

It was the women – fourteen of them down in the last two caravans – who brought what little credibility the Super was prepared to give us. Hard to beat trafficked people roaming free as evidence that the bad guys are the ones on the ground. And hard to beat the sight of a wrecked lab to demonstrate what other lines those people had been into. He nevertheless kept us sitting in their vehicles for forty-five minutes until the tension had eased. After which he pulled us back out of the vehicles and kept us on a leash for another hour, answering questions and giving them the guided tour. Then he packed us off to Lincoln to answer more questions, in my case via A&E to have six stitches sewn into my right cheek. Six wasn't as bad as it had felt, though it would have needed ten to balance the left side. I walked back to the car feeling a little asymmetric. Spent the remainder of the small hours in a room at Nettleham with people pulled in on early shifts. Luckily they had too much their hands with the Albanians to give us more than the minimum attention and they kicked us out at six-thirty a.m. with our diaries inked out for longer sit-downs with the Metropolitan Police, who were already out knocking on *Fizikun's* door. A couple of cars dropped us off at Low Rasen and we picked up our vehicles and headed back to Grimsby, Terry Tickner and all. He'd opted to bill his own client for a room at the Premier Inn rather than head straight home and risk adding an insurance claim to his invoice.

We agreed to catch some kip then meet up late afternoon.

I bypassed the kip. Showered and changed then drove back to Low Rasen.

The day-shift kids were at the cottage looking scared and lost. Seemed the cops had turned up in lieu of the farm shuttle this morning. Handed them their cards.

The five were in the kitchen when I walked in, contemplating their futures and specifically the fact that their next inflated wage packet was now a dream. The bus fare to Lincoln for the chat with the authorities would need to come out of their existing stash. And the kids might be victims of a sort but they were here through the lure of easy money just like the Albanians. I saw the worry as well as fear on their faces as I sat down.

The excitement earlier had deprived me of the chance of a longer chat with Alfie and the answers I suspected he might have. So even if the kids in this cottage had claimed to know nothing last week my instinct said different, and now I was back to press a little harder. To which purpose my change of appearance was just the ticket. The five of them had nearly jumped through the roof when I walked in.

I grinned across the table to scare them some more. Petra and Cookie were standing behind the chairs they'd just vacated and Gangly was behind me, still gripping the door he'd failed once again to shut in my face. The two other boys were backed up in the far corner near an enticing exit door.

I patted the table top in an invitation for Petra and Cookie to sit back down.

'I've got good news and bad news,' I told them.

The kids ignored my invitation. Remained behind their chairs. The two by the far door shifted a couple of inches nearer their escape route.

'The good news...' – I was looking at Petra – 'is that your friend is safe.'

Her eyes widened.

'Alfie,' I confirmed. 'And you were right to be concerned.'

Petra licked her lips and found her voice.

'You know where he is?'

I grinned. The pain in my right cheek was worse than the left. Seemed the port side was healing, though the angry flush maintained the dramatic appearance.

'He's safe,' I said. 'You'll talk to him in a day or so.'

Her mouth opened but she didn't quite have the questions she needed to ask. I moved on.

'Now the bad news,' I said.

I looked at all of them. Cricked my neck to include Gangly.

They all looked back. Gangly shifted nervously. The boys by the far door move another inch towards safety. Petra and Cookie watched wide-eyed.

'The bad news,' I said, 'is that I'm tired of listening to lies. And we're all staying in this room until you tell me what you know about Alfie's friend Chas Abbott. So let me tell you what *I* know about *Alfie* to save some time. Alfie came to work at the farm processing drugs just like the rest of you. He picked up the same nice wage packet as the rest of you – one K a week and a few soft drugs to sweeten things. And he agreed the same contract – invisible and unsigned – as the rest of you. To wit: that you all keep quiet about what you do here and when you finally decide to move on that you give a month's notice. Which, together with the promise of eternal silence, secures you a twenty K golden handshake.'

They watched me in silence now.

'The problem,' I went on, 'was the small writing. The clause that I guess you overlooked in this invisible contract. The one that says that if you ever *do* decide to quit, due notice duly provided, you're never actually going to receive that twenty K.'

I paused. Looked round. They were all listening now like they were learning something new.

'In this game,' I said, 'silence is golden. Maybe a twenty K payoff and a few backup threats *would* keep you quiet but it's a risk your employers weren't taking. So there never was any twenty K handshake. The month's notice was a simple tripwire to let them know you were packing your bags. And when you clocked off and headed over to pick up the cash that's when you'd disappear. If you were lucky they'd recruit you onto their night shift and you'd relocate to the compound.'

I was still looking at them all.

'Did anyone ever wonder what those static caravans were for?'

No one answered.

'If you're not so lucky, on the other hand, if you're seen as a threat or are surplus to requirements, then you'd just disappear. So best case when you quit: you're a prisoner on the farm, working night shifts. You know you're a prisoner, of course, but even then they keep feeding you the sweeteners, telling you it's just temporary. A year or two until it's time to relocate their operation. That's when you'll be free to go with your payout. And even if common sense tells you the thing's a pipe-dream you cling onto that promise, stay cool, work the shifts, hoping things will work out. But there's only one way you're ever getting out of these people's hands and that's a bad way.'

Then Petra spoke.

'What happened to Alfie? Has he been at the farm?'

'From shortly after you last saw him, two years ago.'

Five faces paled in the kitchen. Reality seeping in.

'Alfie didn't tell us he was leaving,' Petra said.

'And we know why,' I said. 'He had a girlfriend, remember?'

'Lynette,' Petra said.

'Lynnette. Well she *did* mention leaving, am I right? She'd made up her mind three months before Alfie disappeared. Decided she'd had enough and gave the bad guys her notice. But she didn't go anywhere. She ended up inside the compound and when Alfie couldn't contact her he smelled a rat. Finally understood the leaving deal. And he did a runner without telling anyone. Headed back to London. He had the hopeless idea of finding Lynette there and somehow staying out of the Albanians' hands. But they caught up with him and brought him right back here. He and Lynette have been living in the caravans since then.'

Faces paled further. Gangly was shaking his head. Looked at Petra.

'Fuck,' he said. He looked back at me. 'What was going to happen to us?'

'If you didn't try to walk away early? I don't know but you might have been all right. These people weren't far from moving the operation elsewhere. That's when you'd get your cards. Maybe a bonus they promised you, along with a warning that if you ever talked they'd come and tear off your limbs. When they moved location that's when they could take the risk of letting go. You'd know nothing about them, hardly know where you'd been working, much less where their new operation was located. The risk they couldn't accept was the person who decided to get out early.'

'We've wages owing,' Gangly said. 'They only pay ten percent up-front. They hold the rest until the end.'

'Well that was probably legit too. Part of their security. I doubt if they wanted you splashing cash around, or building up bank accounts in case any of you had to disappear for any reason. Disappearing broke is one thing. Disappearing with a fat bank balance left behind and evidence of regular top-rate payments going in, is another. Low profile was everything to these guys.'

I stopped.

'But here I am,' I said, 'doing all the talking. When all I'm here for is to hear what you know about Chas Abbott. The truth this time, since this thing is over. '

I was looking at Petra but she shook her head.

'I told you everything,' she said.

'Run it by me again.'

She looked at the others, still adjusting to the new world where she didn't need to sneak out, to talk to people away from prying ears. The others looked back at her like they knew nothing. She finally came round her chair and sat back down.

'Chas was here for just a couple of nights. We had a couple of drinks in the Thistle and he asked about Alfie and I told him that Alfie was gone. Then he left. I saw him hiking out just like I told you. And the people at the farm never knew he'd talked to us. They didn't stop him.'

'That ties in,' I said. 'I tracked Chas up to Scotland. So he was clear of all this. And his pal Alfie, locked up in the compound, never knew he'd called by. But when Chas left Scotland he was talking about coming back, searching again. And my guess is that he did. So there's something you're not telling me.'

'I swear,' Petra said, 'that's the truth.'

She looked at Gangly.

'Tell him, Kenny,' she said.

Gangly-Kenny looked at her for a moment then shrugged. Spoke to her not me.

'I never told you, Petra: the dude came back. A month later. One weekend. You were out. He was still looking for Alfie. He thought something was going on here.'

Petra's jaw dropped. 'Why didn't you tell me?'

Kenny shrugged again.

'For what? It was nothing. He was in and out. Gone.'

'Did he say where he was going? Any plans?' I said.

'He didn't tell me nothing. Looked kind of lost. He just headed off wherever he was going.'

'And no one else saw him? No one's seen him since?'

They all looked blank.

'Okay, let's be clear Kenny: your employers didn't get a sight of him the second time?'

I was watching the kid and saw a light come on. A sudden memory.

'Yeah,' he said. 'Maybe they did. They saw him going out of here. Came in to ask who he was and what he wanted. That was it. They didn't mention him again.'

And there it was.

In the seconds it took Kenny to get his words out the Chas Abbott job reached the end of its road. The jalopy shuddered and bounced, coughed and expired in a cloud of steam on the dusty track.

The trail ended.

Right here.

Or close by. Wherever the Albanians had caught up with the nosey kid asking questions and threatening an operation that didn't tolerate intruders.

When Chas first called at Low Rasen he got lucky. Hiked out unnoticed. But the second time around he hadn't avoided the radar.

He'd brought Hat and his pals scurrying after him to ask their own questions. And they'd seen a threat to their security and fixed it.

Right there, sitting at the table in front of five scared kids, I saw it.

I asked a few more questions but nothing changed. Nothing new came from their answers.

I sat back. Grinned round at them. The stitches tugged my right cheek. The left side was definitely less painful. Maybe I'd have to develop a new style of smiling. Sinister side only. It would suit the job.

I stood up and thanked the kids. They had questions of their own but not the nerve to ask them so they just watched silently as I let myself out into the sunshine.

~~~~~

Back at the hotel Terry Tickner was throwing a bag into the back of his Range Rover.

He greeted me with less enthusiasm than you'd expect from a guy who's just saved your life. But I guess that was nothing personal. Just part of the job. He was at Low Rasen following instructions. And either something from way back spurred him into action when he spotted his quarry about to be eliminated or maybe he just sided with the less-bad crew. I preferred to fool myself that Terry had never forgotten the moment we'd shared back on that old job, lousy outcome notwithstanding.

I threw him a favour now.

'Stand your people down,' I told him. 'Save the expense. I'm going nowhere today.'

Tickner slammed the hatch. Jabbed his hands into his pocket. His jacket shoulder was still ripped. I guess he'd noticed by now. Maybe that explained his sour disposition.

'This,' he angled his head over the traffic in the general direction of Low Rasen, 'hasn't changed anything. My client still wants you in his sights. I'm just wondering how many A&Es I'm going to have to tour before the gig ends.'

'None. The gig ends here. Tell your client: the boy's dead.'

That got him. For the first time he looked interested.

'What boy?'

'Are you going to persist in telling me this is not about Chas Abbott?'

He thought about it.

'We were at the farm looking for him,' I said. 'In case you were wondering.'

Tickner watched the distance then turned back to me.

'Yeah,' he said. 'I was wondering.'

'So maybe we don't need to be coy that the boy was your own business. You were following me to find him. But the kid is gone. He's not findable. So it's the end of the trail for all of us.'

'Is this kosher?'

'Chas fell foul of the Albanians and they put him in the ground. I've no hard evidence but I'm no longer looking for him. You can tell your client that, Terry.'

Tickner turned to rest his arms on the car roof. I gave him a moment.

'I notice you're not denying that you know who I'm talking about,' I said. I leaned my own elbow on the Range Rover. The roar of the traffic washed round us. I listened to it. Gave the cogs time to turn. My cheek hurt and the sun was hot on my neck and the drive back to Town, *sans* shut-eye, beckoned like a dental appointment.

'What I still haven't figured out,' I said, 'is *why* your clients are interested in the boy.'

Tickner stared across the Range Rover at the hotel. Finally spoke.

'My clients' business is their own,' he said. 'But I appreciate the heads-up.'

He pushed himself off the car and walked round to the door.

I pushed myself off and turned to walk away. The long drive beckoned.

'Till next time,' I said.

Tickner pulled the door open then paused.

'Eddie,' he said.

I stopped.

'You're right,' he said. 'They wanted me to bring the boy in. I'll tell them that's not going to happen.'

'Bring him in? You offering abduction services now?'

Tickner lifted a lip. Sneered and slid into the seat.

'Give me a break,' he said. 'There are ways and ways to reel in a guy.'

'Such as?'

But Tickner slammed the door. Fired up and rolled out.

I watched him drive out into the traffic then walked across to the hotel to check out.

CHAPTER TWENTY-SIX
Uncanny Valley

Shaughnessy, Harry and Bernie were heading out for a quick mid-afternoon lunch before driving back. I gave it a miss. The thought of two solid hours on the M1 killed my appetite. The sole positive was that I'd hit London towards the end of the rush. Most of the traffic would be coming the other way.

But two hours is two hours and the M1 is the M1 and the only mitigating factor was Terry St Claire's soothing voice in my ear buds covering the roar of the Sprite's Climax engine and the hood-down wind rush. Rudimentary motoring. Sometimes the only antidote for motorway hell. The downside was the vibration that elicited a sympathetic pain as the stitches tugged the flesh on my cheek.

I hopped between lanes, passed slow traffic, counting down the exits. By Luton I realised that I needed something to counter fatigue. I switched on my phone and called Lucy. She'd been trying to get me for the last hour.

'Hell, Eddie, I was starting to think the worst.'

'You weren't far wrong.'

She ignored the comment.

'Luckily I got through to Harry. He told me everything. Jeez, Eddie, I don't *believe* you got bailed out by Terry Tickner. *That* guy?'

'*That* guy saved my life last night.'

'Sure he did. Doesn't mean I have to like him.'

I grinned. Stretched the stitches. She'd only met the guy once. Trust Lucy for the straight-up viewpoint.

'He must at least have gone up a notch on your scoreboard,' I suggested.

'Half a notch maybe, maximum. And he was only there looking after his own interests.'

I held the grin. How many of us can say we're worth half a notch? I asked what she'd got.

'I know why Tickner is looking for Chas Abbott.'

Attagirl! Fatigue fell away. I wrenched the wheel. Hopped past artics.

Tickner, of course, was no longer looking for anyone but if anyone could fish out the explanation for why he'd *been* searching I guess Lucy could. And this was something I wanted to hear.

'I've been burning out the phones and computer,' she told me. 'I talked to Philippa again and my guy over at the *Standard*. And Eddie, you're gonna love this.'

She was wrong. I was going to love nothing. Chas Abbott was dead and nothing could change that. The kid had set off to find himself, take a year on the road, maybe find the end of that road in a Scottish crofting settlement, but his plans had shredded right from the start when a chance meeting with his dodgy pal put him in the sights of people who saw him as a threat. And when the girl he'd thought he shared something with turned out to have found her own direction the disappointment sent him right back into the path of Alfie's employers. And in a blink of the eye Chas' life was snuffed out by people he never knew. There was little to feel good about whatever Lucy gave me. Still, I needed to know.

'Tell me,' I said.

I watched the gleaming tarmac, the lane markings flicking by, cars and trucks blocking and squeezing. I worked the wheel. Gained the outside lane and raced forward as I took in what she said.

And it finally made sense.

But the knowledge, in the end, made Chas' fate that extra bit pointless. Though I guess you can look at things from both ends of the telescope. Maybe it was all the interest in the kid by his family and by Tickner's client that now looked pointless.

After she was through Lucy listened to engine roar and turbulence coming over the line.

'You still there?' she said.

I snapped back. Dropped back to the middle lane.

'Yeah,' I said. 'I'm still here.'

Though the silence came back.

Then I brought her up to date on Chas, gave her what Harry hadn't known when they spoke, and *that* subdued *her*. She finally saw the thing the way I did.

Lucy's turn to be silent.

'Talk later,' I said. I killed the phone and swung the wheel. Regained the outside lane and planted my foot. Hard.

~~~~~

Five minutes later another call came in.

Susan Abbott, Chas' sister. Looking for an end-of-week update.

But she was way behind and *this* update was going to crash her whole day. It needed to be face-to-face. I asked if she was at the family home but it turned out she was in Town, over in Maida Vale. I breathed a sigh of relief. Cancelled my planned detour round the M25, the slog out to Alton. We could talk in Town. She could pass on the news to her mother herself. We arranged to meet at Chase Street in forty-five.

Forty-five became sixty-five courtesy of a jack-knifed artic after the Orbital that left me crawling Townwards in a jam of heated tempers and tailgaters. I ditched the motorway, diverted, only to hit different hold-ups, the same tail lights. When I got to Paddington Susan Abbott was standing on the street wearing a worried smile. My insistence on face-to-face meant significant news and maybe not good. She was right to worry. I'd have dropped a day's fee to have delivered it to her and her mother together, would have reimbursed the whole lot if it could have changed the news. Luckily for my conscience and bank balance you can't change what's happened.

I keyed the code and touched Susan's elbow, guided her towards the stairs. My silence and touch scared her. She climbed the steps stiffly without asking. At the top landing I opened the door and we went in.

I took her through to Shaughnessy's room. I wasn't ready to refresh my memory of the devastation behind my own door. Monday morning would be soon enough for that. I could arrive nice and early and get the week off to a truly spectacular start.

Shaughnessy and Harry shared a partners desk under the street window and had a little visitors' area in one corner comprising two chrome and leather easy chairs served by a miniature table. I invited Susan to sit but didn't pull the second chair round. Too intimate for someone I barely knew and whose motives I still hadn't fathomed. The news was going to hit her hard but I was no longer sure just *how* hard. And I wasn't in the mood to digest the element of phoney that would be at the core of her reaction.

The best I could do was sensitivity. Sympathy was beyond me.

I walked round Shaughnessy's desk and raised the blinds and got the sash up to let in light and air. On the street below, the last workers were moving home past early evening drifters heading out to bars and restaurants. When I turned back Susan was watching me. She knew something bad was on the way.

'There's no way to break this easily,' I said, 'but our search is over. And your brother isn't there. We're not going to find him.'

Her mouth opened and closed. Her energy sapped to nothing.

'It may take a while to confirm,' I said, 'but you should assume that your brother is dead. He died around two years ago. You might want to prepare your mother for that news.'

I watched as realisation continued to sink in. Her mouth clamped, unable to formulate the questions she needed to ask. Probably she didn't know where the questions should start. So I turned back to the street and took her through it. Explained how her brother had stumbled into the path of some ruthless people. Simple bad luck – if Chas' dodgy friend could be reduced to that epithet – had come his way. I explained how Chas' search for his friend had threatened an operation that was too big to permit threats, and how the people behind it had dealt with the problem.

I gave her a little background to the operation and why I was sure her brother was dead. If the bad guys had felt any reluctance about killing anyone who got in their way then we might have found Chas in that compound working with the other kids. But there was no such reluctance. And the Albanians needed those other kids to keep fooling themselves that they were just working out their contract, that one day they'd be released with a hefty pay packet. So throwing an abducted outsider into the mix wasn't going to work. So the Albanians disposed of Chas. It was going to take a little digging before the evidence – if there was any – surfaced, but Susan's brother was not coming back.

I watched the comings and goings on Chase Street a few moments longer then turned.

Susan was looking at the carpet, mesmerised by its patterns.

'I'm sorry,' I said. 'I'd hoped your brother was findable.'

She breathed quietly, taking it in. Still no words.

'Of course,' I said, 'I'm not entirely sure which part of the news is worse for you. The fact that you won't see your brother again or the consequences of that fact, which I do admit look pretty dire.'

It took her a moment to process my change of tone then her head snapped up. She stared at me in disbelief, waiting for her mind to rearrange my words until they meant something different. But the words were not rearrangeable.

'It's no longer my affair,' I said, 'but you've got me wondering.'

I came round the desk and leaned back on it. Crossed my arms and looked down at her. None of this was my business now. The contract had ended when I confirmed Chas Abbott's fate, leaving only my curiosity. I wasn't looking for truth, which I already knew, just the understanding about what percentage of my fee represented Susan Abbott's love for her brother and what percentage was stumped up for different reasons.

Susan shook her head, still playing the shock and confusion thing. The shock was real but I wasn't in the mood for confusion. I shook my head slowly to dissuade her and finally couldn't hold back an unfriendly grin, though it hurt like hell.

'We know the whole thing,' I said. 'The only question, apart from the one I just asked, is how much your mother knows. Or was she simply concerned for Chas?'

But Susan's face had turned to stone.

'You're right,' she said finally. 'Our motives are not your affair. Just tell me how we can be sure that Chas is dead. Deliver the proof and send out your invoice.'

'Proof may take a little time. But I repeat: you should work on the assumption that your brother is dead.'

'So there's no actual proof?'

I dropped the grin.

'Come on, Susan: there's no hope. Your lottery ticket's shredded. With any luck the police will have something for you in a few weeks but I'd put the Lamborghini and private jet on hold.'

She glared at me then. Then stood, ready to go.

But stopped.

A curiosity of her own.

'What do you think you know?' she said.

'I know that your father had an unconventional start in life. One that stemmed from a brief dalliance on the part of your paternal grandmother. Seems the old lady kept her secret for decades but her extra-marital liaison didn't entirely escape the notice of the society rags at the time, nor of recent researchers, including our firm's resident expert. Nor, of course, of your own vigorous detective work once your radar was triggered. Which is another puzzle. The blip on the screen that sent you chasing after your brother.'

She waited a moment, caught between airing the whole rotten laundry and just getting the hell out. In the end some need to share and to know what we knew, kept her standing.

'It was just chance,' she said. 'After our father died six months ago our mother asked me to help clear out his old belongings up in the loft. It was mostly just junk but I found an old suitcase with some of our grandmother's stuff inside. That's where I found out.'

'...that your family line was not what you'd thought.'

'Our grandmother had an affair back in the sixties. If our father had gone through the suitcase he'd have discovered it himself. I found an old photograph and a letter. The photo was a Polaroid snap of our grandmother in front of Sacré Coeur in Paris with a man. The way they were leaning together it's pretty clear what their relationship was but the man looked a little uneasy at having their photo taken. Probably a tout had accosted them for a hundred franc photo and left our grandmother with a record of what should have been a secret trip. A romantic weekend away. Our grandmother wrote a date on the back of the photograph as if she knew it would soon be just a memory.'

She paused, wondering why she was telling me. But this needed to be out.

'The letter was from someone who signed himself "M". It's dated six months later and is obviously a response to one our grandmother wrote to him. He talks about how you can't always time these 'things" accurately, and how just a few weeks difference would mean that there was no "problem". It's obvious they were talking about a pregnancy. The one that produced our father. The dates coincide exactly. But between the letter and our father's birth our grandmother married the man she'd probably turned to on the rebound when her Paris fling terminated their relationship. Which we now know was illicit, and a big risk to that person.'

'So the Paris guy must look like your father – but you didn't recognise him.'

'No. Just some handsome guy, obviously well-to-do but unknown. I didn't spot the resemblance at the time. The photo was just a piece of family intrigue to push back into the suitcase for the next generation to puzzle over. Family trees are becoming the rage now.'

'Then two months ago the radar screen lit up.'

'Bright and clear. The plane crash that killed the head of the Holland family. Max.'

'His face was in the papers,' I recalled. 'But I guess there wasn't much resemblance to the young man on the Montmartre steps.'

'None. I'd never have seen the connection if they hadn't put his grandchildren's pictures in the papers. Clark and Hillary. The inheritors of the family fortune since their father died in the crash.'

'And Clark Holland...'

'...is the spitting image of the man with our grandmother. Same face, same way of standing, even the same hairstyle. You'd think these things would have changed in fifty years. It could have been Clark with our grandmother if you didn't know that the pictures were separated by half a century.'

'So you put two and two together and realised that your father was Max Holland's son. Giving any of *his* kids exactly the same inheritance ticket as the grandkids pictured in the papers.'

Her face soured further as we came back to the real issue. But she still hung on. Some need to unburden. I grinned again.

'With the old man dead,' I said, 'there'd be a claim for half the family fortune to flow down to the previously unknown side of the family, even if Max had bequeathed the lot to his known son. Which he hadn't.'

'No. There was no will. Max Holland tore it up three months ago after a commercial row with his son.'

'I believe it was to thwart his son's plans to expand the Holland business in directions he didn't approve. His son was on the board but had only a tiny shareholding and was caught pulling in backers to attempt a hostile buy out of half the businesses. Max's will shredding was an unsubtle way of pulling his son back into line.'

'Yes. The old man was ruthless enough to cut his son off without a penny. Sign everything over to some dogs' home if he didn't step back into line.'

My grin held. Dogs on caviar for life.

'So when their plane took a nose-dive,' I said, 'killing Max and his wayward son, the old guy was intestate. Meaning the billions would go to the grandchildren, of whom your brother was one.'

She cursed to the room at large. Glared at me. Anger beginning to bubble.

'So you dug it all out. I'd be impressed if I was interested. If this thing wasn't such a total shit-fest.'

And there we had it.

Anger.

The real emotion.

Stemming from the realisation of what a future without brother Chas looked like.

'I'd be impressed,' she repeated. 'I got everything from my grandmother's photo but how in hell did you get onto the scent? You were just looking for a missing boy.'

'Well, we're good at what we do,' I explained. 'But truth be told we had a little help. Because when I set off after you're brother I was also presented with a connection.'

She was hanging on out of sheer curiosity now. A need to know everything surrounding the disaster I'd just served up.

'Someone started following me right from the start,' I said. 'We found out a few days ago that it was the Holland family looking over our shoulders but the *why* didn't come along until today after we'd traced the paths back, searching for any time or place where the history of a billionaire dynasty and a lost boy might have converged. Things clarified when we found it. Picked up the same affair you found. Your grandmother and Max didn't keep things fully under wraps: a snippet got out which made just the tiniest indentation in the old society columns. We found a feature on a Holland charity event back in the sixties. Max Holland was there with his wife but right next to them was someone identified as Elizabeth Abbott, your grandmother. She was listed under her maiden name then but it was her. And retrospectively you could see it, the way she's standing close, giving old Max a look his wife apparently missed. Maybe the modern rags would have picked that up, dug out the dirt themselves, but there was nothing then. We only found the piece by way of a face-recognition trawl through media archives looking for a connection between Clark Holland and Chas. Our computers were fooled into putting Clark at that sixties' event, even though he hadn't been born. But for us it was the connection we were looking for, just two generations earlier than we expected.'

Susan stared at me a moment longer then puffed out an angry breath. Angry perhaps at her own curiosity. This was just so much trivia that didn't change her situation one damn bit.

'So you had the link,' she said.

'And now that we're all wiser we can look at your brother's photo and it jumps out. He looks just like Clark. Chas was a Holland'

She said nothing now. Steam had run out. So I continued for her.

'When you spotted the similarity in looks between the Hollands and your brother, and between them and the mystery guy with your grandmother in Paris, you took a very close look at the timelines and put it together. Realised that the Holland fortune was due to your side of the family too. Or part of that side: because you're only a step-sibling, Susan. Descended from your mother's family by her previous marriage. Entitled to nothing from your step-father's side. Meaning that Chas was the only way to get close to that fortune. Which if my inheritance law is correct would amount to a straight fifty percent of ten billion. Suddenly you were very keen to get your brother back from his wanderings and fire up the DNA checks. And PDQ. Things were on a timer.'

'You're right. But I paid you to do a job. Not to judge. The inheritance was never my sole motivation for getting Chas back.'

I grinned. The stitches pulled my face like a pin-cushion.

'I believe you,' I said. 'But I wouldn't want to put percentages on it.'

Her mouth struggled to find the right words. But there were no right words.

'You're entitled to your beliefs,' she said. 'I assume cynicism goes with the territory. But keep them out of the report when you invoice us.'

'Sure. We'll keep it short. Update you if the police dig up any evidence in the next day or two. And yes: cynicism goes with the job. But I'm truly sorry we couldn't deliver what you were looking for.'

She waited a moment. Finally turned for the door.

'I'll expect the invoice,' she said.

'Soonest,' I said.

I watched her go out.

My phone rang. I picked up.

'Hi, Margot.'

A moment's silence. Then:

'Is this you or the recorded version I keep getting?'

'It's me. Please leave your message.'

'The message is the same as the last three: call me back, you idiot.'

'Sorry, Margot. Heavy day. Haven't checked voicemails.'

'The voicemails are three days old.'

Same excuse. I'd not checked for a while. And my phone had been on mute the last couple of evenings. My excuses were valid if not praiseworthy.

'Sorry again. I guess I got tied up with things.'

'Did things work out?'

'Not as I'd hoped.'

'Tell me.'

'It's a long story.'

'I've got time. Let's say dinner at Antonio's and bed. That should be sufficient time. And for which you should count yourself lucky or me stupid.'

'I'll be there. Though we may have to hold back on the bed thing.'

'Too tired?'

I thought about it. Didn't know what I was. Too *something*.

'All will become clear,' I promised.

'I can't wait.'

'One hour,' I estimated. Rang off.

I tried to fight curiosity but it defeated me. I went out and opened my room door. Anticipated the shock of seeing it anew. When I opened the door I got the shock but not the one I expected. The shock was that my office looked almost normal.

Almost.

It was recognisable in there but it was like a parallel universe. Things were off. Like that Uncanny Valley you hear about. My desk was upright and functional but where it used to sit on four legs I now had a decorating trestle holding up one end. The desk's back shelf was likewise in place and almost horizontal but the packing tape holding it together was new. Stuff was back on its top shelf but in a messed up order, and the Anglepoise stood like a crooked finger, minus shade and bulb. My clock was clear of its shattered glass and looked like it might be showing the right time, which was six-thirty, but the hands were too precisely aligned, both pointing south towards the stationary pendulum. The thing was dead. A rolled and torn poster on my desk had to be my Trueman, in whose vacated place on the wall was just the stained patch of floral wallpaper and some dents in the plasterwork. And on the bureau beneath the patch the inkjet had morphed into a potted plant that was already looking sickly. At least that detail was right.

But over beyond the desk something even more subtle was off. The window blinds were up and exposed a view outside that was too clear, like the window had just been washed. I finally got it: new glass. Lucy, prioritising repairs. It was going to take a couple of years to get the impressionistic haze back over my view.

Uncanny Valley.

A facsimile of my office, weekend dead. Worse than weekend. Sterile. All the usual mess of paperwork hidden from sight. But when I opened the desk drawers on Monday it would be there, waiting like a cobra to spring.

But that was Monday. Right now it was Friday, and Margot's invitation put a rosy glow on things that good food and a beer would consolidate.

I backed out. Closed the door and went down.

CHAPTER TWENTY-SEVEN
All guesswork

Herbie and I showed up at Margot's barely half an hour late. She answered the door dolled up to go out and looked good. But in an instant her eyes widened. The same reaction as mine when I'd first looked in the mirror.

Then she laughed.

She caught herself and apologised, then lost it again and this time let rip with a belly laugh that was remarkably unladylike. She sought to conceal her loss of control by squatting to fuss Herbie who'd been laughing since I picked him up.

I grinned and sucked it up, though I was puzzled. Margot was nothing if not the motherly type. My fear had been that she'd be all over me, fussing and clucking and talking about career changes. The hilarity was a surprise. More of that Uncanny Valley. London was a different place tonight.

When Margot finally stood she planted a kiss and started the motherly stuff but the effect was ruined. She saw it. Switched to a flirtatious cheekiness.

'I'm so looking forward to hearing this one,' she said. 'Even if I know I'm going to end up wondering why I'm not dating an accountant.'

'I knew an accountant,' I said. 'Nice guy. Nine to five type. Fell into a threshing machine on a farm visit. There weren't enough plasters in the world to patch *him* together.'

But she was already looking at my face with serious doubt. Accountants can always stay clear of threshing machines.

'Let's go,' she said. 'Our reservation was half an hour ago.'

We went.

I was groggy from three tense nights but the food was good and the coaxed storytelling kept me awake. Client confidentiality constraints limit a P.I.'s social conversation but you learn to tell a story without naming all the names, and in the present instance neither the Albanian mob nor Clark Holland's family were my clients and so there was little to hide.

'That's bizarre,' Margot said when I finished. 'To have a billionaire's private investigator investigating you. Why didn't they just hire you directly?'

'That option was gone once I signed up with my own clients. And if they'd hired someone to search directly for the boy they'd have been spotted the instant we tripped over each other, which would have ruined their plan. Their best option was to stay in the shadows and watch me as I did the dirty work. But it was a tongue-in-cheek assignment for Tickner. He knew damn well we'd spot him. The best his client could hope for was that we'd stay confused about what the hell was happening until it was all over.'

'But how did the Hollands know your clients were looking for their relative? How did they know they'd hired you?'

'My clients gave the game away at the start. They'd no idea how long it might take to find the boy and didn't want to risk probate being settled then having to fight a rear-guard action to chase the boy's share. I'd say were worrying unnecessarily: when you're confident of your claim for a few billion then a little time and money spent in court is nothing to fear. But apparently it was their lawyer who got nervous. He'd done his sums: if the family got the kid back and managed to get their own hands on just one percent of the boy's new wealth, and if their solicitor could get his own hands on just two percent of *that* then he'd be looking at a million quid fee when he put his invoice in. A tidy enough prospect to make anyone fidgety. So he advised them to stake their claim smartish, even before they went after the boy. And the family did that. They notified the Hollands and presented their case, which would become irrefutable once DNA checks confirmed the boy's lineage, and the Hollands were caught out of the blue with the prospect of losing half the family estate.'

'I still don't get it. If the boy turned up and his link to the Hollands panned out then there was no way they could hold on to that fifty percent. What was the point of watching the search?'

I grinned. Spooned dessert.

'I've yet to ask them. But my guess is that they wanted to catch up with the kid on the quiet. Watch and wait until we unearthed him then move in on him fast with an offer. The kid was wandering around aimless, no great vision for his life, maybe living hand-to-mouth, out of touch with his family and the world. So maybe if the

Hollands explained the situation, painted a black picture of years of legal wrangling, a bitter fight with the risk of failure at the end, then he might be persuaded to take the easy route and sign an out-of-court agreement to take a payout that *he'd* see as a fortune – say ten or twenty million – in return for relinquishing any claim on the Holland estate.'

'But would the boy have signed up?'

'He might. A payout in the millions would have been a fortune to him, even if it was less than a few percent of his rightful claim. And if the kid had balked they could have upped the offer to a hundred mill. without even raising their accountant's eyebrow. A hundred million in your bank account tomorrow, against the uncertain chance of some greater fortune? Many of us would go for that one. And a hundred million or a few billion are the same thing – either stash is more money than you'll ever be able to spend. A new life. I guess if they'd waved ten or hundred million under the boy's nose they'd have succeeded. All done fast and on the quiet. By the time the boy's family realised what was going on it would have been too late. The waiver would be signed with a hundred legal padlocks in place and there'd be a fortune in the kid's bank account. His family would have had one hell of a struggle to come back from that.'

All guesswork, but when you see only one logical solution to a puzzle then it's probably the right one. I was ruling out, of course, a darker and dirtier plan, which would have seen Chas Abbott re-disappear. Perhaps that was Plan B, ready in the event that the boy declined the easy route.

All hypotheses and speculation. The P.I.'s pockets are crammed with the stuff.

We finally got back to my own condition. I sat back with a strong coffee and took a sermon about caution and common sense and the P.I. business in general.

'You're going to tell me I don't know the life,' Margot said, 'but when your missing boy search ended up at that farm even the novice knows that then would have been a good time to call in the police. You're no longer on the law and order payroll, Eddie.'

'If I'd called in the police it would have been problematic. The links to the London people were circumstantial and whatever *Fizikun* was up to was pure speculation. At best we'd have been looking at a few weeks surveillance in Lincolnshire before the police had enough to go in. I didn't have weeks. There was a chance that the boy was there in the compound, mixed up in their operation. And if that was the case I needed to get him out.'

'So you call in your private army and take a criminal gang out? That's deep water, Eddie.'

'Not so deep. We had the people and we had surprise. And it was the Albanians who'd made the first move, remember. A little strategic thinking and they'd have stayed low profile. Wait for our interest to wane. The number one in gangstering is to look for the quiet life. Fight only with rivals, people in the game. They forgot that rule. Crossed a line.'

'And you were ready to respond. I do so like a hero.'

I grinned. Ignored the barb. I've been a few things but never a hero, except maybe to Herbie and to the occasional client who has nowhere else to go. To desperate people anyone who holds out a helping hand is a hero.

'It's just sad, after all the fireworks, that the boy couldn't be rescued,' Margot said. 'You delivered for your client – located the boy, more or less – but if I know you you're filing the case under "Failures".'

She did know me.

'But don't beat yourself up about it,' she said. 'There's no failure in freeing those workers and trafficked women. Shutting down the Albanians' operation.'

I finished my coffee.

'The woman and workers are free for now,' I said. 'But I don't see any of their paths going in good directions. Half of them will be in someone else's hands in six months.'

Which stopped us both.

'Let's get the bill,' Margot said.

We headed back to her place where the promised bed beckoned. The prospect of eight hours' kip.

We got in and fed Herbie his bowl of milk then showered. Margot pointed me ahead of her towards her room then followed a minute later holding a roll of drawing paper.

'I wasn't laughing at you earlier,' she said. She was wearing a body-hugging chemise that would normally have gained my full attention.

Tonight it took effort even to check out the paper as she unrolled it.

'My first sketch,' she said. 'The proofs I mentioned for my new strip character. Voila *Axegrinder!*'

I looked at her creation. A cartoon character that was a savage take on the private investigator. You knew the guy was a P.I. by the trilby and his lean, dark lines. Margot had drawn up a six-frame strip with a punchy narrative that almost made me laugh and was going to go down great with whichever publications syndicated it.

The guy wasn't me but I couldn't push away a glimmer of recognition. Margot was interested in the *idea* of the private investigator, the absurdity of the profession, the arrogance of its judgements. She was caricaturing the idea. Funny and sad and ridiculous. But it wasn't the real thing. It wasn't me.

Apart from one detail.

You knew that her archetypal P.I. had been in the wars from the very first frame. Something that had left an outsize plaster stretched across his face covering a broken nose. Her guy stepped out of the shadows in that first frame looking the way he was going to look in however many thousand strips Margot would produce, however many decades he lived.

And that plastered-up face had been either divine inspiration or premonition. I didn't know which. It was the face I'd seen in the mirror earlier.

Uncanny Valley.

I started laughing myself until it got too painful. Then slept.

CHAPTER TWENTY-EIGHT
Don't call back

I gave the office a miss on Monday morning. The messed up paperwork and lurking Post-its would be there tomorrow and the sun was shining. I stashed the hood, and Herbie took the shotgun seat and we drove out of Town, beat the rush hour and crossed the Lincolnshire border at eight-thirty. Rolled through Low Rasen a little after ten.

The place was dead, just a dusty road passing through nowhere. The kids' cottage was lifeless, and the Thistle's door looked like it hadn't opened in a decade and might never again. Once Low Farm had been back through the auctioneers there'd perhaps be three or four new locals to prop up the bar, and maybe the odd tourist would continue to take a wrong turn and stop for lunch. Or maybe the place would just fold.

We rolled on towards the farm and checked things out. The main house was quiet under the trees but the police barriers and a van blocking the lane confirmed that a team was busy in there. I pictured Met vehicles parked in Streatham, tape across *Fizikun's* door.

I'd put in a call yesterday to the Lincoln super who'd designated himself as my point of contact. I wasn't going to hear any good news about Chas Abbott but the itch to know *something* had become unbearable. The super stayed polite, resisted the urge to point out that any contact between us was meant to be him calling me. Didn't bother either with false chumminess, just gave me the bare fact that they'd not discovered anything significant related to the boy. No suspicious plots of ground, no signs of disposal, no body. But we already knew that they weren't going to find those at Low Rasen. The Albanians' business model was predicated on leaving nothing behind in their periodical relocations.

The super's information was supplied as a bare courtesy. Our unearthing of a major criminal operation didn't make the cops our friends. They were grateful for the shortcut but a renegade private investigation firm wasn't so far removed in their eyes from the bad guys we'd unearthed. And for all I knew – because the super wasn't saying – the Met might already have been sniffing at the London end of the Albanians' operation. Maybe we'd just short-circuited things. So: no chumminess. No pat on the back. But when it became clear that I wasn't going to be on the guy's back, that my expectations were realistic, he relented and threw me a hint that the Met *had* been prodded by last week's events. That both Lincoln and London were very busy on this thing. But that was it. His curt ring-off delivered the message that if there was more to be said I wouldn't hear it from him. I made do with what little he'd given me. Thanked him.

Chas Abbott: unfinished business.

Even if it wasn't my business any more.

I guess my *itch* had something to do with a sense that I was the only one who'd been looking for the boy with honest intentions. And if I'd begun to care about the boy I might be the only one bar his mother. Sure, his sister cared but that sentiment couldn't be separated from the fact that her sibling might be a very rich guy if only she could get to him.

I rolled to a stop and watched the farm for a moment then continued out.

We drove the local lanes for three hours. Climbed gates, peered through hedges and thickets. Covered most of the area around the hamlet, looking for any remnant of the boy's passing.

Eventually found something.

I dropped Herbie over a gate a quarter of a mile from the farm and vaulted after him. Walked a narrow field too limited for economic agriculture. If the field had been isolated by a mere hedgerow the barrier would have been ripped out decades ago to extend the productive land but the field was bounded by a drainage ditch and the main stream. An acre or so preserved from intensive agriculture, retained for holding stock a few months of the year, left wild the rest. The vegetation had been grazed just sufficiently to keep it manageable.

The field was hidden from the road by its hedge, and from Low Farm by a copse and a quarter mile of barley. As good a location as any.

Herbie scooted up and down, inspecting holes and sheep droppings. I checked the boundaries where the cover of a hedgerow might have attracted a wild camper.

The meadow had seen two years of grazing, two wet winters and parched summers, since Chas was in the area. Time for any signs to have vanished. But if there was any remnant in any field I wanted to see it.

Two years of weathering and trampling. A tall order. This was my sixth field.

I focused. Worked a grid by the hedge. Applied job methodology. The trick is to block out the wider picture, avoid being hypnotised by myriad details: pebbles and shell fragments on a beach; crazy mosaics of cracks on parched earth; stones and tussocks, bursts of thistles in a field. The trick is to be blind to the mosaic, see only what's different, what shouldn't be there.

And down towards the end of the field where the hedgerow curved to align with the stream and presented a concealed corner I found it.

A glint of metal in the grass, with a strand like a muddy shoelace stretching away from it. I squatted to look closely.

The metal was pressed solidly into the soil. I pulled my army knife out and worked loose an aluminium tent peg with two inches of cord attached.

Wondered if I'd found Chas' last campsite.

I searched the area around the peg, treading carefully, but found nothing else. No fragments of canvass or bits and pieces of travelling gear. Just the tent peg and cord. But another skill learned at crime scenes is to see through the ordinary. There's nothing more ordinary than a tent peg unless it's missing the tent. When you pack up and hit the road there's always the risk of leaving stuff but who leaves a peg buried deep in the ground? And how do you de-rig the tent with the peg in place?

Unless you cut the guy rope.

Someone had become impatient. They'd pulled most of the pegs out but maybe this one resisted so they just cut the cord and stamped it into the earth. Bundled everything else up to take away.

Herbie came over to check out the scene. Found nothing of interest. I decided he was right. Moved on and walked, dead slow along the hedge towards the stream. Three or four paces a minute giving the eyes the chance to really *see* each slice of ground. And finally I did see. Something else that didn't belong, trapped under the hedge. I pulled on a pair of latex gloves and knelt to reach in.

I retrieved a crumpled crisp packet. Old and brittle but it had somehow stuck fast in the hedge. The packet's age-opaqued logo was barely readable. I unfolded it painstakingly, hoping for a sight of the sell-by date but there were only specs of ink where the information had been. I tilted the bag, got light from a different angle, thought I saw the impression of an eleven. Maybe 2011. Forensics would recover the rest but my guess was that this was a remnant of Chas' 2010 visit. Then as the packet came fully open it dropped a faded scrap of paper onto the grass. I placed the packet under my knife and lifted the paper to ease it open. It was a till receipt with the transaction detail faded to blank. But the remnants of the date gave me the year I was looking for. And below an illegible retailer name was the barest hint of another name that looked like William. And whilst P.I.s resist the urge to see significance in every tealeaf pattern I didn't see many businesses or places sporting that name.

But Fort William would fit.

I angled the paper this way and that but nothing else came out. Just a blank scrap that could have been anything. But intuition said that the person who'd crumpled the receipt was Chas, back here in Lincolnshire after his trip north to Fort William.

I retrieved the crisp packet and dropped it with the receipt into a sealable bag. If forensics could lift prints that would give the police something to work on. I dropped the tent peg into another bag. That would have my prints all over it but they'd handle it.

I gave it another hour. Walked back and forth across the hot dry grass looking for something more substantial but whatever else had been left from Chas' stay the years had taken. The police would turn the soil. Give it a couple of days' hands-and-knees. Maybe they'd find something.

But I was done. I knew. Chas Abbott had spent his last free night here in this field. Or part of the night, before the people from the farm spotted his light and climbed the gate.

And wherever they'd taken him it was not near here. They had an operation to protect. If they'd been a little more forensic in their clear-up there'd have been nothing at all to connect the missing boy to their operation.

I snapped a sprig off the hedge and planted it in the ground to mark the spot. Herbie was carrying out his own forensic search of a rabbit hole by the far hedge. I whistled and he scampered over and we walked back to the gate.

I repeated my marker trick at the gate with a small branch jammed into the rusty chain.

Guides for the police.

Then I fired up and detoured to Lincoln before heading home. Made a thirty-minute stopover at the Nettleham HQ to hand over the zip bags and receive a little more hostility. Then we left Lincoln behind and drove back to Town.

The M1 was on form and the exits took forever to count down. I played loud jazz to block out the miles, hoping it might ease the journey, but the whole way down I couldn't shake the feeling that I was abandoning the boy, leaving him behind, even if all I was driving away from was an empty field and a few scraps of plastic and metal that had survived the way all material things outlast us.

I realised I was retreating from a shadow of memory. Nothing more.

EPILOGUE
Tell them to hurry

The gates sprang open and eight horses launched themselves onto the track and stormed uphill towards the grandstand. I stood in the open plate glass doors and watched the battle over the heads of the twenty or so spectators lining the balcony rail, absorbed in the distant field as it thundered towards us. Spectacle only, this time round. The excitement would come on the next lap when wagers would be won and lost and when the horse from your own stables would grit its teeth and go hell for leather to see that your colours took the prize. Would bolster your standing as a serious player, quashing the naysayers who doubted your savvy when you'd stumped up two hundred K for the services of the Sultan of Brunei's stud five years back.

And if your chauffeur and butler had a fiver each way on the mount then you'd have a happy household all round when you headed home tonight.

Today a fifty K pot, tomorrow the Gold Cup.

The pack raced by below us and leaned into the bend. The spectators held their collective breath. Binoculars tracked.

The only ones not focused on the field were me and the bar guy. He'd walked up to the glass and was looking across at me with outright suspicion. I threw him a grin. Wondered what had caught his attention. My facial dressings were gone and the fading scars were getting hard to spot. My suit was freshly pressed and the tie I'd bought on the way over was just the right shade of off-amber to put me in the home camp. And my shades for sure looked the part. From a distance I might be any underemployed aristocrat whiling away the day at the races.

But the guy was looking. Some kind of sixth sense.

I moved onto the balcony before he came to any conclusions.

The sun was out and the group round me shone in their full glory. Bespoke flannel jackets and trendy pale shirts, flashes of amber in pockets and neckwear and in ladies' dresses, deference to the host's colours. The women conformed to standard: twenty- and thirty-somethings sporting body hugging micro dresses or summery skirts and jackets, high heels. Amber touches everywhere. A single couple went against the grain with their Middle-Eastern robes and headgear, but their mirrored shades projected the same ethereal confidence in divine privilege as the rest. A smattering of American accents, added to the Middle-East connection, flagged the junket as a business-related affair, one where agendas could be progressed outside the confines of the boardroom and clear of the pedantic recollection of the company secretary.

The horses curved away into the outgoing straight and the excitement subsided for a moment. Just two or three binoculars stayed on the pack. The guy in front of me was one of the few staying focused. He kept his glasses up and had started a quiet chant, some kind of prayer offering, for the horse with the off-amber heraldry which seemed to be nosing ahead. A mount named *Last Laugh* according to my race card. I didn't have my own binocs but the horse looked strong, rippling with a surfeit of power as the jockey wielded his crop.

'Practically in the bag,' I said.

When my voice registered the guy came rigid for a second then dropped his glasses to spin round and face me. And the look on his face almost made me smile.

His movement drew his audience's attention. Heads turned along the balcony. At the guy's side Miss Drop Dead twirled and opened her pretty mouth, and next to us a burly American rotated and cocked a weathered face in my direction. Our Arab friends too stepped back from the rail, pulled their attention from the horses. In my periphery the bar guy was still watching.

'Holy Mother,' Clark Holland said. 'How the hell did you get up here?'

I ignored the welcome. Watched his face. Thought about the life that had put him up here for the sole purpose of an afternoon's primping on the stage of privilege. The privilege that should have kept him safe from the affairs of a young kid, a nobody hitch-hiking to nowhere on a shadowy road.

'It wasn't difficult,' I said. 'I just dressed the part and waited for the right moment. This place isn't exactly Fort Knox.'

'It's a private goddamn suite is what it is,' Clark said. A flush was spreading from the corners of his eyes. 'And you're trespassing.'

He gestured inside to the bar guy. A practised movement, natural or nurtured. The staccato summons of a guy who's stumping up a half million per annum for the exclusive view and the champers.

The bar guy started to move but Clark didn't wait. Anger suddenly caught him. He came to the boil rapidly and without warning. Planted his reddening face in mine and jabbed his palms in my shoulders to bounce me backwards. I stepped away. Sometimes you've gotta give a little.

Out over his own shoulders the field was shifting and reforming in the distance. One horse was a head clear, though it was too far away to make out the colours.

'Your horse is consolidating,' I noted. 'At least I think it's yours. They all look the damn same to me.'

Clark ignored the diversion and came back into my face. The hue on his own contrasted spectacularly with the cream and off-amber of his clobber. It was the kind of hue that's usually followed by a stroke. Or a fist. I sensed the latter on its way but luckily we were interrupted.

'Oh my! Our handsome detective is back.'

It was Hillary Holland. She'd abandoned her cohorts to come over to her brother's side. She was still every bit Clark's sibling. Now I had two sets of sharp blue eyes pinning me with the their steely superiority. Where they didn't match was face colouring. Hillary wasn't as easily worked up as her brother. I picked up a scent of expensive perfume that made for a heady experience in combination with the spectacular allure of her body-hugging dress. Hillary Holland was as good-looking as Miss Drop Dead, whom she'd just nudged aside. Any billionaire's catch if she wasn't already loaded herself.

I smiled, still watching for moves from Clark. The smile didn't come from inside.

'The pleasure's all mine,' I said.

'Of course. But if you're here to cause trouble you're making a mistake.'

I held the smile.

'Perhaps,' I said. 'But here I am.'

'And now it's time to leave.'

'Don't you want to know what kind of trouble I'm bringing?'

'We don't want to know anything,' Clark said. 'You don't know a damn thing that would interest us. You don't even know enough to know that you don't come near us. *Ever.*'

His face was still a knot but at least his fists had stayed at his side. Hillary turned to smile up at him as if this was prime entertainment.

'Clark, darling, we'd better let the authorities handle this.'

She took his elbow and drew him back a step to let the bar guy through. He was just a kid dressed up in the course's catering clobber. His job was mixing cocktails not manhandling punters. Credit to him, he stepped up.

'Sir,' he said, 'I need to ask you to leave.'

I kept my eyes on Clark.

'Request noted. Now scarper. You don't want to be part of this.'

The kid drew himself up. Stood his ground but didn't move closer. This wasn't his job even if the company's suit obliged him to take a stand. There was a strain in his voice when he switched to the only initiative he could rustle up. Demanded to see my pass. Which I didn't have.

'Then I'll need to call security,' he concluded.

'Tell them to hurry,' I said.

The boy hesitated. Out on the track the field was rounding the distant corner.

'Go!' Clark spat. The bar guy shifted and fled for the phone. The American and Arab guys moved closer. They didn't know what the hell this was about but if moral support was needed they were good for it. Probably good for fisticuffs too. One of the Middle Eastern guys looked like he'd seen a few skirmishes.

But Hillary came back in to keep the tension from turning into something else.

'What's all this about?' she said. 'Just tell us. '

'It's about unfinished business.'

'You *have* no unfinished business here. You've no business with any of us. Never will have.'

'Strictly speaking you're right,' I agreed. 'This isn't my business. So I guess you'd call it personal. I'm here with a message.'

Clark shook his head. The flush was fading from his cheeks as the shock of the intrusion faded. Feeling a little more in control, the way he'd been in control most of his life and always expected to be.

'You're off your rocker, mister,' he said. 'This can't be about that Abbott kid.'

'Could be and is.'

Something like genuine shock came through this time. Maybe he'd thought I really might be here for something else. He exchanged a puzzled glance with his sister then inched closer again. I stayed put this time.

'As much as I'm intrigued,' he said, 'this is a private suite and I'm not in the habit of wasting time with fruitcakes. So when the joke that passes for course security arrives you can unburden yourself to them.'

'Security will be a couple of minutes,' I said. 'So why don't I say my piece to you?'

'The Abbott affair is over,' Hillary said. 'What could we possibly need to hear from you?'

Clark still looked ready to take me on but a sense of decorum held him back. Punch-ups are not the thing in corporate boxes at Ascot. The world up here was all about wealth and power and the avoidance of such inconveniences.

'Partly,' I said, 'I just wanted to take a look at your day, see how life goes on when a nonentity kid falls by the wayside.'

Clark's mouth opened but his sister beat him to it.

'The boy's death was unfortunate. But it was none of our affair. There've been no tears shed here.'

'That I understand,' I said. 'Chas Abbott's fifty percent stake in this family would have been quite an issue. If you didn't manage to buy him off and if he opted out of joining the clan then we'd have been looking at the forced break up of the company. In that respect his death was quite a stroke of luck.'

'See it how you want. It never was and still isn't your affair.'

'And the fact of the kid being your cousin, your own blood counted for nothing. Excess really does make monsters of us all.'

Clark was colouring again. He pushed his face closer and looked set to forgo the assistance of security.

'Who the hell do you think you are?' he said. 'You're just some cheapskate private dick scratching around in the dirt, poking into people's lives. But here's the thing: there's a ceiling. Poke around in the mud as much as you want but this...' – he rotated a finger that took in the little party, the balcony, the suite with its tables piled high with canapés and caviar and champagne – 'this is another world. One you're not part of.'

'Sure. But I'm happy with my mud. Especially when I see the kind of dirt that sticks to people like you. But I guess money trumps everything in your world.'

'Please just go,' Hillary said. 'We're all sorry for what happened to that boy but it's *our* business. We don't want your sermons, Flynn. My brother's right: you don't belong. So let it rest.'

I smiled at her.

'Your own cousin. Just an inconvenience?'

'The Abbott kid was *no* cousin,' Clark said. 'We didn't even know he existed. That line of baboons was never part of this family.'

'That *line* was no different from your own apart from the fact that no one knew about it.'

Clark flapped his palms out.

'And there we have it. The pertinent fact. They were never part of us and yes, if the boy hadn't met his untimely death he'd have been a problem.'

'You've still not told us,' Hillary said, 'why you're here. We're not going to cry over what-ifs and what-might-have-beens if that's what you hoped.'

I thought about it. Realised she'd just answered the question I'd asked myself a few times on the way over.

'I'm here,' I said, 'because the boy deserved to be more than a might-have-been.'

'But it's over. And the boy wasn't even your client.'

Her brother spoke slowly. 'Go home, Flynn. You despise our world and we despise yours. Let's agree on that. Then you can take a hike.'

'I'll be gone in two seconds,' I said. I was speaking to Hillary. 'But since you're puzzled about why I've stuck with it let's say it's an itch. I just needed to know a couple of things. I guess I wanted a better ending than walking away from the few tatters of a campsite that was all that was left of Chas. I was looking for something that might make his death more than just a convenience for you people.'

'So you've scratched away,' Hillary said. 'Has the itch gone? I'll bet it's not. Or did you just come here to let off steam?'

I thought about it again.

'A bit of both,' I said. 'But I need to put you right: the itch is gone. I guess that's one of the things I came to tell you.'

'And why would we give a damn?'

'Because the scratching has affected you.'

Clark pulled an ugly sneer across his face, shook his head..

'You're wrong,' he said. 'Nothing you know or do and nothing you *think* will ever affect us. But my horse is out there right now and I'm going to miss seeing her take her third Class 1 if you don't get the hell out. And I'm going to play absolute bloody hell with security.'

'They dug up remains,' I said.

'What remains?'

'Of people who've crossed the Albanians' path over the last few years. Out in Essex. A source spilled the beans and took the police to the site. The cops have been keeping a lid on things so you haven't read anything in the press.'

'And so?'

'One of the bodies was Chas Abbott.'

'That's sad,' Hillary said. 'But we already knew he was not coming back. So forgive our indifference but so what?'

I opened my mouth to reply but Clark beat me to it. His face had switched to a broad smile. The flush had faded to pale peach.

'So what,' he told his sister, 'is that the lid is now closed. If they've made a positive ID then hallelujah! The boy won't be rising. And excuse,' he said, 'my own indifference.'

'Do they have a positive ID?' Hillary said. A hint of curiosity had kicked in despite her words.

'Dental records and DNA match to his mother.'

'Well then.' Hillary's eyes flashed. She gripped Clark's shoulder. 'It's all over darling. And as you say: hallelujah and goodbye.'

She threw me one last glance and turned away, waving the audience back to the railings. Clark stayed with me, enjoying his moment. His American and Middle Eastern pals stayed too. They didn't know exactly what was up but they were enjoying the moment of shared superiority. Then Clark's mind went back to his horse, coming hell-for-leather round the final bend. The field was leaning into the rails. I couldn't say which horse was out ahead but I assumed it was Clark's.

'I understand that the family's solicitors will be in touch,' I said. I'd raised my voice to re-snag Hillary's attention. It worked. She turned back, sensing something.

'All these probate rules,' I said. 'Formalities to check. Apparently they're gonna request samples from one of you. Help establish that Chas' lineage goes back to your grandfather.'

Hillary looked puzzled. Her brother switched back to angry.

'The kid is dead,' he said. 'The claim on this family died with him. They can request what they want. Now get the fuck out.'

I grinned. Shrugged. Felt the final vestige of my itch ease to nothing.

'If only life were that simple,' I said.

'What do you mean?'

'Chas has a daughter,' I said. 'So she'll take her father's share. That's fifty percent of the Holland estate if I have it right.'

'Bullshit.'

But Clark's face suddenly looked scared. And Hillary's mouth had dropped. She came back towards me with a sudden, terrible suspicion that the hand grenade I'd just tossed was live.

'They've still to test the child,' I said. 'She's kind of remote, way up in Scotland. But the woman who had a brief fling with Chas the summer he disappeared was quite clear about who the father was when I went back to talk to her. And the family lawyers have already contacted her. On a one percent commission I'd anticipate a good old fight from those people if you want to hang on to your grandfather's billions.'

Hillary stood at her brother's shoulder. Her face now matched his. Two porcelain studies in horror as they looked at my own face, which didn't look like the face of a practical joker. And I guess they'd never seen a more authentic grin on anyone's face.

'Sweet Jesus,' Hillary said.

'I guess you'll fight,' I said, 'but you'll lose. Fifty percent of everything. My crystal ball shows Holland International heading for the breakers' yard.'

They stood like statues for five seconds. Then ten. Until the realisation was locked in. A new reality burning through their brains.

'Get out,' Clark said.

'On my way,' I said. 'I just wanted to break the news. I suspect I was the only one trying to find the boy for honest reasons and I think he'd maybe appreciate my popping by to close things off.'

We could feel vibrations now as the horses galloped up the final straight.

'A race isn't over till it's over,' I said.

There was a roar from the stands as a sudden confusion of colour and flying clods sent the three front runners stumbling and falling into a roiling mass taking two more horses with them. Clark and his sister turned instinctively, as if the race could still have significance. I looked and spotted the jockey with the Holland colours rolling clear, protecting his head. The three remaining horses rounded the melee and cantered for the line. I sensed a few outside bets coming in.

I left them to it and walked across the box. Let myself out. Skipped down the steps and headed for the car park, thinking how a detective with any kind of savvy would have put a fiver down on the way in.

But we're all wise after the event.

THE END

ACKNOWLEDGEMENTS

No author writes alone. We all feed off the works of others, consciously or not. No writer *should* be writing unless he or she has absorbed a myriad of stories or documentary works across their selected genre. Every book I've written has been infused with the spirit of dozens, maybe hundreds of works I've read, both memorable and long forgotten. And some of the world's major authors, past and present, would be astonished to hear that they'd had a hand in my writing.

But sometimes it's one specific book whose theme has been consciously embedded into a writer's latest story. In the case of *Shadow Road* the work in question is Jon Krakauer's 'Into The Wild'.

That book is the non-fictional account of how Krakauer picked up on the mysterious vanishing and sad end of a young American boy and decided to follow retrospectively in the boy's tracks to uncover the route he'd taken to his final resting place and perhaps to gain some insight into *why* it happened. As an adventure in investigative journalism the book can't be beaten.

My own fictional account of the search for a lost boy is very different from Krakauer's – not least because crime novels tend to reach for the sensational elements missing in real life – but readers will perhaps notice the similarity of spirit in the apparently hopeless quest to find someone who may not be findable. In Krakauer's case, actually, the boy had already been found. But the *journey* and the *why* promised to be much more elusive. In Eddie Flynn's parallel universe my aim was to present a picture of a missing boy who had no particular reason to be missing, and to sustain the mystery until (as is my wont) perilously near to the end. Is it possible to get to within a chapter or so of a mystery story's end without a solution in sight? More specifically, to do it without bringing in a last-minute deus ex machina – in plain English, a dirty trick – that just annoys the reader? Could I throw Flynn right back to square one as the last pages are turned and still satisfy the reader? That's now up to the reader to decide. All I must do here is thank Jon Krakauer for the inspiration.

Those of you who wonder whether Flynn's *vodka* settlement actually exists might be interested in Margaret Leigh's *Spade Among The Rushes* which is the non-fictional book that his lost boy had picked up on his travels. I read the book myself after I'd accidentally stumbled into the settlement a few years ago as I followed my Ordnance Survey map round the Scottish west coast, not realising that the place in front of me was apparently quite well known. If you ever go there yourself be aware that you'll likely get your feet just as wet as Flynn did, even with better gear.

My main thank you goes to crime-buff lawyer Kerry Davies who cast a corrective eye over the technicalities of the inheritance wrangle that underlies this story, although out of consideration for her career I did not ask her to endorse the legal implications of Flynn's early-pages diversion into the darker side of death. Any errors there are mine and are entirely deliberate.

As always, I'm grateful for the dirty trick detection skills of my wife who read the early draft without crying foul at the puzzle's late resolution and assisted with the later proofreading. If her judgement is correct then my plan worked. And if I do put Flynn back at the start of the shadowy road so late in the story it's nevertheless true that he couldn't have got there and gone on to resolve the mystery without taking every step of the preceding trail, so no reader should feel they've been taken for a ride...

SO DO WRITERS NEED REVIEWS ?

A message from Michael Donovan

The answer to that question, of course, is yes. Especially for a writer published independently of the big houses.

In today's digital reading world a book series is only as good as its exposure which is determined by the obscure marketing algorithms of retailers like Amazon.

But obscure though those algorithms are one thing is clear: positive reader response, and in particular a strong list of positive reviews, is a key ingredient for pushing a writer's work to the top of promotion listings where the books will be seen by a new set of potential readers.

And positive reviews also help those readers decide to give the books a try.

So if you did enjoy the latest Eddie Flynn investigation, and if you think others would appreciate the stories - and if you'd like to see titles appear more frequently - then why not take a few minutes to return a positive review on your retail platform or other review site?

As few as ten additional reviews can make a measurable difference in sales and therefore the prospects for future titles. A few tens of reviews can massively boost a book's visibility and ensure it reaches many readers who'd otherwise never read about London's coolest detective.

So is the latest in the Eddie Flynn series worth a couple of sentences? Would you feel you were doing other readers a favour by letting them know? If so, please consider taking a few minutes right here and now...

Meanwhile, I'll keep on bashing away at my keyboard, working always on the next one.

Michael Donovan

www.michaeldonovancrime.com

THE P.I. EDDIE FLYNN SERIES

1 BEHIND CLOSED DOORS
Their teenage daughter is missing. Why don't they want Flynn looking for her?

2 THE DEVIL'S SNARE
Baby-killers or victims? They've hired Flynn to prove their innocence. But why are they lying to him?

3 COLD CALL
A killer's in her house. She's moments to live. Somehow gets to a phone. But why call a private investigator's number?

4 SLOW LIGHT
If her husband is cheating there's a black Christmas coming. But not knowing is killing her. She needs to find out. A quick job for Eddie Flynn - until the husband turns up missing.

5 THE BLACK FIRE
An empty hotel room. An absent guest. No name in the book. But someone wants the stranger found. And they've chosen Flynn as their hit-man.

6 DOG WALTZ
Her father recalls the Jill Dando affair. Wants his celeb daughter protected from a circling predator. But where is the threat coming from? And why is his daughter not helping?

7 SHADOW ROAD
A young graduate. A nobody. Vanished in his gap year. His family want him found. But why are people with knives, guns and Lamborghinis closing in?

www.michaeldonovancrime.com

THE WATCHING

Michael Donovan

It's every woman's nightmare.

Kate walker is a criminal lawyer with a crushing caseload and clients who rarely appreciate her efforts. But if her job is more purgatory than career she's not about to give up on it. Helping the underdog and the vulnerable is her passion.

And even if the job leaves little time for herself she can't complain. After all, she has great friends, a beautiful home and a new lover. Life outside the office and courtroom is pretty good.

Maybe too good... because someone has noticed. Someone who'd like in on her perfect world.

Now they're watching her, calling her, tormenting her with their increasingly dark games. And as Kate's life slides insidiously from disbelief to nightmare she realises that no one can help. She's alone in her dangerous new world.

Soon she's watching every shadow, avoiding empty places and late trains and scurrying home each night to her locks and barricades.

But what if locks and barricades aren't enough? What if her tormentor, like a ghost or demon, can just walk in?

"Chock full of suspense ... infused with dread ... Highly recommended"
Best Thrillers

www.michaeldonovancrime.com

Printed in Great Britain
by Amazon

32814491R00152